Limerick For Death

LIMERICK
FOR
DEATH

Gregory C. Randall

Windsor Hill Publishing, Inc.
Walnut Creek, California 94596

ISBN: 978-0-9987083-4-8

FOR MY MUSE,
BONNIE

Chapter 1

There once were two smugglers from Cork,
Who fell for a wench named O'Rourke.
While they fought 'or the lass,
With sharp knives they slashed,
She ran off with a Yank from New York.

1a

March 1944
Off the Coast of County Cork, Ireland

Standing on the iron bridge of the conning tower of his U-boat, Commander Kurt Struble, with binoculars tight to his weary eyes, scanned the black Irish coastline. His impatience rising, he turned to his lieutenant and ordered in clipped German tones: *"Noch einmal, Herr Hess."*

The officer raised the signal gun, with its narrow focus lens, and again aimed into the dark coast of County Cork. Two flashes, a two-second pause, two more flashes, again a pause—and then one short flash. They waited.

Overhead, a million stars painted the sky and the slivered ghost of the almost new moon held fixed as the U-boat bobbed softly on the flat, glasslike surface of the Celtic Sea. The waters were unusually calm for this time of the year; Struble considered that a good omen. The early spring breeze coming from the land reduced the thin marine layer to almost nothing; the air smelled of verdant hills seasoned with the brine of the sea. Two seamen standing on the lowest step of the conn, their binoculars also pressed to their eyes, looked starboard and port for the faint telltale lights or dark silhouettes of British patrol boats. But only the submarine's faint diesel gurgling of its exhaust, and the vibrations of the boat, disturbed the night.

The commander looked at his watch: 02:35. They had been signaling for five minutes. Five minutes more and, if no response, they would submerge and wait until the next night. It was critical that their human cargo get into Ireland. Struble had been given two days to make it happen according to plan. If not, they would put the two men on the beach without the critical assistance from the Irish Provisionals. Either way, the two men would be on their own.

"*Captain, sie antworten,*" Lieutenant Hess said. "The response is correct."

"Get the raft on the deck," the captain said.

A forward hatch was opened, and faint light from the sub's interior shone on the six men who emerged. A large bundle was quickly pulled up. The captain listened as compressed air filled the inflatable assault boat. No words were exchanged between the experienced seamen.

"Captain Struble, thank you," a voice said from the deck of the boat.

"You just do your job, Doyle. That's all we ask. I've done my part, now you do yours."

"Yes, sir," Rian Doyle answered. "After four years, it's time for a little payback."

"Vengeance is cheap and will blind you. Do your job; that is the best way to get even. When that boat hits the beach, we are done. My orders are simple, to leave you and your associate here. That is all. My crew is paramount. Good night and good luck, sir."

"Captain," Doyle answered. He tossed off an informal salute and walked the wet steel deck to the rubber boat.

"Colm, m'boy, we are on our own."

"We have always been on our own, Rian, even while we lived with these fine masters of the human race," said Colm Casey softly in Irish. "I do not trust them." Like Doyle, the younger man's throaty accent marked his Irish as originating in or around Cork.

"I would rather trust a Protestant with my sister," Doyle said without a laugh.

Casey placed their waterproof rucksacks into the boat and secured them with ropes. They adjusted and tightened their life jackets and secured their personal weapons in the waterproof pockets of their coats.

One of the crewmen cupped his hands to his mouth. "Ready to release," he said in a soft voice.

"Granted," the captain said from the tower. "Gunther, you have one hour. Look for our signal. If you do not return in ninety minutes, we are gone, and you will have to take your chances with the Irish. Remember, the signal light is set at the top of the cliff. It is a narrow focus. Do not lose sight of it. If you do, only God will know your ugly face after you wash up on the rocks."

"Yes, sir, Captain," Gunther answered and turned to his partner, Dolf. "One hour, comrade. You will get your exercise tonight."

"The fresh air will do us good."

Without a sound, the boat slid down the side of the submarine and floated noiselessly against the hull.

"Secured. Good luck," the deck watch said to the men. Even though they were standing five feet away, they were black shapes lost in the dark. The two Irishmen and the boat's two crewmen, one after the other, slipped down the side and into the bobbing boat. The single hawser, held by another crewman on the deck, was dropped into the smaller craft. The four men struck the sea with their paddles, and pulled quickly away from the submarine. A green immovable pinpoint of light, mixed amongst the stars, a hundred feet above the sea and one thousand feet away was their goal.

They pulled hard with their paddles against the slack tide and set a quick pace. They reveled in the open air after being cooped up for fourteen days since leaving Bremen. Their course had taken them through the North Sea and around Scotland. For the two German seamen it was their third patrol, a lifetime in the

Kriegsmarine. For the two Irishmen, walking again on Irish sod was now almost a reality.

Doyle set the pace with a bawdy limerick.

There was a fine lass from Blarney,

Who'd tilt up her ass for money.

Me name is ol' Nancy,

Come tickle me fancy.

Lass, there be not enough gold in Killarney.

The sea slowly lifted and lowered the boat. At the top of each swell, Gunther called out the bearing to the green speck floating among the stars. "Two degrees to port, men. We are almost there, another five hundred feet."

They heard the swell of the surf strike the base of the hard cliffs. The whooshing of the ocean climbing the hard coast of Ireland was enticing to almost soothing; the men in the boat knew different. One mistake and they would, like thousands of others over the millennia, drown amongst the rocks. Doyle aimed a flashlight at the green light, clicked it on and off twice.

"Pull, lads, we're almost there," Doyle urged. He looked again at the spot of green light on the top of the cliff; it flickered and then disappeared. He shifted his eyes immediately to the sea's horizon and the surf ahead.

As if answering an unsaid prayer, a crisp white light appeared in the wall of blackness a hundred feet below the extinguished light. They paddled hard and fast.

"It's certainly not like the days when we were running guns into our fellows," Casey said. "Yes, my German comrades, ol' Doyle and I have been up this narrow slot more times than quickies with Miss Lucy. Hold fast here, we'll feel a quick push from the left, and then slide right in." The inflatable slid to the right on the rise of the swell, then corrected. "Hard left—now!" The small boat slipped across the flat calm of water trapped inside the inlet.

"Ahoy, ahead," Doyle called out. His voice echoed off the sharp cliffs that rose on either side of the narrow cove.

"Is that the pirate Rian Doyle I hear bleating like a rutting sheep?" a voice answered from the blackness.

"True, true, Paddy. 'Tis I, returned to the bosom of me home."

As soon as Doyle answered, a floodlight washed the beach that terminated the cove. Beyond the reach of the ocean, four shadowy figures were visible on the sand.

Sliding up the shingle, the rubber boat beached itself. The two Irishmen jumped into the shallows. Casey grabbed the hawser and pulled the boat farther up and away from the water. In the boat, the two Germans stood. Gunther, his Schmeisser casually held with two hands, watched as the two passengers embraced the four men. Dolf, now also holding a weapon, stood at his side.

"*Schnell, müssen wir gehren,*" Gunther said.

"Absolutely," Doyle said. "Paddy, these fellows have to get back. There are a few things in the boat we need, then up we go."

He and Casey retrieved the waterproof rucksacks, said their thanks and goodbyes, and pushed the rubber boat back into the cove. They stood silently as the two German sailors rowed hard into the oncoming swell. When they were past the narrowest portion of the inlet, Paddy turned off the floodlights. The boat and its small crew instantly were swallowed by the night.

1b

Paddy switched on a flashlight and panned it across the natural stone face at the back of the cove. They had the ocean behind them, but above and to the sides, rock enfolded them like two cold hands framed for a black prayer.

"Do you still remember the way, Rian? It has been a long time, and I know your memory wasn't that good 'for ye left."

"One never forgets, like a first love. All the way back, past the witch's breasts," Paddy said, meaning the two pillars they would encounter as they proceeded up the narrow trail that had been cut into the stone. "And then on to the iron door. I assume it is still there?"

"It is, m'boy—little has changed in two hundred years." Paddy played his flashlight on the stone wall; the number 1749, along with numerous initials, was carved into the stone face. Ahead, just as Doyle had recalled, a massive iron door, rusted red by salt and tide, blocked their path. "I've often wondered how many have climbed these steps over the centuries. I've done my share, so have you Casey, but thousands, maybe more, have left their boot marks on this stone," Paddy said, speaking as much to his companions as to himself. The steps up to the door were cupped from the wear of uncounted hobnailed boots. Paddy tapped four times on the door with the butt of his flashlight. A clank from beyond echoed throughout the cave, followed by the sound of iron sliding on iron. Paddy stood back, and the door swung open.

A young woman, not more than twenty years old, stood in the light of four flashlights. Her flaming red hair was as tangled and wild as the prickly gorse that filled the Irish hills a hundred feet above them. Her green eyes flashed in the lights. A massive Irish setter stood close to her side. When the dog saw Casey and Doyle, he let out a low growl.

"You took your bloody time, Uncle Rian," the girl said, her hands on her hips. A gas lamp sat on the floor behind her sputtering and hissing.

"And you, Brona O'Bryan, were not much taller than half a mare's withers when I saw you last. You have grown up quite nicely, lass."

"And you keep a civil tongue about you," Brona said. "If my da were to hear you, he'd knock you down a peg or two." She said this with a devious smile. "And you, too, Colm Casey," she added in response to his grin. "I know your reputation. So, my remark holds for you as well."

"Yes, ma'am," Casey said, his smile growing wider. Both he and Doyle knew that Brona O'Bryan could damn well take care of herself. "And how is Dergo?" he asked her. "He was but a year old when I left."

"The dog is fine, but be watching your tongue," Brona said.

"I believe the devil's in him and will be in his heirs. By the saints, he's more faithful than any of you fine gentlemen."

That brought a snort of laughter from the men. They knew Brona well, and the dog fit her personality.

Two of Paddy's men slipped the rucksacks over their shoulders, and the troop followed Brona as she held the gas lamp high and led them up the stone steps. Dergo went ahead of his mistress. Five minutes later, both Doyle and Casey were gasping for air.

"Didn't those jack-booted Nazis keep you in shape, Uncle?" Brona said. "There were times, when I was but a child, I watched you make a dozen trips in a night. And carrying a bundle of rifles every time."

"I was younger and more handsome," Doyle said, taking in a deep breath of free Irish air.

"Back in the day, weren't we all," Paddy offered. "Then again, we were fighting for our freedom."

"And our lives. Now, not so sure what the hell we're doing," Casey said, his heart rate finally slowing. "Those Nazis may say we are their friends and comrades, but I sure as hell do not trust the bastards. If we didn't need rifles and ammunition, I would tell them to fuck off."

"But we do, and train us they did," Doyle said. "So, boys, this is the least we can do to throw the Brits out of the north."

They climbed until they came to another door, this one made of wooden timbers and held together with exquisite wrought-iron hardware. Brona lifted the iron latch and pushed the heavy door open. They entered a small room with a stone floor, masonry walls, and heavy beams and rafters crisscrossing overhead. A small incandescent light barely illuminated the chamber. In the corner, a wooden stairway led to the underside of a door built into the ceiling.

"For the rest of tonight and tomorrow," Paddy said, "you two stay here. Brona has prepared a feast as well as beer and whiskey, your choice. We will contact the agent in Cork who has your identification papers. He will come and collect you tomorrow afternoon. You will go north with him. He knows everything and everyone. There should be no problems, and the two of you will be on the Dún Laoghaire ferry tomorrow night, Holyhead the next morning."

"Then the fun begins," Casey said.

"Yes, if you count as fun a couple of old Irish Provisional IRA members," Paddy said, "who, most probably, are still on the English wanted list, trying to outfox MI5 agents and the British regulars guarding Holyhead dock."

"Better than being shot climbing over barbed wire while sneaking onto some beach on the fucken' coast of Cornwall," Doyle said.

"I like my odds better on the coast," Casey answered. "A lot better."

Paddy and his boys climbed the stairs and left. Doyle looked around the room. A single table and two chairs had been placed to one side; two cots with pillows and blankets sat against the opposite wall.

"Reminds me of my six months in Dublin's Kilmainham Gaol," Doyle said. "But then again, then there were fifty stinking lads layin' shoulder to shoulder on the stone floor."

Brona pulled a basket out from under the table and set it on top. She extracted two loaves of bread, chunks of cheese, a large sausage, and a quarter of a ham.

"Jesus and Mary, girl, do you have enough?" Doyle asked.

"Uncle, this isn't all just for you—and besides, this is all you get until you leave."

"Yes, ma'am," Casey said, his stomach growling.

She poured whiskey from a jug into two heavy glass tumblers. "Welcome home, Uncle."

"Thank you, lass, it is good to be home," Doyle said.

"What is it like there, in Germany? We get so little news, and what we do hear I don't believe. The BBC is all propaganda and bullshit."

"Same in Germany, so it is hard to believe what we hear. According to the German press the Nazis are winning everywhere, but as we were driven from outside Berlin to the docks in Bremen, much of the vaunted German fatherland was bombed rubble and blasted villages. Sure didn't look like they were winning anything. They tell their people little about what's happening, but probably the same here."

"Then why don't you tell 'em to just fuck off? You two can disappear into the dales and be gone. You hid from the British once; they never found you. Here, no one would look for you. You are heroes to many of the folk around here."

Doyle and Casey exchanged looks. Brona couldn't know how tempting her suggestion was after everything they'd seen during the last year.

"Our brothers up north need the guns," Doyle said, unsure how much she already knew. His niece was no longer a child to be protected from the truth. Still, it pained him that one so young should already know the realities of war. "The Nazis promised five thousand rifles, mortars, and ammunition for our work," he told her. "That's a lot of incentive, lass. Besides, they let us know that the three other Irish lads they were training might meet with accidents if we did not hold to our part of the bargain. They truly are bastards."

"And what work is this exactly, Uncle?"

"The Americans and the Brits are planning to invade Europe. Everyone knows that. Our job is to find out when and where."

1c

Doyle and Casey sat on bags of barley in the back of the rusted shell of a lorry as it trundled up the coastal road to the ferry at Dún Laoghaire. The two days in the smugglers' hole, under the O'Bryan estate, had been like a vacation, and even as impatient as they were to start, for the first time in years they relaxed. Maybe it was the whiskey—instead of that god-awful fruity flavored schnapps the Nazis favored—possibly the cheeses, but most probably it had been the company of Brona O'Bryan. She told them everything that had happened in the county since they had left. Who died, who had children, who were up north in Belfast fighting against the British, and, sadly, who were fighting and dying for the British in the Orient, North Africa, and even Italy.

As he walked around at night, Doyle had been disappointed to see that the O'Bryan estate had begun to fall into disrepair. Poverty, never a stranger to the Irish, had settled in and left little for the upkeep and management of handsome properties and most especially large estates. The house with its sixteen rooms and surrounding lands consumed every Irish pound Brona could scrounge. She did as well as she could. Her parents, infirmed and sequestered in the upper rooms of the house, spent their days caring for each other. The house and grounds were left to Brona, a few field hands, and one elderly housemaid who doubled as the cook. The hands and staff stayed and helped because they had nowhere else to go. The few pounds the local smugglers paid for using the tunnel helped.

During the eighteenth century, the tunnel had provided a route for bales of Irish wool en route to France and, in exchange, wines and brandies to Ireland, all driven by the punitive taxes and tariffs imposed by the British landlords. While the Provisional arm of the Irish Republican Army had fought against the British some forty years, thousands of guns and millions of rounds of ammunition had been carried up the tunnel and through the safe house adjacent to the estate. Although after the truce in 1921, the tunnel lay unused for a decade. Unused until the war in Europe exploded, when the passageway then again became a two-way conduit for everything from information to weapons.

"What are you going to do after the war, Colm?" Doyle asked. He lit a cigarette and braced himself as the truck bounced against the pocked road.

"I've been fighting so long, I'm not sure what you mean," Casey answered.

"This war, the one between the Brits and the Nazis."

"Don't forget the Americans. They've changed everything. I believe that Hitler doesn't have a chance now."

"So why are we doing all this?" Doyle asked, echoing Brona's earlier question. "We could pull over to the side and just walk away."

"For our brothers?" Casey said.

"It's a reason, but not the best. Ireland has been cursed and pissed on so long, I'm not sure we'd know what to do with this freedom we've gained. Even with the partition and the peace, we've gone on killing each other. The Catholic Church controls Irish society and politics to boot, and for good measure you throw in the conviction we Irish are against the world and you end up with a fucken' bloody mess," Doyle said. After the welcome break of the last couple of days, he felt the strain of the last years resettle in his neck and shoulders. Casey always seemed to handle it better, and now his friend laughed softly as if realizing the true source of Doyle's rant. Doyle had only known fighting, first on the dirty streets of Cork, then the British, then the time in the north, then the *Cogadh na Saoirse.*

"We are a fucken' crazy people," Casey said. "We still believe in witches and fairies and all sorts of shadowy things living in dark places. But I'm glad to be home, if only for a few days."

"Me, too."

An hour later the lorry slid to a stop, the double doors were pulled open, and the agent, who had provided their passport and travel documents, stood in the shadow of the setting sun behind him.

"Out, lads, we are here. You know well the ferry—nothing much has changed. All the security is on the English side. Wales is a wee bit sympathetic to us, but the British army controls the dock. The suitcases I gave you have clothing and some personal things—you are workers imported to help with fortifications and construction. There will be a bus waiting to pick up you and a dozen other lads on the other side. It will take you to a work camp about two hours south; there you will change your papers. They are hidden in the lining of your suitcases. The fellow on the dock who keeps the immigration lists works for me. When you get to Shrewsbury, the bus will stop. Get off and walk the two blocks to Saint Chad's Church. There will be a car waiting to take you to Bristol. From there you are on your own."

The agent handed Doyle a card.

"Remember this phone number. Memorize it, and then burn it. When you need to get back, dial that number—they will provide transportation to Holyhead."

Doyle nodded and held out his hand. The agent shook hands, started to turn away, and then turned back.

"What you are doing for those German devils—I do not want to know," he said, looking into first Doyle's and then Casey's eyes. "I lost two brothers to the British in 1920. Hanged they were, so my vengeance goes deep. May the saints travel with you."

Doyle and Casey walked down the quay to the ferry, suitcases in hand. There were maybe forty people in line waiting to board. They showed their papers and tickets, and crossed the ramp to the ferry's deck. An hour later they immersed in inky darkness as the boat headed east across the seventy miles of open sea to England.

The two Irishmen sat uneasily on the wooden pew-like benches that filled the main passenger cabin. They had not been given one of the small yet comfortable berths; they took it in stride.

That night the Irish Sea was a vicious bitch. Passengers went to the rails as often as they went to the ship's heads. The two Irish spies weathered it well. Their two weeks in the submarine had conditioned them to the ocean. They watched their fellow travelers and felt both luck and sympathy. They managed an hour or two of troubled sleep. As the ferry rounded the rocky point of Holyhead Island, the rising sun danced between the piles of clouds blown across from Ireland. To the relief of the passengers, the sea instantly calmed as they passed the breakwater. Nearing the dock, they gathered in the large salon on the main deck and waited in ones and twos. Many seemed nervous. They were about to land in a country at war; every one of them would be considered a potential threat to England. To the German bomber pilots, they were as much a target as the English. Everyone had their papers ready in one hand and their luggage in the other.

Doyle looked through the windows and down to the dock. A dozen soldiers walked the stone quay; all carried rifles at the ready. Two sandbag bunkers, one at each end, were fortified with manned machine guns. Doyle took a deep breath and joined the queue waiting to present their papers. Casey stood five men back.

"Papers," the lieutenant asked when it was Doyle's turn at the impromptu customs station table. The officer held out his hand. There was an impatient flick of his fingers.

Doyle said nothing and handed over his papers.

The officer looked at the papers and then checked a multi-page binder on his desk. He looked up at Doyle and then at a series of pages with photos. He looked again at Doyle's identification papers, and then nodded to one of the soldiers. "Take Mr. Reardon to the hut. I will be there shortly."

Doyle knew something was wrong; he had been through too many of these inspections not to notice the signs. Two soldiers, their rifles aimed at Doyle, motioned him away from the remaining passengers in the queue. He followed their directions and stood off to one side. He took a passing look at Casey, and then looked down at his shoes.

Casey shuffled his way to the table and offered his papers. The officer repeated the same process with the papers and then motioned to a soldier to approach. The soldier leaned into the officer, who whispered something.

"You are coming with me," the soldier ordered Casey. "Stand next to him"—he jerked his thumb in Doyle's direction— "and do not move or say anything."

Casey looked at Doyle for a long moment and then began to walk toward his partner. Doyle shook his head. Casey looked past the soldiers and slowly reached into his pocket.

"No, Colm!" yelled Doyle. "For the love of God, no."

Casey pulled a pistol from his pocket and fired at the soldier directly in front of him. The man fell. He turned to the other guards and fired. One after the other, they dropped. Casey screamed at Doyle to run. He then swung his pistol toward the officer at the desk, and as he brought the weapon to bear, three rifles barked. The bullets struck Casey and spun him to the stone pier. Colm Casey lay still.

Doyle turned and began to run the fifty yards to the end of the pier, praying with each step. His prayers never reached God. The guards opened fire at the fleeing Irishman, knocking his legs out from under him. He tumbled fifteen feet across the pavement, crashing heavily against a sign that welcomed ferry passengers to Wales. The last thing Rian Doyle saw of this world were the grey clouds scudding across the magenta morning sky, an English sky.

Chapter 2

They fled their emerald island,
To America, their new homeland.
There they were called Micks,
No more than dumb hicks,
None failed to dream of their Ireland.

2a

Present Day
Lafayette, California

Geno's Bar is one of those institutions that every American town has or should have. For the quaint village of Lafayette, east of San Francisco, it is the titular political, libational, and judicial center of the town. From lunch through closing, politicians (in favor, and not), cops, lawyers, and average working Joes use it as the place for rest and recovery before heading home. The Bay Area Rapid Transit station, with its rail connections to Oakland and San Francisco, is a short stroll away. And up the street stand city hall and the police station. The proprietress of Geno's is Gina Cavelli, a comely woman who many believe to be the embodiment of two of Italy's greatest cultural contributions to the twentieth century: Sophia Loren's looks and Gina Lollobrigida's style. Ms. Cavelli's hair—usually piled high in a curly salt-and-pepper-colored mountainous confection—suggests family roots somewhere in the Genoa region of northern Italy. Her grandfather Geno moved the establishment's mahogany bar from San Francisco to the Lafayette location after the 1906 earthquake and later passed it on to his son and then to Gina. The place is, as some of the locals say, an institution of high social and historical value. Some have even suggested that a plaque be mounted on the door. Gina said no, it might scare away the loyals. Others, mostly mirthless progressives in town, say it's a tawdry place of ill repute. Gina believes, if that plaque is even posted, that sentiment should be inscribed on the plaque as well.

Sharon O'Mara sat at the bar swirling the icy contents of a tumbler.

"You okay, girl?" Gina asked as she wiped down the wooden bar with a white towel. "You have been in the mopes for the last week. While, at times, it is annoyingly you, it has now just become tedious. What's up?"

Sharon let out a deep sigh; yes, she *had* been in the mopes. She knew it could only be one thing: "I'm getting old."

"That's what's getting you down? You're . . . getting . . . old?"

"Well, maybe that's not it entirely, but it's part of it. I'm sitting here on the ragged cusp of turning very old, ancient in fact, and for some unexplainable reason it's pissing me off."

"What is?" a voice asked from the doorway.

"Good God, look who's now sharing his time with us, his royal lordship Mr. International Consultant himself," Gina said. "Out—we can't afford your hourly rate."

"Really?" Kevin Bryan said as he pulled out the barstool next to Sharon. He dropped his six-foot-six frame onto the padded seat.

Gina smiled. "The usual, your lordship?"

"Seeing this girl here, with that look on her face, make it a double, Gina. I need the courage." He placed a stack of mail, wrapped in a rubber band, on the counter.

"Double Jameson coming up."

Two seconds later, a tumbler full of ice and whiskey dropped in front of him. "Thanks, sweetie."

"Find out what's got her panties all in a twist. I can't seem to get anything out of her. She's mumbling something about getting old."

Kevin leaned over and gave Sharon a kiss on the cheek. "All

right, tell me what's the problem."

Sharon took a sip of her scotch and said, "The clock. I can't stop the clock. Every day I get up, do the same old crap, and then do it again the next day. Going to the farmers' market and Costco seem to be the high points of the week. The gym is becoming annoying; all the members seem younger, stronger, prettier, and have nicer boobs. Even Basil is beginning to sense it. When I suggest a walk, he just harrumphs and stares at me. Then there's the weight thing and the . . ."

"Weight? You look as great as you always do—and I'm not going to say anything about the boobs thing—so all the rest of it is just bullshit. You're delusional."

"I know what I see on the scale in the morning. A woman knows. Even the extra hours at the gym don't seem to help. Then there's the gravity thing."

"Don't talk to me about gravity," Gina said, interrupting. "For some of us more endowed, Newton and his infamous discovery have been less than welcome. So, that's what this is all about, your vanity?"

Kevin crooked his finger to Gina; she came over and leaned in. He whispered in her ear.

"You have got to be kidding. That's it?" Gina turned to Sharon. "This hangdog act is all because you are turning forty? I've literally watched you chase bad guys down the Grand Canal in Venice in a green ball gown. And, from the stories I've heard—sitting at this very bar—even the ghost of Fidel Castro is looking for you. And you sit there bitching about turning forty? Where's my pity towel?"

"A lot of help you are, Mr. Kevin Bryan," Sharon said, turning on Kevin. "That is supposed to be a secret, something I need to go through all by myself."

"Significant life events must be celebrated together with friends and liquor," Gina insisted. "You do not turn forty by yourself—that is a rule. Besides, I've had that date circled on my calendar for almost a year. Maybe we can go somewhere exotic?"

"Like to your Cheesecake Factory?" Sharon said to Kevin.

"I like the place," Kevin said in protest. "What's wrong with—"

Gina, ignoring Kevin, said, "No. I mean exotic, different—maybe even dangerous. How about big-game fishing in Mexico? You like that."

"Not in the mood, and besides the season's not right, although maybe later in the year. And not everyone likes to spend hours in the hot sun chasing big fish."

"I'd do it for you," Kevin offered.

"I may be old, but I'm not a charity case."

"Then stop acting like one," Gina quipped. "No, something that's a once-in-a-lifetime thing, perilous to get to, and where the water's not safe to drink. However, after the last few years and your travels to all the top bad-guy spots like Cuba, and Mexico, and Germany, and . . ."

"Don't forget Amsterdam and London," Kevin chimed in. "Could do London again, minus the kidnappers and the smoked kippers. Clive Barrington still has that open door at his estate in Kent. Now that would be fun."

"Fun but not exciting," Sharon said. "And the guy is so British, stiff upper lippish, and all that rot. Gina, is the game on?"

"Ten minutes ago—Giants are playing in Atlanta."

"Hand me the clicker thingy. I'll find it."

Gina slid the remote down the bar. Sharon aimed it at the flat panel and began clicking; five stations later, she stopped. The Giants were up to bat.

Kevin sipped his whiskey, pulled off the rubber band wrapping his mail, and began to sort through the stack. One pile, on the left, for important stuff, the other pile for the junk.

"How come you don't get catalogs?" Sharon asked, looking at the accumulation on the right.

"You have to order something to get them," Kevin said. "Life is so much simpler if you don't shop online."

"You never shop online?"

"See, it works."

He picked up a thick business envelope made with high-quality paper and studied it closely. It was covered with postal stamps from Ireland. In the upper corner, the name *O'Shaunnessy, Little, and Lynch, Solicitors*, and then underneath, *Dublin, Ireland*, was printed in black ink.

"Strange," Kevin said. "This doesn't seem like junk mail."

Sharon took the envelope and felt its thickness. "Too thin to be an IRA bomb." She then sniffed. "Lawyers—I can smell them by the stink they leave."

"It says it on the envelope."

"Yes, but you can still tell by their musky skunk-like scent."

Kevin extracted a small penknife from his pocket. He slid the blade along the envelope's edge and retrieved a sheaf of unfolded documents. His friends watched as he read the papers, growing agitated as he finished perusing each sheet and placed them one on top of the other. He pointed to his drink, then to Gina. "Another, please."

"What's up?" Sharon asked.

"My great-aunt passed away, my Aunt Brona O'Bryan. I haven't seen her since I was twenty or so. To be honest, I'd almost forgotten all about her. My folks took me to the old country and County Cork when I was maybe eight or nine. We traveled all over the south of Ireland, then one day—it was raining, as I remember—we stopped at a massive house. All dark stone and, for me, quite scary. Thinking about it now, it was like Downton Abbey."

"Scared? You?" Gina said.

"Shush, I'm listening," Sharon said.

"Dad said that this was the old family estate—*Baile O'Bryan* he called it. Translates roughly into 'home of the O'Bryans'—been in the family for more than three hundred years. When I was there last, soon after college, I thought it was a falling-down wreck of a building; some of the windows were broken, a real mess. Hell, I haven't thought about that place in years. We were never close to the Ireland O'Bryans, such as they were then. Not much has changed."

He accepted the drink Gina proffered, nodded his thanks, and took a few quick sips.

"Brona was in her mid-seventies then. Quite a woman, reminded me of Maureen O'Hara, even to the eyes and red hair, though her hair was well greyed by then. I thought she was beautiful, probably a knockout when she was young. She was aloof. Even when I was there, she kept to herself. I saw her only in the evenings; she had a cook or something that served some of the most awful Irish food. Spent three days there, and now that I think of it, that's when I developed my aversion to lamb or anything from the sheep family."

"You wear wool," Gina reminded him.

"I don't eat my sweaters, do I?"

"She lived in the big house?" Sharon asked. "Was she married?"

"She never married, and yes, upstairs. Soon after World War II, her parents died—my great-great-aunt and uncle. Brona inherited the estate. I am the great-grandson of one of the brothers of her grandfather. He was the one who shortened the O'Bryan name to Bryan when he arrived in America. That was sometime in the 1890s. I'm a loose connection at best. As a result, this letter is quite a surprise."

"Why's that?" Sharon asked.

"Because she left me the Baile O'Bryan estate."

2b

The Giants were up one to nothing after the first. Kevin Bryan was up one castle to none.

"You have got to be kidding me," Gina blurted. "You really are an earl or a duke or something?"

"Hardly, but it is a big pile as they call it in British parlance," Kevin said. "And a pile is what it was more than twenty years ago. I can only imagine what it's like now."

"She may have fixed it up," Sharon added hopefully. "Where

is it?"

"On the rugged coast of County Cork, maybe thirty miles from Cork City. I remember views out to the Celtic Sea and knee-deep green grass and sheep—lots and lots of sheep."

"Sounds beautiful," Gina added.

"Maybe, but even today everyone lives on the edge in that part of Ireland. Nothing has changed over the last twenty years."

He told them that after the Rising of 1916, the partition, and Ireland's eventual independence, the O'Bryans, according to Kevin's father, were put on a list. The British made sure that those who may have played some part in the war were prevented from entering into any serious financial ventures that involved England. All business interests and connections were terminated.

"They were left out to dry, so to speak," Sharon mused.

"Exactly. It destroyed what little income the estate had. The civil war then took its toll; the Irish Republican Brotherhood and the Irish Citizen Army fought it out after the British left, even setting brothers and sisters against each other. All extremely nasty: the Catholics made sure the local Protestants were uncomfortable, and many of them fled to Northern Ireland. The Protestants then made it tough for Catholics in the north. The Irish Republican Army—that gang came out of the civil war—eventually became the terrorists that we know now. The worst were the Provisionals, the Provos. Very nasty, more like gangsters than freedom fighters."

"What's that have to do with your estate?" Gina asked.

"It's not my estate, yet," Kevin said. He held up one of the papers and pointed to a section in the middle. Both Sharon and Gina looked, and then gasped.

"My God," Sharon said. "Really?"

"Yes, it's all mine. All I have to do is pay the one and a half million euros in back taxes—due for the last thirty years."

"And for your lordship, I assume that is a problem?" Gina said, setting another Jameson on the bar.

Kevin gave her one of his patented looks that, at one time,

told criminals during his days as a Lafayette police detective that their smart-ass remark was not going to be tolerated.

"I know, I know, I get it. But wow, what a cool thing," Gina said.

"Yes, maybe. But obviously this tax lien is a slight bump in the road to my future as an Irish lord and manor owner."

Sharon pointed to her tumbler. Gina nodded. When the refreshed glass was set on the bar, Sharon said, "I have an idea, a little crazy, but hear me out. First, our friend here may have to go to Ireland to sort all this out. Two, I know quite well he does not travel well and will need care and assistance. Three, I have never been to the country of my own family's roots. This"—she used both hands to gesture at her red hair and pale, pinkish complexion—"came from somewhere on that island, and it would give me a chance to check out my heritage. And five, it is my birthday, and I think it would be a great place to have a party."

"I have been told the Irish do not take second place to anyone who is celebrating almost anything," Gina said.

"An expert speaks," Sharon said, smiling at Gina.

"Really?" Kevin said. "I have no desire to go and deal with some shyster Irish lawyers who are probably out to rip me off. And the plane ride will be a literal pain in the ass."

"You survived the last two trips as security consultant to that diamond importer."

"They provided first-class tickets—not steerage."

"Sharon, this is an idea that needs exploring," Gina said.

"Maybe we can invite some others to come and join us," Sharon said. "Stay at the castle, walk the hills and dales, look at the sea, watch the grass and sheep grow. It could be fun and not like riding shotgun through the hills of Cuba."

"Sharon, please don't make more of this than it is," Kevin pleaded.

"We can invite Claudette LeClair, Jean-François, Evelyn Lucca."

"Totally forgot," Gina added. "Evelyn had a meeting out

here this afternoon. She said she'd stop by."

"How is she?" Kevin asked, looking for any reason to change the subject. "I haven't seen her in months."

"Doing well," Gina said. "Says her business is up with the economy turning around, and they have opened three new stores, one in Vancouver. We trade emails and Facebook. It will be good to see her."

As if cued, Evelyn Lucca walked through the door and gave Kevin a big hug around his middle. Evelyn being five-foot-five and Kevin being six-foot-six made for a fascinating picture of contrasts. Evelyn and the Lucca family owned the STIA international chain of shops that sold their own brand of exclusive and very high-end handbags and leather goods. Headquartered in Florence, Italy, a STIA Leather Goods boutique was now in almost every major city on every continent, except Antarctica. There were rumors in the *Wall Street Journal*, seemingly every week, about some suitor or conglomerate trying to buy the company. Evelyn swore that would never happen, only she and her family could control the operation to the level of quality they demanded. Evelyn lived in San Francisco but spent weeks at a time at the family villa outside Florence. Her days often would go to eighteen hours, and she loved every minute of those hours.

Sharon slid off her barstool and gave Evelyn the classic cheek and cheek kiss. Evelyn took a seat on the open stool next to Sharon.

"Evelyn?" Gina asked.

"Just a glass of Chardonnay, then I need to go home and get some sleep. My brother is in town tomorrow on his way to Japan. We have a lot to discuss before he leaves; we are looking at Beijing and even Chengdu for stores. Who would have believed that fifteen years ago?"

"To STIA, still love their handbags," Sharon said as she fondly stroked her own dark green bag on the bar. "Congratulations."

"Are you still in the dumps? Gina said you've been . . ."

"Gina, is my personal life a book you open to everyone?"

"It is—for some of my friends—if you sit at this bar. I manage the support groups."

"I'll remember that. Evelyn, what do you know about Ireland?"

"Other than a future store location in Dublin, very little."

Sharon told her about Kevin's new inheritance while he unsuccessfully tried to downplay the whole thing.

Evelyn looked at the man and smiled. "My condolences. Our family has a couple of these things floating around Italy, France, and even something in Croatia. They are all a pain in the butt."

"A nice pain, I'm sure," Gina said.

"Sometimes, but still expensive pains. I can recommend an attorney that could be helpful if you need them. Due to the growth in Ireland and before everything went sideways, we had some warehousing there. They could be helpful."

"Thanks, that's appreciated." Kevin gave Evelyn a kiss on the cheek.

For the next ten minutes, the friends discussed the Giants and their first-place standing only a game ahead of the hated Dodgers. At a commercial break, Sharon asked that Gina pour a round for everyone on her, and then she announced to the three friends: "I have come to a big decision. I have decided, for my fortieth birthday, *we* all absolutely shall go to Ireland."

Gina, noting how Sharon had brightened, spoke up. "A brilliant idea, anything to get your sad butt out of here. However, what do you mean 'we,' *kemosabe*?"

2c

Kevin asked, "What the hell are you talking about?"

"Yes, I think it would be great," Sharon said. "Places we have never been, things to see and do; it will be—how did you say it in Venice, Gina?"

"*Spettacolare?*"

"Exactly, spectacular."

"I can't say that it wouldn't be fun," Evelyn said. "I could use a vacation, and besides I would only be an hour and a half away from Florence. Sounds enticing."

"Don't do it, Evelyn. You are falling into her trap. It's all too crazy, if you ask me," Kevin said.

"Well, it's a thought, and the more I think about it—it will be fun. Something totally out of normal," Sharon said. "And we can deal with your castle at the same time."

"That is the problem. It is out of the normal—even for you," Kevin said.

The Giants won the game, and ten minutes later Sharon pulled into the narrow driveway next to her Walnut Creek cottage. Basil sat patiently in the window, watching. He hurried to greet her at the back door.

"Down, down, I have only been gone a few hours, you're fine." She let the German Shepherd–Rottweiler hurry by her and out into the small garden behind the house; he returned a few seconds later. She put a large bowl of kibble on the floor that he quickly wolfed down. When he finished, he found Sharon sitting at her computer; the image on the screen was the Google Earth view of Ireland.

"What do you think; could you let me go for a couple of weeks while I tour the home of my ancestors with friends?"

As if reading her thoughts, Basil turned and headed to his bed, spun three times, and then collapsed. His head hung over the side of the bed as he stared at her.

"Don't give me that look. It's as strange as the one Kevin made."

At the mention of Kevin, Basil's eyebrows raised then just as quickly lowered.

"Great, now I have to figure out how to keep you happy, too."

She turned back to the screen and started pounding away on search sites. Yes, a vacation would be nice.

The images of Ireland looked fascinating and exotic, and above all completely safe. Dublin, Trinity College, lush green hills, dramatic cliffs overlooking the surrounding seas, cute villages nestled in glens, all beautiful. As for the cost, her two-year-old business as a facilitator, taking on odd contract jobs to help friends and friends of friends, was doing well. She had rescued a kidnapped family of one of the Giants' baseball players, saved enslaved Chinese women from some expatriated Tongs in Oakland and San Francisco, but nearly got killed by some leftover Nazis from Hitler's German Reich. Over the last few years, she'd put away a nice, tidy sum of dollars, and on top the surprise inheritance from one of those clients. Her finances were now better than ever.

Basil's ears perked up when Sharon's phone began to chime an old Italian operatic overture.

"You've not gone to bed?" Sharon said, looking at Gina's name on the screen.

"Just getting home," Gina answered. "You know my hours are the least normal of anyone you know. And besides, after what you said tonight, I just knew you would still be up. What you suggested sounds great. Kevin needs all our support. With us there, we can keep him out of trouble."

"And who is going to keep you out of trouble? It does sound like fun. I can help you with expenses if you need it."

"Not a chance."

"It's a serious idea," Sharon said.

"More like an insane suggestion," Gina answered.

"Well then, a suggestion, but I meant it all the same. And I'm getting excited, too. It would be fun to do something without the chance of being killed or at least maimed."

"Stop saying that. Tell you what, I'll stop by in the morning and we can talk about it. Get some sleep, I'll bring pastries at ten, and then we can have a girl-to-girl. Okay?"

Sharon thought for a moment. "Okay, you know which bakery?"

"Yes, I do. Go to bed—I'll see you in the morning."

* * * *

Morning arrived with Basil's face a half inch from Sharon's nose at 6:30 AM.

"It's too damn early. Go lay down."

Basil had heard that admonishment more than once; he would not be dissuaded and continued to breathe heavily into her face.

"Dog, give me a break, please."

When nature calls, it calls. Basil, being the excellent product of years of good training and less than respectful breeding, did his best, but there came a point. A point that even Sharon knew could not be denied—a dog will do what a dog will do. As such, a few minutes later, she found herself padding down the hallway with the big mutt more than thankful for her attention. After opening the back door, Sharon leaned against the frame and sighed. Time and gravity could not be stopped.

She quickly dressed in her gym clothes and drove the half mile to the fitness center. This morning it was aerobics and stretching. Ninety minutes later and soaked in sweat, she threw a protective towel over the leather seat of her Jaguar sedan and headed home. Coffee perked as she showered, and at precisely 10 AM, the doorbell rang. Basil, trained not to bark, stood at full attention halfway down the hall, looking back and forth at the front door and then at his mistress as she walked to the door. A quick glance through the glass window showed only the top of Gina's head.

"Good morning, sunshine," Gina said as she scratched the top of Basil's head. "And how are you, big guy?" Basil's tail swung back and forth with great sweeping arcs almost touching the walls of the hallway.

"Coffee's ready," Sharon said.

The two friends followed the dog into the bright kitchen; Gina placed the bag of bakery goods on the table. "Have you had a chance to come back to reality?" she asked.

"I still think it's a great idea. In fact, I want to make it even more fun," Sharon said.

"How so?"

"More people than just us four, and besides I think that Kevin would be more amenable if there were a few other guys along. If it were just us girls, he'd probably find a way to say no.

So, we invite a few others."

"One should be Claudette LeClair," Gina said. "At least then Kevin will have someone to talk to. She's sweet and plays well with others, and I like her."

Claudette was the granddaughter of one of Sharon's former clients, Alain Dumont. He had hired Sharon to return some very valuable Impressionist paintings to a Jewish family in Los Angeles after he found out that the art rightfully belonged to them. During the war, Alain and some fellow soldiers had discovered the paintings in an underground cave in the German countryside where they had been hidden by the Nazis. Alain had passed away a few years earlier and left Sharon a significant bundle of Apple shares in his will. She went from living month to month to being set for life.

"Yes, Claudette would be perfect," Sharon said to Gina. "We could see if JF and your friend Fidor Balanca are available?"

At the mention of Balanca's name, Gina blushed.

"I knew it," Sharon said. "Look at you, all pink and pretty. Yes, definitely Fidor. You were one very naughty girl if I remember."

"Me? What about JF?"

Jean-François Voss was another of Sharon's clients. JF, as his friends called him, had been recommended to her by Evelyn. He hired Sharon to investigate the mysterious death of his twin sister, Catherine. Fidor Balanca was a friend of JF's from Saint Petersburg. The Russian was rumored to be involved with the mob or politicians; it wasn't easy to tell the difference in Russia. While in Venice during the America's Cup sailboat race preliminaries, Gina and Fidor had a heated fling.

"What a group," Sharon said, avoiding Gina's question. "But now that leaves Evelyn odd woman out. How are we going to fix that?"

"Well, there is that policeman from London, Clive Barrington. When Clive was here, after all the chaos of the All-Star Game and the arrest of Marta de la Vega, Evelyn seemed to enjoy his company the night of the ball game."

"That might be an idea."

Gina thought for a moment. "Well, there's only one way to find out," she said, looking as pleased with herself as if it had been she who had come up with the idea of the trip to begin with. "Let's call them."

Chapter 3

There was a lass, her hands full of gold,
An angelic dancer, truth be told.
She whirled in delight,
Flung the coins to the night,
Then tumbled, her sweet face—now ice cold.

3a

A hundred feet above Clonakilty Bay, Molly O'Rourke braced herself against the cold gusts of wind that whipped up the ragged face of the cliff. Her black hair whipped about her face, the wind brought tears, and the long woolen cloak she wore pushed tight against her lanky body. The sizable Irish setter, Dergo, stood close to her leg. His red fur rustled in the wind. She had inherited the dog from Brona O'Bryan. She did not want the farm animals, the worn and weathered house, and she certainly did not want the debts associated with all of it.

She raised the binoculars she carried and scanned the sea, her eyes traveling to the far cliffs across the bay and up the Clonakilty River. There was a time when ships with shallow drafts would slide up the river and across the bar during high tide, unload their cargo, and then drift back to the sea on the next outgoing flow. But no more; that era had passed, and the sandbar had filled in across the cove.

The ship she now watched for was late.

The life she lived was not one she would have chosen if God had given her a choice. Nonetheless, it suited her, and besides, the ghosts of Ireland hadn't given her much of a choice. For more than three hundred years, her people had earned a living from the sea. Not by fishing with a net or a hook; the O'Rourkes and their kindred were smugglers. The rationale was simple: there always would be those with needs, and there would be those who would provide for those needs. And, when those in power—the elites, the royals, the landlords, even the church— wanted more money, they would tax the citizens or, even worse, outright steal it. Call them vices, or sins, or just nasty habits—if common people wanted to enjoy themselves, they had to pay, and the powerful would tax them. Many in the past were hanged for not paying the rich their due.

A fact of the twenty-first century was that one nasty habit, smoking, was the most easily punished. Every country in Europe imposed a "moral" tax, purportedly to curb the poor choice of their citizenry to use tobacco. And there were no higher taxes levied in Europe than those imposed by Britain and Ireland. Driven by the resultant high prices and insatiable demand, there would be those who would provide the product to the people—the market—at a significantly reduced price. Call it the free market. The pages of the *Irish Times* and the London papers made out that smugglers were rich as bloody kings. The papers said those selling black-market cigarettes, drugs, and other illicit and illegal goods made millions. Molly O'Rourke knew better; the numbers the police posted on their Internet and news sites as well as what the newspapers reported were all blown-up lies and exaggerations. *Who the hell do they think I am, a fucken' bloody Columbian cocaine cartel?*

Molly was not alone on the bluff. Now she turned to one of the two people standing behind her. "When is she due, Sean?" It was a question for which she already knew the answer.

"Sundown. She will signal with a series of flashes, then maneuver into the lee side of the bay. Our boats will motor out to her, transfer the boxes, and then slip back into the bay. They will unload at the usual inlets and beaches. Approximately a third of the boxes to each boat. Should be over in less than an hour."

"Then where the hell is she?" O'Rourke said, again scanning

the sea.

As the sun neared the horizon, she spotted the black bow of a low-slung freighter rounding Galley Head Point. Five minutes later, as the sun disappeared into the sea, a light flashed from the bridge of the ship.

"The signal's correct, ma'am."

"Call the boats. Make the rendezvous."

"Yes, ma'am," Sean answered and began to punch in a text message on his phone.

Molly watched the ship glide into Dirk Bay, and even at this distance she heard the anchor chain as it played out. In the gloaming that overtook the pastures, quietness fell across the rugged cliffs of County Cork. The richness and aromas of the earth and grass washed across the three people watching the action below. Dergo sniffed.

Three speedboats crossed the bay, each from a different direction. In minutes, they had tied up to the freighter. Through night-vision binoculars, O'Rourke watched as box after box of cigarettes was transferred to each speedboat. Sean's phone pinged.

"They are done, ma'am. Shall I signal the bank?"

"Yes and tell our boys thanks." Sean already was texting as Molly added, "And inform the captain we enjoyed doing business with him."

So far, so good. Fifty cartons in each case; fifty cases in each boat; twenty-five hundred cartons. She calculated everything in English pounds. She had paid two hundred and fifty pounds for each case. If the market held, she would sell them for five times that in England. She might clear a hundred thousand pounds. She looked at the boats as they each headed in a different direction. After her people were paid—maybe seventy-five thousand pounds. *Shit, what a stupid way to make millions.* If they were pinched, the press would announce that 7,500 packs of illegal cigarettes had been recovered worth more than a million pounds. *I can only wish—assholes.*

"The captain says thank you. The account transfer is

verified."

"Excellent, let's get out of here."

Dergo leading the way, they walked back to the rusted and beat-up delivery van parked on the blind side of a stone wall hidden from the local two-lane highway. The lettering on the van's side read *Clonakilty Bakery*. Sean Doyle took the driver's seat and his younger sister, Corinne, climbed in the back. Molly O'Rourke took the left-hand passenger's seat and lit a cigarette. Dergo curled expertly next to Corinne and watched Molly.

"The boys will meet tomorrow morning at the warehouse," Sean said as they pulled onto the dark, empty lane.

Molly didn't answer right away but looked out into the Irish night as they headed back toward Clonakilty. She then asked, "Which of the boats is going to the O'Bryan tunnel?"

"Tommy's," Corinne said.

O'Rourke didn't say anything.

"He'll be fine, ma'am. Tommy can get a little crazy, but he will be all right."

"Who was with him?"

"Mac," Corinne said.

"At least Mac will keep him out of trouble," Sean said.

Tommy O'Rourke was Molly's twenty-two-year-old nephew, the son of her dead older sister who was found with a needle in her arm in a Dublin woman's room when Tommy was five years old. Molly was sure the drugs had fucked up the boy before he was born. Molly was all he had, and he was more than a handful; in fact, he was as dangerous as a snake under your shoe. Ready to strike at a moment, he had lived by his fists in the housing projects of Cork until, when he was fifteen, Molly finally got him out.

Adam MacLeish, Mac as he was called, came from an old Cork family and was one of the few men who could control the boy. It was a makeshift father-son relationship that tenuously held itself together. Tommy calmed when Mac was around, but then Mac had his own sad story. Born in Skibbereen, he was orphaned when he was twelve years old and had, with help from his grandmother, raised his two brothers and two sisters. Self-educated and a pledged bachelor, MacLeish eventually fell in with the local gang, run by Brona O'Bryan, that smuggled everything worth a penny into Ireland. "Anything for a shilling," Brona would say. Mac never talked of his younger years, but the rumor was that he had spent ten of them in the north with the Provisional Irish Republican Army. Few people talked about the Provos, especially in the far south of Ireland, and never once had Mac mentioned any association with the IRA. If Brona O'Bryan knew anything about the man, she took it with her to the grave, a grave that Adam MacLeish dug by himself in the old St. Mary's cemetery.

Mac quickly realigned himself with the younger Molly O'Rourke. The joke going around was that Mac needed the strong arm and will of a woman to keep him on the straight and narrow. Mac contributed to the joke—his humor was ribald and raunchy and added much to late-night backroom tavern meetings. His limericks voiced the realities behind the grey vale of Irish life. Truth be told, Mac enjoyed the steadiness of a woman's thinking; he thought they were the better half of the human species. After Ulster and Belfast, he was certain of it.

"Text Mac," Molly said to Corinne. "Tell him I'll meet him at the O'Bryan cottage, twenty minutes."

3b

It took Mac, Tommy, and another young man named Albert an hour to move the fifty cartons up from the beach, to the tunnel, and up the stairs to the room under the Baile O'Bryan cottage.

"Why did that woman never put a fucken' elevator in this tunnel?" Tommy complained.

"If she had, it would not be a secret tunnel, now would it, Tommy?" Mac said as they stacked the last of the cartons against the wall. "That tunnel has been under this house since before the landlords. God knows how it's been kept secret, but it has. Some say that more than a few have died keeping it safe from the ears of the English."

Mac's phone pinged, and he looked at the screen.

"Then they were idiots," Tommy said, lighting a cigarette.

"You should quit those things. It will be better for you," Mac said to Tommy.

"Helps to calm me jitters."

"You are far too young to have jitters," Mac said, turning to Albert. "The boss is on her way. Go upstairs and wait for her. No lights, mind you; use your torch."

Albert Corrigan had been with MacLeish for fifteen of his twenty-four years—another one of Mac's orphan projects. Albert had been found sitting in the last pew of St. Mary's Church in Clonakilty. He said he was nine years old and had taken the bus south from Dublin. No parents ever claimed him; none reported him gone. Mac raised him like he was his son, but Mac also understood the boy was damaged—a bit slow, not a lot, just a little around the edges.

Albert never left Mac's side unless dispatched on some errand. Now he waited in the dark recess between the main house and the old cottage. The stone and wood cottage had been built over the hidden basement where the tunnel up from the beach terminated. Two hundred years earlier, the house proper had been strategically placed to afford the best views from the high windows to the east, north, and west. A tower to one side provided an elevated view to the south. At the building's back, a hundred and fifty yards away, the cliff's edge overlooked Dirk Bay and the Celtic Sea. The tunnel, used for centuries by County Cork smugglers, was a crack in the cliff that, for uncounted years, provided a subterranean connection between the top of the cliff and the sandy cove at its base.

As Albert watched, headlights bounced along the narrow two-lane road and then veered onto the driveway that coursed its way down the gentle hill above the farm. A delivery van silently rolled to a stop in the courtyard. Three people emerged and began to walk toward the old house.

* * * *

"Late evening, ma'am, isn't it?" Albert said.

The sudden movement of Sean Doyle drawing his pistol was more of a surprise than Albert's greeting.

"Yes, it is, Albert. And put that away, Sean. You know better," Molly said.

Chagrined, Sean slipped the pistol back into his coat pocket. "Sorry, ma'am, just a little edgy."

"You are always edgy," Corinne said. "You should cut back on the coffee, especially at night."

"And you, Sis, should keep your tongue still," Sean answered. She gave him the finger.

Dergo, his gate measured and lithe, went to Albert and put his big head in the young man's hand. Albert reciprocated by scratching the hound's head.

The four walked to the arcade built to connect the older building with the newer cottage. O'Rourke pushed the door open into a small foyer. Albert shut the door behind them and clicked on the four wall sconces that illuminated the room's wooden paneling. A large painting of an O'Bryan ancestor hung on the right-hand wall. Its gilded frame trapped the image of a handsome man in an Irish kilt and jaunty cap, broadsword hilt in his hands. Three Irish wolfhounds surrounded his long legs.

"Your lordship," Molly said with a bow to the painting. She then pushed the lower right corner and rotated the painting about four inches, left. A moment later, the wall panel moved and began to open. It slid sideways into a narrow gap in the wall, leaving a narrow man-sized door. Another wall sconce in this new chamber cast a light down a steep wooden stairway.

"Is that you, ma'am?" a voice called up from below.

"Yes, Mac. It's me. We are coming down."

They gathered in the cellar under the cottage. It smelled of old wood and salt air. The cigarette boxes were piled five high and ten wide across the far stone-faced wall. Two cots were stacked against the opposite wall. There were no windows in the cellar, and if they turned off the light, it would be as dark as the last dungeon cell in Limerick Prison.

"You know the drill," Molly said. "Mac, make sure the other cases are collected and taken to the Clonakilty warehouse. Once there, Corinne will handle the distribution to Dublin and England."

She handed him a thin stack of envelopes. "Make sure these get where they are supposed to."

"Have I ever not, ma'am?" Mac said with a wink.

"No, but these are strange times, so watch the others when you collect the boxes. Tommy will have your back." She looked at her nephew.

"No worries," Tommy said.

She handed out more envelopes to the four men and one woman.

"Albert, you be careful now about this, understand?"

"Yes, ma'am," Albert said. "Mac and I have talked it over. Besides, I give it to him so he can take care of it. He knows I can be forgetful."

"We have it covered, ma'am," Mac added. "Are you returning with us?"

"No, I'll walk—much to consider. Go home; I will call you when I need you."

Dergo at her side, Molly watched as the others climbed the stairs. She waited until the door slid to a hard close and she heard the click of the lock before crossing to the massive door on the far wall. Even though more than two hundred years old, the iron bolt slid almost noiselessly from its seat in the door's frame. The door had been built to withstand almost any brute human force that might try to force it open. It would hold long enough to give a few minutes time and some distance from pursuers coming up from below and the sea. Using the iron loop handle, she pulled the door open and ran her hand down the door's edge. Not for the first time, she wondered what it had seen over the last centuries. Who had come up this stairway or who had escaped? Every smugglers' tunnel runs both ways.

Picking up a lantern, she clicked it on, and walked into the passageway. Electric lights had never been installed, but approximately every fifty feet a cut-stone ledge protruded from the face of the tunnel. Old wax drippings hung from the shelves; in spots, the damp floor had collected a small cone of melted candle wax. After one hundred yards, Molly abruptly stopped. Without her knowledge or a light to warn her, she would have tumbled more than fifty feet down the steep stone stairs. With no one to find her, she would probably die a painful, broken death. Two electric lanterns sat on the ground near the top step; she turned one on and, leaving it there on the floor, began her descent. The setter, his vision better than hers, led the way. When she was a child, she had counted exactly one hundred and five steps to a landing about halfway down. On her first trip down the stairs, she was frightened.

"Just stay close, Molly. I will protect you."

Molly had followed behind the tall woman. The hiss from a gas lantern filled the stairway. The noise was like a thousand snakes were sliding down the stairs with them. That was thirty years earlier. Another Irish setter, the great-grandsire of Dergo, had led the way.

"Do you have that piece of chalk I gave you?" Brona had asked.

"Yes, Auntie," she said affectionately, even though Brona was not her relation.

"I want you to write your name right here." Brona pointed to a spot. "Just below my name. I wrote that many, many years ago. Put yours right under it."

Ten-year-old Molly O'Rourke did as instructed.

"You have very nice penmanship, Molly. The sisters teach you well."

"I try very hard, but they sometimes called me hopeless. Auntie, I have lots of hope."

"It is those ladies in their stiff outfits who are hopeless. You have your whole life in front of you. Make something of it."

"I will, Auntie. How much farther?" Molly asked, trying to muster a brave sound to her young voice.

"We are almost there. How many steps did you count?"

"One hundred and five."

"Excellent. Now, remember that number, and let's begin again."

"One, two, three," Molly said as they began the final leg of the descent.

3c

After Molly O'Rourke returned from her inspection of the stairway, the tunnel, and the narrow sand beach and landing, she secured all the doors and locks. As a young woman, she had been impressed by the ancient artisans who had built this intricate system of locks and doors; she still was. She knew that, today, mechanical brute force and explosives would easily foil the system, and in the process, destroy all this beauty. This was designed and built by an artist. Only the initials WCW appeared on a few of the locks, initials for a name lost to history.

The morning sun was high over the empty paddock that paralleled the entry drive when she left the cottage. Three barns flanked the sides of the fenced area. Unmowed grass filled the old pens; in places, the wooden rails had fallen. Molly could not remember the last time she had seen an animal in the paddocks.

After removing a large biscuit for Dergo, she slipped a canvas bag over her shoulder and headed to the path that wound its way through the stone walls and fields back to Clonakilty. After the long night, the fresh air invigorated her. She had thought about staying at the cottage, as the nineteenth-century addition was called, but she was unsure how the Dublin solicitors would take it. Since the death of Brona O'Bryan, four months earlier, she had heard stories and speculations about the disposition of the house and estate. Rumors, to be sure, but they concerned her. There had been talk of selling the house and land off at a discount. Some were sure the taxes were more than any of it was worth. The most intriguing was that Brona had left everything to her only living relative, a man, who lived somewhere in California. Molly wondered about the man, who he was and why someone would want this old wreck of a farm.

She stopped on the crest of the hill that looked down on the baile, the cottage, and the farm buildings. The house had developed a swayback along its ridgeline, windows were broken or missing on the ground floor, and weeds choked the once beautiful gardens that Brona had revived during the war. In many ways, the buildings had taken on the appearance of Auntie Brona in her last years. From a distance graceful and elegant, but in close, tired, worn out, lost, and broken.

If only I had a million euros, Molly thought. *Yes, just a million.*

* * * *

The warehouse stood just outside of Clonakilty's colorful downtown. Disguised as a functioning auto repair shop, it was surrounded by dozens of old cars, providing a makeshift battlement that enclosed the one-story building. It, or another similar building, had sat on this site since before the Uprising a hundred years earlier. As with the cottage at Baile O'Bryan, inventive technicians had built storage under the floor of the warehouse as well as tunnels that extended to two other buildings. These buildings were residential duplexes; their basements provided additional storage. Molly O'Rourke lived in the upper unit over one of these storage cellars. To all in town, she was a businesswoman who ran one of the best bakeries in West Cork. Her scones were gobbled up by the tourists, and her bread was found in the local grocer and in the restaurants of two of Clonakilty's finest resorts. Some days, how she kept her two disparate businesses separate in her head amazed even her.

The delivery vans had come to the warehouse, dropped their cargo, and gone. Mac had thanked the men and paid them. He trusted them with his life. Some had been with him in Belfast, the others he had grown up with. They all had family histories that interconnected and interbred for hundreds of years. Smuggling—as well as silence—was in their blood.

The next few days would require Mac, and a few of the boys, to move some of the boxes to specially constructed lorries that would transport the contraband to the ferry terminals at Wexford and Dublin. From there, the two trucks would travel separately to Liverpool and Pembroke. Molly O'Rourke had learned never to put all her eggs in the same basket. The return trip would be trickier. For every carton of cigarettes sent to England, twenty-five English pounds would return to the warehouse. Her people in England handled the distribution of the cartons of cigarettes and the collection of the money. Molly and Mac were the only ones who could open the truck's smuggling compartments in Ireland. Molly could only guess, hope, and at times pray for how long their secret would stay hidden. Only she and McLeish knew about the cache of money in the basement safe.

Molly had slept through the day. Now she poured herself a whiskey and settled into one of the large chairs in the parlor. At the sound of the doorbell, she activated her mobile and tapped in a set of numbers. The screen showed Mac casually standing at the front door. She clicked through the other cameras that displayed the grounds as she walked to a panel at the top of the stairs. She buzzed him in.

"Did ye enjoy your stroll, ma'am?" Mac asked as he handed her a bag. The smell of Italian food filled the entry.

"Thank you, Mac. I did," she said, taking their dinner. "How is Albert?"

"The lad is well. He's home watching the tele. He is a fan of the gardening shows; maybe that's something I can get him interested in. The boy could make a good gardener. It would be something that he could do if I weren't in the picture. There's some meatballs for the mutt in the container."

Dergo had already smelled the meatballs and sat staring at the box as Molly began to take the cartons out of the bag.

"Are you planning to leave us?" she asked.

"In this line of work, we all need contingencies. The boy would not do well in prison."

"Pleasant thought," Molly said as she set the table. "It is good that you think of him. There are a few estates around here and just as many golf courses and resorts that could use a lad like him. Would you like me to make a few calls?" She set a bottle of wine on the table.

"That would be kind of ye, the calls I mean," Mac said later, as he twirled his spaghetti. "The boy must be taken care of. Though, I think he could manage being on his own now."

"I'm sure that he could."

They finished their dinner in silence, each lost in their own thoughts. The two had worked together for more than twenty years. Since his return from the north, Mac had steered away from any additional entanglements with the Provisionals. They stopped and talked a few times, but he told them the past was past. He had responsibilities. The boy and driving deliveries for the bakery were more than enough, he'd told them. His monthly trips to England with a van full of packaged baked goods allowed him to cover their living expenses. Mac and Albert paid for everything with cash. Keeping a low profile was enough of a bother; Mac did not need the sticky fingers of the IRA meddling in his life again.

"Next week we need to make two trips. The warehouse is full, and product needs to be moved. Will that work with your schedule?" Molly asked.

"Yes, no problems. Sean and Corinne will take one of the trucks. I'll take Tommy with me in the other. Albert will stay at the bakery."

"Good," she answered. "Albert could work with us in the bakery."

"Yes, but I think, in time, he should keep his distance from us. You know that all this could be gone in a day or even a moment."

"Yes, I understand. I'll make the calls."

They rinsed the plates and stacked them in the sink. After refilling their glasses, they took the stairs to the basement, where they passed through a pair of locked steel doorways to enter a small room hidden behind a wall that resembled a poured-in-place concrete panel. Like the foyer door in the entry to the cottage basement, the panel slid quietly to the side, revealing a massive wall safe. Above the safe door and cast into the steel panel was an inscription: *BANK OF DUBLIN — 1904.*

Chapter 4

This Irish lad, a grandson of O'Bryan,
Flew with friends o'er the sea to Ireland.
After enduring the hassle,
They teased: Where is this castle?
"On a cliff, entirely made of sand."

4a

The Aer Lingus A330 banked gently over the River Liffey and Dublin City as it made its approach to Dublin Airport. With the last payment from his consulting work in London finally in the bank, Kevin splurged. He, Sharon, and Gina bought seats in business class. Sharon insisted that she front the difference for Gina to sit with them. Gina did not argue.

Using her birthday as an excuse, Sharon had enlisted Jean-François Voss, Claudette LeClair, Fidor Balanca, and Evelyn Lucca into her international birthday party. Kevin tried to get London police superintendent Clive Barrington to join them, but, for now, Barrington demurred.

"A big case here, Bryan. Can't leave just now," Barrington said. "Why don't you join me in Kent when you are done in Ireland? There's plenty of room."

Kevin, with group approval, tentatively accepted the offer. "I will send you an email if there is a change. I'm not sure what I'll find in Cork."

"Good luck with that. County Cork is pretty, but be careful with that estate. I know what you are getting into with an old pile of brick and stone."

Barrington's country estate was located near Tunbridge Wells in Kent, south of London. The county has been called the Garden of England, and his was in the running with some of the best for grounds and gardens. The estate had been in his family since the days of King Henry VIII; its history was as rocky as many of Henry's marriages. The Barrington family had managed to retain the property after World War II when taxes put hundreds of other estates on the block. It still cost a small fortune to maintain, the result being that a portion of the house had been turned into a luxury bed-and-breakfast, restaurant, and must-see garden. A bachelor, Clive Barrington lived on the upper floor with his two beagles, an untold number of cats, a valet, a housekeeper, and a cook. He spent his weekdays in London and his infrequent long weekends in Kent. Barrington was a London copper; his current position was as a specialist in the Economic Crime Command and put him at the forefront of international police operations and liaisons between London and European capitals and business institutions. That is where he met Kevin Bryan.

Claudette LeClair owned a software company in Paris. Her business worked closely with high-tech machinery and robotics. Kevin had a soft spot for the woman. While their association was not fully romantic yet, he always enjoyed her companionship.

"Really? No way, I pay my way," Claudette said when Sharon offered to cover her expenses. "That is one thing that Alain always said: 'Be indebted to no one.' But I would enjoy the time away from Paris. Is that lanky skyscraper of a fellow really inheriting a castle?"

"Yes, or so he thinks. However, there's a lot of very expensive what-ifs. Please, let me cover some of the costs," Sharon said.

"Not a chance. Besides, I think it's a fifty-nine-euro flight from Paris on Ryan Air. Don't say anything more, just give me the time and place."

Jean-François said yes but also would not hear of her paying. He was sure Fidor Balanca would come along, too; seems that the Russian fixer had acquired a small Citation jet during the past year, compliments of some oil tycoon in Azerbaijan. They would arrive together.

Evelyn's schedule put her in London that week; she would take a short flight late in the day. They all would meet at the

Shelbourne Hotel on Dublin's famous city park, St. Stephen's Green.

The three Californians piled into a Toyota minivan and, with Kevin driving, managed to get into central Dublin unscathed. After driving on the left side of the road and navigating all the intersections and roundabouts backwards, they passed relatively unmolested through some of the worst traffic of Dublin. Kevin demanded a drink in the hotel bar before they even found their rooms.

"Fine bit of driving there, Mr. Bryan," Gina said as she sipped a pint of Murphy's. "Luckily, I also remembered the words to 'Hail Mary.' Probably said a rosary and a half on the way in."

"I wondered why you were so quiet," Sharon said, joining Kevin with a tumbler of Jameson.

"Do I ever complain about your driving, ladies? Ever?" Kevin said with a huff. "Sure, the first few minutes were scary, even frightening, but I quickly got into it. No harm, no foul."

"What time is your meeting with the solicitors?" Sharon asked.

"Tomorrow, at 10 AM. According to their directions, it's only a five-minute walk."

"Me, right now, I'm taking a nap," Sharon said, finishing her drink. "The time change drives me nuts, and I know what it does to our chauffer here. I need a shower, four hours sleep, and then dinner. Meet here at eight? I'll get an idea from the concierge about restaurants. That work?"

"A take-charge woman, that's what I like," Gina said. "Eight it is."

The three were given rooms on the upper floor. While not adjacent rooms, they all faced St. Stephen's Green.

* * *

Gina's hours were the most unconventional of the three friends; such is the life of a bar owner. While Sharon and Kevin professed exhaustion, she was wide awake, and, after putting away a few things, she headed out into the midafternoon sunshine of Dublin. She crossed into the park and wandered past the small lake and brightly planted garden beds. The riot of colors and rich greens of the gardens challenged her California eyes. Trading the West Coast's brown hills for Ireland's emerald green was almost too much for her. But she reveled in every moment of sensory overload. A tourist sign at an intersection pointed to Grafton Street, Dublin's preeminent shopping thoroughfare. She walked its length, making mental notes about return visits to particular shops. Every alley that abutted the street had at least one pub that announced an Irish trio or singing group. This could turn into a busman's holiday, she thought. Every bar a research opportunity.

At a tavern called Paddy O'Toole's, she stopped and read the menu. The usual bar foods, appetizers, and drinks were listed. Her stomach growled its presence, and she pushed her way in. Music that sounded like the iconic Chieftains echoed inside the nearly empty pub.

"Miss, what would ye like?" a young woman asked as Gina sat at the long wooden bar.

"Murphy's, if you have it."

"Sorry, but this is a Guinness-owned tavern. Guinness?"

Gina smiled. "That would be fine."

She watched the girl slip a pint glass under the spigot and start the slow process of filling it with the most famous beer in the world. She noticed the specials on a chalkboard and the liquor bottles all hung upside down with gravity spouts. There were mirrors everywhere. Maybe she could use a little more color in her own place, she thought, maybe more live music, maybe a larger selection of local beers. Lord knows there had been enough boutique breweries opening in the Bay Area. She sipped the beer and was not surprised that it was warmer than she would have preferred. Such is the way of the Irish—and the Brits for that matter.

She looked past the bottles on the shelves and into the mirror as two young men walked in. They scanned the empty bar, and then turned their attention to her. Gina looked back for the bartender; the woman was gone—probably in the kitchen. The two men, both dressed in black T-shirts and black leather jackets, took the seats immediately to Gina's right. She was more annoyed than upset; all she wanted was to talk to the bartender for a few minutes. Now these two.

"You from the States?" the nearest asked.

Gina took a sip—ignoring them.

"Quiet type, aren't you?"

She continued to snub them.

"And rude—it's like what I've told you, Louie. Yanks are too full of themselves."

"You lads stop bothering the lady," the bartender said as she walked back behind the bar. "Order or leave. I've too much to do than to deal with the likes of you boys."

"Yes, your royal highness. Louie, I don't think we are wanted here."

They pushed their stools back and stood. Both men looked Gina up and down, and then Louie raised his hand and, pointing it like it was a gun, faked a shot at Gina. They turned and walked out into the street.

"That was strange," Gina said. "Thanks for the help. I own a bar back home. Had to do that a few times myself."

"No worries, local riffraff. They come and go, think they are hot shit. Really just assholes. Need a refill?"

"No, thanks. I'm good. Nice place—yours?"

"No, one of a chain that Guinness owns. But the pay is good, hours I like, and even benefits. You sure about the beer?"

"Positive. Thanks. I'm Gina." She extended her hand.

"Laurie." They shook. "You here on holiday?"

"No, with friends. We just landed, and they are napping. I was too keyed up, but I am starting to drag."

"We are open late. Bring your friends back. There is a great singer tonight with a small group behind him. He sounds like a young Van Morrison. The crowd is lively. So, if you feel like it . . ."

"Thanks, we may just do that."

"Here, we are okay, but mostly pub food," Laurie answered when Gina asked for dining recommendations. "Down the street and on the corner is a good Italian restaurant. You might try that."

"Always Italian; those are my people. Thanks. And maybe we'll see you later."

Gina finished her beer and paid Laurie, who accepted the American bills without a second thought. "Close enough, Gina. Later."

Gina pushed open the exit doors and had to squint. She was facing the early evening sun, and for a second she was blind. In that second, hands grabbed her arms and pushed her toward a yellow van that was skidding to a stop at the curb. A second man joined the man who had grabbed her. The van's side door slid open with a loud bang as the men shoved her toward the open interior of the van. Gina saw a hooded man waiting inside.

"No fucking way, asshole," Gina yelled and tore one arm free and swung her fist at the first assailant. She connected with his nose and cheek; the blow staggered him. She twisted toward the other man who now, with a vice-like grip, pushed harder. She tried to turn and drive her knee into his jewels, but she was lifted completely off the sidewalk by the man whose nose she had bloodied. With no traction, she was helpless. Still she continued to kick and struggle, doing everything she could to stop the men from shoving her into the blackness of the van.

It was as if a runaway lorry hit the trio. Just as the two kidnappers reached the van's open door with Gina, a dark blur slammed into the three. The two muggers were split away like pins in a skittles toss; they tumbled across the sidewalk. An arm swept Gina up and pulled her away from the assailants. Her savior delivered two swift kicks, and the would-be abductors remained on the ground. Within seconds, Gina and her rescuer were fifty feet down the sidewalk. From that distance, she saw the hooded man emerge from inside the van and quickly help his partners to their feet. Unsure if she had been saved or just passed along to another kidnapper, Gina struggled against the strong arms wrapped around her middle.

"Let me down, damn it. Let me down!" Gina yelled. "Now, or I'll scream to high heaven for the police."

Her champion stopped and lowered her gently to the walk. Gina looked about; a dozen pedestrians stared at them. Down the street, the yellow van jerked its way into the city traffic. It wove in and out of the cars until it disappeared. She looked at her liberator. He was a little taller and more athletic than normal: jeans, black T-shirt, a black motorcycle jacket, and brutally handsome. Handsome like one of those romantic novel covers, handsome. Black hair with an errant strand over his forehead, dark eyes, black eyebrows, and a dark tan. One of those tans that, by Irish standards, was a mixture of wind and a lot of time outdoors. Gina realized that she was shaking.

"Are you okay, lass? I didn't think ye wanted to go with those bastards," the handsome man said. "I hope I guessed correctly and didn't just mess up some strange elopement or something."

Gina just stared at the man and managed a soft, almost inaudible, "Thank you. I have no idea who they were and why . . ."

"Are you staying near here?"

The crowd was pressing in; a woman asked if everything was okay.

"We are fine, ma'am. All's well, I'm a police officer." He pulled a leather packet from inside his jacket and held it up. The badge flashed in the sun.

"I'm staying with friends at the Shelbourne," Gina whispered, everything a blur.

"I'll walk you there." He took Gina's arm, and they headed up St. Stephen's Green Street. The hotel was a few blocks away. They stopped alongside the park's garden wall, where a fence enclosed the green.

"Do you know who those men were?" he asked.

Finally regaining some composure, she looked up at him. "Who the hell are you?"

"My manners, sorry. Inspector Liam Donovan, with the Dublin Garda, the city police."

"The police?" she echoed, even though she'd seen him flash his badge. "What just happened? Why would those guys try to kidnap me?"

"Kidnap? I have not a clue. Today is my day off. I was heading to a pub to meet some friends. When you threw that punch—and a good one, mind you—I realized that this was not some kind of lovers' spat. So, tell me what happened, Miss . . ."

"Gina Cavelli, Inspector." Gina told him about her arrival, her friends, and walking down Grafton Street, the beer, and then being accosted. "I have no idea what they were after. I wasn't even carrying my purse. My passport's in my pocket as well as about a hundred dollars. That's it."

The inspector pulled out his phone and made a call. He talked for a minute then took Gina again by the arm. They reached the hotel's main entrance and walked into the lobby. Gina looked around and did not see anyone she knew. "Inspector, there's a bar they call the Horseshoe," she said. "It is supposed to be somewhere around here."

"Call me Liam. I will show you, this way."

They headed down an elegant hallway into what could have been the set of a period movie about the late Queen Victoria era; rich paneling and leather furniture lined the halls and filled the various function rooms.

"Your choice?" Liam asked.

"Pardon me?" Gina said.

"The hotel, was this your choice?"

"A friend's recommendation."

"Your friend has excellent taste."

"You have no idea," Gina said, thinking of Evelyn Lucca.

They turned into the Horseshoe Bar with its historic U-shaped bar. Sitting at the open end were Sharon and Kevin, each with a tumbler of whiskey. Seeing Gina, Sharon raised an eyebrow and gave a slight nod that meant *who's this?* Gina nodded back, and as she and Liam drew closer to where her companions sat, she said, "Liam, I want you meet my friends: Sharon O'Mara and Kevin Bryan. You two, I want you to meet my very own Irish copper and champion."

4b

Sharon asked, "Are you okay?" when Gina finished her story. "Not even a scratch, thanks to this guy."

"Thank you," Kevin said, and then briefly told the Irish inspector about his own experience as a police officer and detective. "Do you have a problem here in Dublin with kidnappings and ransoms?"

"No, and why ransoms?" Liam asked.

"Why else would someone try to kidnap Gina?" Kevin put his arm around her and pulled her close.

"What are you implying, Mr. Bryan?" she said. "I'm not worth being kidnapped? I'm not good enough for the sex-slave traffickers?"

"Not at all, you would be a fine catch," Kevin said. "It's just that your being in this city for less than three hours hardly seems enough time to set up a kidnapping let alone all the machinations of grabbing you and throwing you in a truck. Maybe mistaken identity?"

"No, I'm positive that the two who grabbed me were the same two that hassled me in the bar. They marked me. When I swung at the moron's nose, I remember realizing that the face was familiar. I am certain they were both the same guys. After they left the bar, they had ample time to confirm who I was, make sure I was the right target. It is all too weird."

"I agree," Sharon said. "You had to be the target. The big question is why? Inspector Donovan, you have CCTVs?"

"Probably ten thousand of them in Dublin, and there is one outside Paddy's. I'm having my people check them."

"Paddy's?" Gina asked. "Was that the place I was in?"

"Yes, Paddy O'Toole's. It's an okay place. I was heading to a bar near Trinity College to meet some people when I played the

Sir Galahad role."

"And I'm glad you did, Sir Knight," Gina said.

"I'm late. Here is my card with my mobile number. Ring me later. By then I should have some answers to my inquiries at the station. Not sure what we will find, but it is a place to start. Do you have mobiles?"

"Yes, and they will work here in Ireland," Kevin offered and wrote down the numbers on a napkin.

"Never asked—business or vacation?"

They all said at the same time, "Both."

After Donovan left, Sharon and Kevin bombarded Gina with questions. Her most common and coarse answer was: "I haven't a fucking clue."

"After I went upstairs," Kevin said, "I called the solicitors and told them that we were in town and that I would stop in around ten tomorrow morning. The woman I talked with was the same lawyer that sent the letter and who I talked with a few weeks back, Ms. Sinead O'Shaunnessy. She said she would be assisting me; she was about as pleasant as some criminal attorneys I dealt with. She came across as hard and a little too sharp; almost seemed annoyed that I was here."

"Great, this may be the shortest real estate deal in history," Sharon said.

"She also added that her law firm had been assisting the O'Bryan family for years, and she had met Aunt Brona a few years earlier and had helped prepare the documents."

"I'm going with you," Sharon said.

"And me, too," Gina added. "After today, we travel in pairs or more. It might be more than me they are after."

"Who's 'they'?" Sharon asked.

"No clue. That's my demand, and you guys are going to stick to it, like it or not. The bartender at O'Toole's suggested an Italian restaurant a few blocks from here. I'm going to shower and put on something fresh. Then your lordship can buy us ladies dinner."

Later, as they were sitting at dinner, Kevin's phone buzzed.

It was Liam Donovan.

"I'll put you on speaker," Kevin said.

"I sent a couple of the Garda out to ask about the cameras," Liam began. "The woman at the bar said they were for show, no recording, typical for many places in town. With all the government cameras, they say, why bother. Unfortunately, from the other cameras on the street, all we got was the van pulling through the intersection at the end of the road, but we did read the plates. Yesterday, a woman reported that the plates had been stolen from her van, no help there. The tech guys followed the van for another few blocks, and then it disappeared into an industrial area along the waterfront. Lots of warehouses and offices—it never showed again. They are running additional searches that might turn up something, but it looks like these guys are pros. Educated guess—the van is now a different color or pushed into the river."

"Thanks, Liam," Gina said warmly.

Sharon and Kevin looked at each other and silently mouthed the man's name. Gina saw it and gave them the finger.

"You are most welcome. If anything shows up, I'll let you know."

"Pros? Not good. Something is happening, and it is all too weird," Sharon said after Donovan clicked off. She turned to Gina. "The only thing that even remotely connects you to Ireland right now is Kevin's little adventure. But why you?"

Gina's phone began to ring. The ID read *Anonymous*. "Hello?"

She listened for a minute and said, "Yes, lunch tomorrow would be delightful. My friends have other things to do, so I'm free . . . at the hotel? . . . See you at noon."

"Really?" Sharon asked as soon as Gina ended the call. "Was that Mr. Cute Irish Inspector calling you back for a date?"

"Well, he did save my life."

Sharon looked at Kevin. "Aren't you going to do something?"

"Me? Why are you asking me? I think it's kind of sweet, the whole Sir Galahad thing. She might have been killed. I'm damn glad he was there."

"Thank you, your lordship. See, if old stuffy Bryan can accept it, why can't you?"

"The subject isn't Donovan," Sharon said. "It's who tried to kidnap you, and why. I don't believe in coincidence—you were targeted."

"Thanks," Gina answered, a slight flicker of fear on her face. "So it's even better to have a cop on my arm, don't you think?"

Sharon put her fingers on Gina's hand. "Yes, you are right. We don't travel alone now. Even when the rest of the gang shows up, we let them know. Not to be too paranoid, but if there is something bigger going on, someone just showed their first card."

* * * *

After an excellent Irish breakfast, Kevin and Sharon walked the ten blocks to the modern edifice of the law offices of O'Shaunnessy, Little, and Lynch, Ltd. The building sat in the center of the newly renovated Grand Canal Dock complex; its blue-green glass façade reflected the marina and the surrounding towers. Known, unaffectionately, by locals as Silicon Docks, this half-mile square chunk of north Dublin now housed the European headquarters for Google, Facebook, LinkedIn, and many other dot-com businesses. For the two Californians, it was a bit of a shock to see so many of the same names and logos that lined the freeway from San Francisco to San Jose hung on one-hundred-year-old buildings.

"Small world," Sharon said as they stood at the railing on Pearse Street Bridge overlooking the Grand Harbor.

"And getting smaller every day," Kevin said. "This is nice though. I can feel Irish strings pulling me, like I've been here before. In my case, it's a warm feeling. Not cold."

"I'm getting a little of that, too, but my family history is so jumbled up, I'm not sure what I'll feel if it happens to me. Besides, your family only left Ireland about a hundred years ago."

Kevin's great-grandfather Robert O'Bryan had immigrated to the United States. He'd been the one who shortened the name,

Kevin told Sharon. His son Robert, Kevin's grandfather, spent his eighty years in the Bay Area. Robert was good with his hands and worked in a wooden mold shop making forms for the iron-casting industry. Later he had a cabinet shop—"A lot of the kitchen cabinets on San Francisco's west side came out of his shop," Kevin said with some pride. "Until my father got married, he worked for Gramps. In the late 1970s, just after I was born, they moved to Orinda. You know the rest. I guess the Irish in me pushed me toward being a cop. Now, I'm not sure what the hell I am."

"I love your father. He is like you, a true person. Kevin Bryan, you have hundreds of friends that love you dearly. There are many troubled young men and women who owe you their lives and their futures. The world is a safer place because of you. And, most especially, because you are my best friend. This trip is giving us a chance to just slow down the pace, to rest and think. I won't get all psychobabble on you, but you need this. Take advantage of it; that's why Gina and I are here."

"I thought it was to keep me out of trouble and to celebrate your birthday. Thanks—we do make a good team."

"Like the Bickersons—as we have been told more than once." She leaned in and kissed him on the cheek. "I haven't any idea what will happen with these attorneys. Listen, ask questions, but I suggest that you be a little vague. Maybe some of the questions should sound dumb, even naïve. Not sure if they know you were a cop. It might be best to leave that out for the moment."

"I was thinking late last night that Gina's abduction attempt, assuming it was not random, has to be connected to my inheritance. Who else even knows we're here? And if that's the case, we might be walking into a hornet's nest." Kevin looked at the wall of glass; the building had to be twenty stories.

"I had the same thought. I assume, then, that we probably have been followed. And someone is up there looking down on us, wondering what the hell we are doing. How's that for paranoia?"

"I love it. You suggested playing dumb; I can go with that.

Can I buy you a cup of coffee?"

"Love one," Sharon said as she looked up and down the bridge. Dozens of young people were going about their lives. Bicycles filled the empty spaces in the congested traffic lanes. Two hundred feet away, a lone man leaned against the railing talking on his phone, a cigarette in his hand. Like clockwork, every fifteen seconds he looked up and passed his eyes over them. "Three o'clock, grey jacket," Sharon added.

"Not very good, is he?"

"I see a coffee shop across the wharf. Let's be late. I love showing up late for attorney's meetings."

"I'll buy."

For twenty minutes they sat enjoying their coffee, their shadow watching them. He bought a newspaper from a vending machine and took a bench facing the harbor. Sharon and Kevin ignored the man.

"My grandfather passed away when I was ten. That was a few years after my parents took me to Ireland; that's when I met Brona. They were also the reason I came back here a few years later. Dad told wonderful stories that his father told him of the old country. I'm surprised I've not been back since then. Those Irish strings still pull, but being a cop gave me a lot to deal with. Glad you talked me into this."

"This is the least we could do—any excuse for a party."

"Shall we go kick the hornet's nest?"

"Love to."

Chapter 5

A mean woman was this Sylvia Boyle,
Who wanted a plot of Irish soil.
She held all was hers,
A prize to be sure,
Till her greediness all embroiled.

5a

A Few Months Earlier
New York City, New York

Eighty-eight floors above the Uber- and taxi-clogged streets of Lower Manhattan, Sylvia Boyle looked out the corner window of her office in Donald Boyle Development—DBD, Ltd. Across the Hudson River in Jersey City, she could see their derelict property and imagined the new city she would add to the skyline opposite Battery Park and Lower Manhattan. When she wasn't tearing things down, she was building them. She had inherited DBD, Ltd. from her father when he suddenly died during a big-game safari in Africa. "Suddenly" happened when an enraged Cape buffalo pounded Boyle's Irish-American carcass into the African veldt after his .50 caliber rifle shot bounced off the beast's magnificent upturned horns. It was the senior Boyle's intent to mount the beast's head in his new office in the building planned to replace one of the World Trade Towers lost on September 11, 2001. He had guaranteed a lease for three floors of the new building; the beast's head would sit proud and large in the lobby. The Cape buffalo itself guaranteed nothing. After stomping Boyle to death, the buffalo chased Boyle's guides to their truck, which he then overturned. Two of the guides were severely injured. The Cape buffalo was last seen marching back into the thorny bush, no worse for his inconvenient meeting with the Irish-American developer. That could not have been said about many of Boyle's clients.

The new and exceptional Trade Center Tower was now finished, and the three floors were occupied by DBD, Ltd. There was also a Cape buffalo head in the lobby. It was rumored that Sylvia Boyle personally shot the beast from one hundred feet with a shoulder-held Barrett M82 .50 caliber rifle. The animal was intent on repeating his dance act on the daughter of Donald Boyle when she knocked him to the ground with one shot. The taxidermist did an excellent job repairing the hole the bullet drilled in the center of the buffalo's head. To deal with DBD, Ltd. required a person to stand under this massive head while he or she waited in the lobby for an audience with Sylvia Boyle. The hallway to her office also was lined with other deceased members of Africa's Big Five trophy group. To say that it put off many would be putting it mildly. For Sylvia, it was just a part of doing business. Where Google offers their mantra "Do no evil," Sylvia's was "You will be next."

DBD, Ltd. had, over the previous fifty years, developed dozens of high-rise mixed-use projects in the metropolitan areas of New York City and New Jersey. The company also built resorts in Las Vegas and partnered with two Native American tribes to build casinos in the Midwest. Three massive apartment complexes, with over eight thousand units in each of them, provided affordable housing in Queens and the Bronx. The firm's ruthless reputation preceded them, and while losing some battles, they won more than they lost. Pictures of the developments, like the game animals' heads, also lined the walls.

Since leaving Harvard in the early 1970s, Sylvia Boyle, multibillionaire and now sixty-six years old, had worked closely with her father. While she never practiced law, she knew every legitimate (and some say illegitimate) legal venue and process to gain approvals for the company's development programs. She also had attended City University of New York and Rhode

Island School of Design. She played golf exceptionally well and was women's club champion more than a dozen times during the 1980s at the club her father built on Long Island. A golf club that had hosted two PGA tournaments. The rumor was that the reason they never hosted one of the majors was that Donald Boyle was a pain in the ass. The professional golfing associations would have nothing to do with him. Sylvia Boyle didn't care one bit what the world thought of DBD, Ltd., or herself, for that matter. All that mattered was the deal and the project. All else was simply envious bullshit and in her way.

Her affection for Ireland—the ancestral home of the Boyle clan was near Bantry—materialized when she was in her forties and after the divorce from her third husband. One summer, long before the death of her father, she took the company jet to Shannon Airport with two of the children (the third, the oldest, was in college), hired a car, and spent a week traveling the backroads of Southern Ireland. As hard as her heart was in business matters, she fell in love with the land and the people of Ireland. It was then she decided she would build one of the greatest golf resorts in the world right there in Southern Ireland. One that would rival Gleneagles in Scotland and Doral in Florida, maybe even Pebble Beach in California. Money was not the issue; the issue was finding the right piece of property.

The call came early in the morning, a month after Brona O'Bryan had passed.

"Ma'am," Sylvia's assistant announced after tapping on the doorframe. "Ms. Sinead O'Shaunnessy is on the phone. She wishes a few minutes of your time."

Boyle walked away from the window and her dream for New Jersey, thought for a moment, and then smiled. *Maybe this time.*

"Good morning, Sinead. How are you?"

"I am very well, thank you. And you and the children?"

"Extremely well, and the children are hardly that anymore. One now works for me, and the other two are doing as well as can be expected. Much is underway, and as always a week behind."

Two of Sylvia's children, both in their thirties, had distanced themselves from their mother. They felt her influence was too difficult and damaging for their own children—Boyle had not seen them in three years.

"I understand," Sinead said. "Running companies can be such a bother, a comfortable bother to be sure, but nonetheless, a bother."

"I assume that you finally have found me a property?" Boyle said.

"It is a gem, if I may say so myself. It has everything."

"County Cork?"

"Yes, south County Cork, near the village of Clonakilty," O'Shaunnessy said. "It has a half mile of cliff frontage overlooking the ocean. It also has an old, worn-out house and a few outbuildings that are worthless. But that is no matter; it is the property that holds great promise."

"Is it the O'Bryan estate?"

"Yes."

There was a pause. Boyle smiled again and asked, "The price?"

"It is not on the market yet. It is one of my firm's legacy clients from the days of the firm's founding by my great-grandfather. The last remaining family member died, that being Brona O'Bryan. We are completing the probate, and I hope to recover some of the hundreds of thousands in fees that were never billed. Unfortunately, the old lady threw us a curve, to use an American expression. There is an heir no one knew anything about, one of your people, an American. He lives in California."

There was a longer pause this time. "An heir? What the hell are you talking about?"

"A nephew of the dead landowner. He lives near San Francisco. His name is Kevin Bryan. My people are working on completing his dossier."

"And what did he say when you told him?"

Again, silence. "Sinead?"

"We have not informed him yet. There are a lot of back taxes due as well as considerable costs to fix the house."

"But this is the property we've talked about?" Boyle asked.

"Yes, the same. I know that you have waited for this particular piece of land for a long time."

"Yes, I have."

"I sent you the location in an email; it should be in your box. It conforms to the information you sent a year ago. It just took time to be sure."

"Give me a minute," Boyle said, moving to her computer. Two minutes later, she was looking at an aerial view of the property.

"And you said that this heir has not been told?"

"No, this is between us for now. Our research has found that Bryan is the direct descendent of one of the brothers of Brona O'Bryan's grandfather. There may have been some contact between them during the last twenty years, but nothing that we can find that's recent. He is an ex-cop who worked for a city near San Francisco. Our investigators found that he currently is unemployed but does some security consulting work. He has, as we like to say, nary a pot to even piss in."

"Thank you, Sinead," Boyle said, her excitement growing as she zoomed in on the property and studied the ground in three dimensions. "It does show promise, and you said there is no price yet?"

"None, and outside of a few people in my firm, you are the only other person aware of it."

"Again, thank you for your discretion. How would you like to proceed?"

"Sylvia, I am quite aware that you do not like to work with partners. I fully understand. Partners can be such a pain in the ass. But in this case . . ."

"Say no more, I understand. I believe we can work something out. I currently am involved in some delicate negotiations that require me to be in New York for the rest of the week. Suppose I fly over and meet you next week. We can look at the property and have a more businesslike conversation."

"That is all I was hoping for. I cannot sit on this much longer; I have a responsibility to inform Mr. Bryan. Two weeks at the most."

"That can be met," Boyle said. "You have been very good to work with in the past, and this may be our greatest adventure yet."

5b

Boyle's Gulfstream G550 rolled to a stop at the private business terminal at Cork Airport. The tarmac was wet from the early morning rain as a Range Rover pulled up to the door of the jet. The driver opened an umbrella for Sinead O'Shaunnessy as she climbed from the back seat of the vehicle. They watched the stairway unfold from the body of the plane. A single passenger came to the door. She also opened an umbrella and immediately descended the stairs. Halfway down, Sylvia Boyle waved to O'Shaunnessy; the solicitor waved back. The American was dressed for the weather and carried a camera.

They headed to Customs and a few minutes later emerged, climbed into the SUV, and headed out of the airport.

"There are some sandwiches and sparkling water in the cooler, if you like," O'Shaunnessy said. "Your flight was uneventful?"

"I love that plane. It does make life so much easier. Thank you for the sandwiches. I am here for the rest of the day. I intend to fly back tonight."

"I understand. My staff knows only that I am away for a few days. No worries there."

Boyle tilted her head at the driver.

"I trust him explicitly," O'Shaunnessy told her. "We are free to talk."

The driver took the back roads of County Cork and headed south toward Clonakilty.

"I never tire of the countryside of Ireland, especially County

Cork," Boyle said. "My family is from near Bantry; the old house is gone. It will be nice to reconnect to Ireland again after a hundred years. Thank you for the additional information, the photos, and land surveys. My golf course architect already is making some preliminary sketches."

"Do you trust him?"

"Her. A retired professional golfer who has an eye for this sort of thing. I supported her during her career. Yes, I trust her."

"And?"

"She is as excited as I am. There may be room for two eighteen-hole layouts. The building holds some promise as the clubhouse, but many additional improvements will be needed."

"I understand. This would do wonders for the local economy, jobs, and prestige," O'Shaunnessy said. "Always a point to be made with the locals. However, there will be some resistance. This part of Ireland always has been a source of irritation to Dublin. Some of the leaders of the Uprising and Ireland's Independence came from the area. They tend to want to be left alone."

"Then we have our work cut out for us, don't we, Sinead?" For Boyle, the golf course and the development of the property were secondary. Her own family's legends identified this region and this property as an important part of their past—a past that had been stolen.

An hour later, they turned onto the narrow road that led to the old house. Hedgerows hemmed them in on either side; through breaks in the thick green growth, they saw sheep grazing on the open land.

"Some of the locals have used these pastures for years," O'Shaunnessy said. "We could find no written agreements. Just one more issue, albeit small, to deal with."

The overcast had cleared to tumbling piles of clouds and blue sky; sunlight streamed in great shafts of brilliant light across the green countryside. The house stood under this billowing mass, as if lit with a spotlight.

They parked near the cottage and began to explore the area

around the house and the ancient garden. It was evident that Boyle was becoming even more excited.

"Wonderful," she said, taking photos. "Even spectacular."

"It is that."

"Far more than I expected, although the house can wait. I need to stretch my legs. Which way to the coast?"

"This way," O'Shaunnessy said, pointing to a trail.

They walked the quarter mile to the cliffs. At every step, Boyle gestured and mentioned something about a tee or a green. She took more photos as they hiked the narrow path. She waved her hands about like a schoolgirl on holiday. At the cliff, she stood and stared in wonder.

"Sinead, you have outdone yourself. I believe we can make something here that will be the envy of the golfing world. It may not be a true links course, but it would rival Pebble Beach. Thank you for thinking of me."

"You are welcome," O'Shaunnessy said. "And my offer as partner?" She had waited until this moment, knowing that it would be the best time to broach the subject.

Boyle stood looking out to the sea for a long moment. The breeze off the water pushed her wildly cut auburn hair away from her face. She turned to O'Shaunnessy.

"You ask a lot. Thirty percent and a seat on the board of DBD."

"Twenty-five percent would be acceptable."

Boyle stared at O'Shaunnessy. "Never back away from a percentage, Sinead. That is what I learned from my father, and it has served me well. I will give you what you asked—it is fair, especially for thinking of me before anyone else." She paused. "There isn't anyone else, is there?"

"No, Sylvia, no one else. I, like you, have been waiting for such an opportunity. I've grown tired of the legal business. I am sixty-one years old, and it is time to make my mark. The firm is in good hands. It will continue long after I'm gone. This property is an opportunity that seldom arrives. I will handle the legal issues here in Ireland. I have friends and politicians who understand what a development like this can do for the region. I can make that work. With your expertise and guidance, this will be something that both of us will be proud of. And, I can handle this American; he is of no consequence. I will inform him of his inheritance and meet with him. I will make him understand the issues he faces, and then offer him alternatives. Alternatives he won't want to let pass."

"Excellent," Boyle said, looking back to the sea. "I do believe I can see New York from here."

They finished the tour of the house and the adjacent cottage. The mood had not changed; Boyle remained exuberant. However, O'Shaunnessy was a tad less excited. She'd known that Boyle would love the property, but she also knew that securing the proper approvals to develop it as envisioned would be difficult. It would be in the presentations and discussions with local governments that the deals would be made. Deals that would include arm-twisting, campaign contributions, and a few carrots and sweeteners.

* * * *

The clouds thickened and scudded in from the ocean. Sheets of light rain danced across the fields and the itinerant flocks of sheep as the Range Rover turned back onto the main highway.

At the top of the rise that overlooked the pasture and the house, a lone figure dressed in an oiled greatcoat and slouched hat stood in the rain and watched the Range Rover leave. A great red dog stood next to her. Molly O'Rourke slipped her camera back under her jacket and wondered why the O'Bryan attorney was here and who the woman was that toured the property. She did not trust the Dublin solicitor. She knew the history and the law firm's connection to the O'Bryan family. It was one of the last things that Brona had said to her before she died: "Be very careful of that fucken' O'Shaunnessy woman. I use her, but don't ever trust her."

5c

O'Shaunnessy watched as the front landing gear of the Gulfstream left the runway; a few seconds later the rear wheels left Ireland's soil and folded into the jet. The plane banked south and headed into the sunset, breaking through the remaining clouds of the daylong storm. She took a deep breath and slowly exhaled. Yes, the visit had gone well, better than she had expected. She had known Sylvia Boyle for more than twenty years; in fact, they had done some business together soon after she opened the New York City office of O'Shaunnessy, Little, and Lynch. The reason for the New York office was practical and pragmatic. So many Irish citizens moved back and forth across the Atlantic, Sinead knew there were going to be opportunities for her firm to be well situated on both sides of the ocean. Her strategy had paid off exceedingly well. She also enjoyed her personal trips to the financial and retail center of the Western world.

Her initial contact with Boyle had been during a St. Patrick's Day dinner hosted by a local branch of the Irish Provisionals in New York. One of O'Shaunnessy's contacts was a senior member of the board of directors of a charity that had been formed by the Provisionals to aid the children of Irish patriots killed or injured in the Troubles in Northern Ireland. She knew the man was also a conduit for money moving from America to Ireland as well as a source for arms and explosives. It was not her place to inform the authorities; after all, he was a client. The gentleman introduced her to Sylvia Boyle that evening.

"Ms. O'Shaunnessy," the man had said. "If there is one woman you need to know, and become friends with, in this godforsaken city, it is this one, Sylvia Boyle. She's a daughter of the sod, and her father and her grandfather have been very helpful to us. I've known the lass since she was as tall as my knee."

The two women shook hands and further acknowledged each other with a nod.

"There, I have done my job, I can go home now. However,

you two lasses must talk. You both are strong Irish gals and have much in common. Good night."

The two women watched the patriot walk out of the private dining room. The restaurant had been a fixture of the Hell's Kitchen neighborhood of New York for fifty years.

"Hard to believe that man is the retired Irish ambassador to America," Boyle said.

"I would have thought that he would prefer Ireland to live in," O'Shaunnessy said, "especially after that remark about New York City."

"Seamus is as Irish as the cold stone at Blarney Castle," Boyle said. "And just about as flattering as the gift the stone gives. Yes, his skills at negotiation are legendary. I also think he stays here in America because there are more than a few on either side of the Troubles that would prefer him dead. He has, as we say, a significant price on his head."

"Your family has known him for some time then?"

"Yes, my father and he have done business."

"And that business is . . ."

"We are builders and developers. In fact, we are developing a mid-rise apartment building not two blocks from here. My father has a strong affinity for this neighborhood; he grew up here."

The two women talked for another hour, astonished at the many common connections and people they knew. Why they hadn't met before surprised them: Gstaad, London, even Vail, Colorado. It was in London, years later over lunch at the Savoy, that O'Shaunnessy discovered something else about Sylvia Boyle: she was enamored with a particular piece of Irish property with which O'Shaunnessy's firm had a long association.

* * * *

After Boyle left for New York, O'Shaunnessy began composing the letters and supporting documents that Kevin Bryan would need to understand what Brona O'Bryan had left him. It was purely an unemotional process. After thirty years of law, and uncounted probate and estate settlements, she approached this settlement no differently. She was aware of her family's connection to the O'Bryans. Had things turned out differently, the O'Shaunnessy line would have died off in the last years of the nineteenth century, and she, Sinead O'Shaunnessy, would never have existed.

Christopher O'Shaunnessy was a twenty-one-year-old Dublin volunteer in the anti-British Irish commandos who aligned themselves with the South Africans in the Boer War. When the Boer army came under attack during the siege of Ladysmith, O'Shaunnessy was wounded by fellow Irishmen of the Irish Fusiliers under the command of the British army. Michael O'Bryan, a thirty-one-year-old Irish commando in O'Shaunnessy's unit, had dodged Fusilier rifle fire and rescued O'Shaunnessy. He protected and nursed the young man back to health, and the two eventually escaped east into Portuguese East Africa. When they eventually made it back to Ireland, Christopher returned to Trinity College and acquired a law degree. Michael O'Bryan returned to smuggling and his home along the coast, south of Clonakilty. O'Shaunnessy never forgot the debt that he owed O'Bryan. When he asked O'Bryan what he could do for the man who had saved his life, all O'Bryan asked was, "Keep the forces of the law and the British off my back. That's all I ask, for if there is one thing the British fear more than a Zulu and a spear, it is a solicitor with a writ." For the next hundred years the firm of O'Shaunnessy, Little, and Lynch never sent the O'Bryans a bill for legal services. For the recent thirty years, even though Sinead deeply respected her late great-grandfather (who lived until she was twelve years old), she had tried to find a way to recoup what she thought her firm was due. She now believed that Mr. Kevin Bryan might just be the opportunity.

The morning her assistant said that there was an American on the phone, the same Mr. Kevin Bryan, Sinead had been pleased. She was certain about the past-due taxes and made sure that they were prominently highlighted in the letters she prepared. The photos included in the initial letter were taken to put the house and other buildings in the worst light possible. O'Shaunnessy couldn't control all the available public information, assuming that the unemployed cop even had a clue as to how to do additional research on what she had sent him. Her goal was to control the information about the property to the extent possible. She was in the process of constructing an offer on the property on Boyle's behalf when the American ex-cop called.

"Ms. O'Shaunnessy, Kevin Bryan. How are you? With the time difference it is early morning here in California."

He did not sound at all like she thought he would. He was confident, clear, and to her trained ear, educated. "I am very well, Mr. Bryan. It is a pleasure to hear from you. I hope that the letter did not confuse you. I assume that you have a thousand questions."

"Yes, I do. Far too many to discuss over the phone."

"I understand."

"So, some friends of mine and I are coming to Ireland for a vacation and to do some research on the house and property. I hope you are available on the fifteenth or soon thereafter. I would like to meet you and visit the property."

O'Shaunnessy tightly clenched the phone's receiver. This she had not anticipated.

"This is not necessary, Mr. Bryan. To be perfectly honest, I was not sure, with all the obligations on the property, that you would be all that interested."

"Frankly, I agree, there is a lot up in the air. But since this friend of mine has been quite insistent about seeing the property and Ireland in general, we have decided to spend a few days. This should help me make a better decision."

"A decision? And what kind of decision might that be?"

"The possibility of paying off the tax liens and fixing up the property, Ms. O'Shaunnessy. I will call before we arrive in Dublin to set up an appointment at your offices."

That call was three weeks earlier. Today, Christopher O'Shaunnessy's great-granddaughter looked out the window of her corner office down to the plaza where the late Michael O'Bryan's son sat with a red-haired woman near the coffee shop. Sinead's investigator had followed the three Californians from the airport to their hotel the day before. He had also attempted to throw a scare into the group when his men pretended to kidnap one of Bryan's friends. They weren't going to detain the woman, just throw in some uncertainty. They had not expected the woman's violent reaction, the broken nose, or the able assistance from a passerby. The investigator followed Mr. Bryan when he left the hotel the next morning with the other woman in the group, one Sharon O'Mara—he learned this from his sources at the hotel. Where the third person, Gina Cavelli, was spending the morning, he was not certain. The investigator left one of his agents at the hotel to watch for her.

Bottom line: O'Shaunnessy was pissed at Mr. Bryan. She looked at the clock on her desk, then back to the plaza below. She now had to deal with the impatient Sylvia Boyle, this American and his family ties to the O'Bryans, and her family's obligations to them. Bryan was being intentionally late, trying to put her off. *Well, he will see how this game will be played.*

5d

Molly O'Rourke laid out the photos she had taken on the table in her small office. Two showing the women's faces, even in the rain, were quite clear. She knew the solicitor; O'Shaunnessy was her name, the witch. She did not recognize the other woman; maybe in her sixties, auburn hair, stylish, and, from the quality of the outdoors clothing, well off. Her Barbour outfit and boots would cost at least a thousand euros. She carried a high-end Nikon—those sold for about three thousand euros. In fact, O'Rourke was quite familiar with the brand. She had brought in two hundred of the same model a few years back. They sold quickly, and she had made a nice profit on each.

She studied the face of the unknown woman. Why was she looking at the O'Bryan property? From the appearance of her face, Irish to be sure, but she carried herself like an American. All swagger, even for a woman, walked quickly, seemed exuberant. She might be a buyer or connected to the inheritor. Knowing O'Shaunnessy, she leaned toward this woman not being associated with the new heir. She studied the photos again. Twice during the walk to the cliffs, the attorney and the woman had stopped for several minutes while the visitor looked around, pointed, and pantomimed an imaginary golf swing. Interesting.

O'Rourke turned back to the computer on her desk and went to work. In the search window, she typed: *woman, developer, golfer, America, images.*

She scrolled through the hundreds of photos of young professional female golfers until she began to see the faces of older women. Why images of Donald Trump showed up she wasn't sure, but she did smile—maybe it was his haircut? As she scrolled through the images, the photo of an older woman in golf attire surrounded by younger women holding golf clubs caught her eye. She clicked the image and asked for more like this. Dozens of photos popped up, one the cover of *New York Magazine.*

"Well, I'll be damned," O'Rourke said aloud. She looked back at her photos and the woman on the magazine cover. The caption read: *Sylvia Boyle, wealthiest woman in New York.* Ten minutes later, after reading three bios and numerous social postings in various newspapers, including the *Wall Street Journal* and the *Financial Times,* she was certain. One article pointed out that Sylvia Boyle's family was from Bantry. Molly knew a few Boyles from the western part of the county; they were a shady lot. There was only one conclusion: Ms. Sinead O'Shaunnessy was trying to find a buyer for the Baile O'Bryan. It also meant that this Sylvia Boyle, a developer of massive projects and golf course resorts, might be one of these potential buyers. *Not good, not good at all. Aunt Brona, you were right.*

Chapter 6

With caskets of gold they came from Spain,
To the coast of Ireland for bribes arranged.
Four chests wrapped in steel,
For the rebel, Hugh O'Neill,
Alas, they all be caught and then hanged.

6a

Late Summer, 1601
The Headlands South of Clonakilty, Ireland

Juan Flores de Mendoza held tightly to the hawser secured to the ring at the bow of the longboat as it slipped silently toward the double lanterns set high over the headlands. He intently watched; the lights were stacked one over the other. If he kept this line, he knew he was on the right and exact heading.

"A degree to port, helmsman," he prompted. The boat moved imperceptibly.

Half a league behind them the square-rigged caravel *Santa Anna de Cordoba* was anchored, every flame aboard extinguished. She would wait until morning to retrieve the crew of the longboat. If they did not return by midmorning, she would leave them to their fate in Ireland.

"Row, strike the water, men. Be quick if you wish to return to Spain," Mendoza admonished.

After a fast trip across the Celtic Sea from Santander on the northern coast of Spain, the *Santa Anna de Cordoba* had slipped into the arc of Clonakilty Bay late the previous afternoon. To the west lay Galley Head. She set her anchor, and as soon as it was dark, the longboat was lowered with its cargo and crew of ten.

Mendoza had watched as the four chests were slowly lowered into the boat and secured

"Lieutenant Mendoza," Capitan Valdes said. "You know your orders; do you have any questions?"

"No, sir. I am honored that I was chosen for this important mission. I will not fail you."

"You would not fail me; you would fail your country."

It had been thirteen years since the defeat of the Spanish Armada. The captain did not need to remind Mendoza how many good men had been slaughtered and executed by the English after the disaster. "Here in Ireland, we will regain our glory," the captain said. "Here we will show them the might of the Spanish. *Buena suerte.*"

Mendoza saluted his captain and climbed down the ladder to the longboat. The helmsman set the course. Now an hour later, the caravel was hidden in the thin mist that had formed over the smooth sea. The lights on the headland above the haze still beckoned.

He was the first to hear the soft sound of the surf. He was also the first to pray that the information and orders he had been given were true. They followed the lights on the headland until they rose about forty-five degrees above the water, and then Mendoza raised a single lantern and flashed it four times. They waited. A new signal lamp appeared just above the waterline. Mendoza was to follow that line until the rocks enclosed the boat; then he should look for more lights. The men pulled the oars. Not a voice or sound was heard until Mendoza said softly, "There, helmsman, there. To the light."

They rode in on a swell, through the sharp-edged pinnacles that rose from the shallows of the narrow cove. Above, a ceiling of rock sheltered them. Three lights directly ahead illuminated a shingle of sand. As the bow of the longboat slipped up the beach, five shadowy figures stood their ground. Mendoza leaped out; two more sailors jumped into the shallow water and held the gunnels.

"Lieutenant Juan Flores de Mendoza at your service," he

said in English and saluted the first man that approached.

"Captain Padriq Doolan," the Irishman said. "Pull the boat up. The tide is receding. We can unload, and then you and your men can return to your ship."

"Captain, I am to stay with the chests. The men will return."

"That is not part of the deal, Lieutenant."

"It is now. Wherever those chests go, I go. After they reach Hugh O'Neill, I will return to Spain. Until then, they never leave my sight."

"That was not part of the agreement," Doolan argued.

"It has changed. My men need to leave. The gold is in the chests. Either remove the chests, or we will return to the ship." At a subtle gesture from Mendoza, long rifles were produced and aimed at the men on the beach.

Doolan turned to his men and said something that Mendoza didn't understand. He assumed that they spoke in Gaelic, the Irish tongue. Doolan's men laughed.

"It's your boney Spanish ass, Lieutenant Mendoza. Remove the chests."

In minutes the four chests, heavy with gold escudos, sat on the sand high above the line of the surf. The Spanish officer said goodbye to his men and the helmsman and watched as they slipped out of the cove and into the black night.

"Gentlemen," Doolan said to his men. "These chests are heavy with the future of Ireland. I suggest that we start them up the stairs."

The men grabbed the handles and began the climb; it took almost an hour to complete the ascent. They carried up two of the chests and then went back for the next two. In the broken-down and abandoned stone cottage that masked the entry to the tunnel, they rested and ate a meager breakfast of dried meat, bread, and hard cheese.

"I would kill for a dram of whiskey," one of the men said.

"Aye, me as well," said another.

Mendoza silently agreed. His stomach rebelled as he chewed a piece of dried meat.

"Captain Doolan, how do you expect to carry these to Hugh O'Neill?" he asked. "You will need a wagon and mules. I do not see any."

"They are hidden in a stable in a village a few miles north of here. We will leave and retrieve them. By late afternoon we will return and collect the chests. We then head north. O'Neill's men are to meet us in Limerick; they are marshaling their forces near there."

"And the English?"

"We have not seen them in weeks, but they are rumored to be east of here in Cork. We should reach Limerick in four or five days. We will have to go west through Killarney; there's too many English around Cork."

The Irishmen left Mendoza and the four chests in the small room under the wooden floor of the stone house. Doolan hadn't argued, but if he had, Mendoza would not have budged. His duty was to remain with the treasure, and his first charge from his admiral had been simple: "Never let them leave your sight."

He watched the five men cross the pasture beyond the cottage and disappear over the crest of the green hills. He had never seen a country so green and lush, very different from the dry hills of his native Toledo. And much nicer than the jungles of the Americas. He wondered what his wife was doing, and how his three children were. It had been eighteen months since he had been home.

By midafternoon, the sun broke through the clouds drifting in from the sea. Doolan had left him with some food. From his own pack, Mendoza retrieved a goat's skin bag full of Madera wine, a gift from the captain. He had thought about sharing it with the Irish but decided that it was all that he had of Spain. It would comfort him for at least the next day or two. He chewed on a chunk of the cheese: it was bitter yet filling. By his reckoning, six hours had passed since the Irish had left. He wished he'd brought his pipe, one more thing he'd forgotten. A smoke would have complemented the wine.

The noise of horse hooves pounded out a staccato din that

filled the still afternoon. Mendoza knew the sound, and it was far more than what he expected from Doolan and his men. Through the window, he watched two-dozen riders crest the same hill he last saw Doolan cross. Many of the men held lances, their tips raised to the sky. They spread out and encircled the house and waited.

One man in officer livery, his helmet polished and bright in the afternoon sun, rode up to the cottage.

"To the Spanish officer in the house, come out immediately."

Mendoza did not answer. He quickly raised the hatch over the tunnel and secreted himself under the floorboards. He'd left no trace of any of his things. A few minutes passed. He then heard boots scuffling across the floor above and muffled voices, English voices. More time passed, and then the ground vibrated from the hooves of the English soldiers' horses as they left. Mendoza waited until it was almost dark, but Doolan did not return with the wagon. Mendoza dragged the chests farther back into the tunnel, scratched out a small cubbyhole with a piece of planking, and then covered the boxes with stones and straw. Back in the cellar, he slowly raised the hatch and, after making sure the room was clear, looked out the tiny window. He saw no soldiers nor heard any horses.

The sun was half an hour from setting when Mendoza gathered up his pack, took a long pull of wine, and headed up the hill. Staying close to a low stone wall, he climbed, and at sunset reached the summit. To the south, the sea extended out to the rim of the world. The sun stood three fingers above the horizon. To the east, the green hills of Ireland rolled on into the approaching night. Looking to the west, his heart stopped; a massive oak tree blocked his view of the hills beyond, and hanging from its huge limbs were five bodies twisting in the breeze that blew in from the sea. Captain Doolan's face was the first he recognized. After that, the others who had greeted him on the beach rotated into view. The shock turned to panic as he heard horses. He removed his pistol from his waistband and drew his sword. He would not end up like the rebels behind him, hung like ornaments from a tree. Juan Flores de Mendoza would die a soldier.

6b

Spring, 1734
The Headlands South of Clonakilty, Ireland

The three Boyle brothers stood on the crest of the hill. To the south, the Celtic Sea churned and boiled. Sea mist bathed the cliffs like smoke rising from an inferno. Laid out below them were small fields, enclosed by stone walls that wandered away to the thicket of woods beyond. A small stone hut, collapsed and abandoned, sat in the higher and drier corner of one of the pastures.

"There, boys, we'll take cover there," Miles Boyle said to his brothers as the rain continued to pummel them.

The brothers, all in their twenties, quickly ran down the slope, scattering sheep. Each carried a sack and, hanging on his belt, each brother had a dagger and sword. Miles had a flintlock pistol pushed through his belt as well. Slung over their shoulders and hanging from a strap, each man also had a leather bag with all his possessions and two days' worth of victuals.

In the dry shelter of the partially collapsed roof of the hut, they spread out the rewards of their thievery: some tin plates, a few pieces of clothing, a small hand mirror, a broken dagger, and a hairbrush. When you steal from the poor, poor pickings are what you get.

"We can sell the brush and dagger for a few shillings; for the rest, we trade," Miles said.

"Yeah, your trading is what got us here—first the horse, then the mule," Conal said.

"We had to eat," Miles said.

"We could have found another way. Stealing will only get the locals outraged and after us. Maybe even the English," Kyran said.

"Hardly. They don't care what one Irishman does to another. Only if it hurts their lordships do they fucken' care."

"I wish we was home. I'm tired of sleeping in barns. Miles,

in three days we could be home."

"We are outcasts. Don't you remember? They threw us out, never to return, they said. If we do, they'll throw us in jail. I'd rather be free."

"Yeah, free and starving, and possibly find ourselves with a noose around our neck due to some misunderstanding about something. I sure as hell don't want to be sent to the Americas," Kyran added.

"God, I'm cold. I'm to start a fire, if your lordship doesn't mind," Conal said to Miles.

"And what are you going to burn? Sheep's dung?"

"There's some boards on the floor. We can pull a few of these and see if they burn."

"They be as rotten as the king's heart. But go ahead, try if you can. A little heat would be welcome."

Conal pulled up and tossed aside rotting boards until he found a few pieces that might burn. "Kyran, there's a nice piece of oak there," he said and pointed.

His brother ducked under a beam of the collapsed roof and pushed away the straw and debris. One moment he was standing on the floor of the cottage, the next, after a sharp crack and splintering, he disappeared. Conal and Miles crawled to the hole in the ground where their brother once stood.

"Kyran, are you okay?" Miles yelled into the hole. "What the hell happened?"

"The fucken' floor gave way, you idiot. What else do you think happened? Pass me a bit of candle."

Conal retrieved a two-inch piece of candle stolen from the vestibule of the church in Clonakilty and dropped it to his brother. A moment later, a small glimmer of light appeared in the hole.

"What's there?"

"A hole. It may be the asshole of hell—what else do you think? Wait, there's a breeze, and I smell the ocean. Maybe this tunnel winds its way down to the sea."

"Conal, get your things, we're going down," Miles said.

"I've heard of these smugglers' tunnels. Maybe that's what this is."

"And maybe it's a hole that leads to nothing."

"Won't know 'til we find out."

The three brothers, carrying bits of candles, explored the tunnel all the way to the sea and back up. Halfway down, they found an empty tin oil lantern as well as other signs that the tunnel once had been used.

"I think this was lost and forgotten," Miles said as they climbed back toward the surface. A dozen steps from the hatch, they stopped and sat on a rough pile of rocks.

"Now what?" Conal asked. "This land has to belong to someone and so does this tunnel."

"I haven't a clue what to do," Miles said as he balanced his piece of candle on the edge of a rock near his right hand. He pulled a wad of tobacco from a pouch and stuffed his pipe. He raised the candle to light it. "I do know that this tunnel hasn't seen a soul in years."

"Miles, move the candle over a little, I thought I saw something," Kyran said. "Good, there. Pull that rock away, now the next. What's that?"

In minutes, they'd cleared away the rocks and debris that had accumulated during the one hundred years that the chests more than one brave man had given his life to protect had remained undisturbed. With each removed rock, more of the heavy wooden boxes were exposed until all four sat free and clear. One by one, they hauled the chests up the tunnel and into the cellar.

"Jesus, what do you think?" Conal said.

"Only one way to find out. Do you still have the pry bar in your bag?"

"Yes, sir."

The Spanish chests were well made, all metal sheeting and reinforced corners and edges. It was dark by the time they sprung open the lock on the first chest. All three brothers knelt around the box as Miles slowly lifted the lid. When the first escudos and doubloons appeared, the brothers turned to each other not knowing what to do.

"The others," Miles said after a few moments.

They worked until their candles burned to nothing. They tried pieces of wood, which proved to be impossible to keep lit. Finally, Miles said, "We will have to wait until daybreak to finish. It's too dark. Conal, see if you can close off the entry a little. In the morning we'll try and figure this out."

In the scant shelter of the tumble-down roof, the three brothers talked quietly into the night, speculating about what to do next. If they could find a way to remove the chests and get them to a safe place, they would be rich beyond their or anyone's dreams. However, they all knew that it was almost impossible to walk into a shop and pay for anything with a Spanish doubloon. Miles said that if they used any of the gold, they would have every English revenuer, magistrate, thief, and taxman after them. They needed a strategy that would allow them to convert this gold into something useful, and considering that none of the three could read or write, it would be a formidable challenge.

The chests being too heavy to carry, they agreed to rebury them. Later, once they had a solution, they would recover and relocate them to someplace safe. As they climbed the hill above the stone hut, they passed under a massive oak tree, now in its fourth century. The tree dominated the views of the hill from the surrounding countryside. The walk into Clonakilty was uneventful. There in the village they hoped to trade their stolen tinware, the dagger, and the hand mirror. They paid little attention to the small posters tacked to signposts and the walls of buildings: *Wanted, Three Brigands for Stealing, Names Unknown. Last seen in Bantry. Reward.* A description of the three Boyle brothers followed. Illiterate, they ignored the notice.

A schoolteacher, known for her nervousness and suspicion of everyone she did not know, saw the three strangers. She immediately went to the local authorities, who then organized a group of citizens and, along with an armed English soldier, confronted the three men. A fight ensued, and Conal Boyle was killed by a lance to his heart. Miles and Kyran were arrested. The leader of the posse sent to arrest the men was the protestant leader of the small community, William O'Bryan. He questioned the two surviving brothers about their illegal activities and threatened them with hanging if they did not confess. That night, in the dark of the cellar they were locked in, the two brothers agreed to admit to their petty thievery but pledged to each other not to say anything about the chests of gold. After numerous witnesses perjured themselves, claiming they saw the men steal the worthless objects, they were held for trial. They were detained in the local jail, or bridewell, until a trial date could be set before the magistrate

"Brother, when we get out of this, we will go back for the chests," Miles said to Kyran. "Hold fast."

The men were sentenced to ten years in the Cork County Gaol. Kyran died in prison from smallpox; Miles managed to survive the pox. For the next eight and one-half years, he thought about two things: the chests hidden in the tunnel, and the protestant tormentor, William O'Bryan. After his early release, he wandered the roads of County Cork alone, working odd jobs for a cup of soup and a potato; sometimes he would be given old clothes and worn shoes. Months after leaving the gaol, he made it to the pastures in the headlands south of Clonakilty. As he walked under the great oak tree, his heart began to race; he knew he was near the stone hut. At the hill's crest, under the great tree, his heart almost breaking, he discovered that during the years he'd been away, a manor home had been built near the wood. Where the old stone hut once stood, a stable and paddock had been constructed. He walked to the narrow carriage road that led from the main road to the house and sat on a log. He removed his pipe, and after expertly stuffing it, lit it. The smoke rose and hung as a cloud around his head. Prison had aged him. Now in his late thirties, he appeared to be twice that. From the direction of the house, he heard a horse; Miles Boyle sat and waited.

The horse and its rider stopped. Their shadows engulfed

Boyle. He looked up and recognized the man who had put him in prison, William O'Bryan.

"This is private land, be gone," O'Bryan said, not recognizing the man. "Get out. Leave or I'll have you arrested."

"Just resting, Captain. I be heading north to my family. Been away for a while," Boyle answered.

"What's your name?"

"Of little consequence to you, sir. I be on my way." Boyle slowly rose, tapped his pipe on the log, and turned to climb the carriage path back to the main road.

"Don't I know you?" O'Bryan asked as Boyle reached the road.

"I don't think so, Captain. Obviously, our paths would never have crossed. Good day, sir." Boyle waved at the man he held responsible for the deaths of his brothers and the theft of more gold than any of the leprechauns of Ireland could ever have imagined.

William O'Bryan raised three sons and two daughters on the estate. Through the plagues, famines, and diseases that marked the seventeenth century in Ireland, he had managed to keep his family healthy and his businesses profitable. As a protestant Irishman, his connections to England and Dublin allowed him to help the poor, and with the assistance of the Catholic Church, he came to the aid of many in the county. It did little to stop the emigration from the region and Ireland, but he did what he could. When William O'Bryan was fifty-three years old, he was found dead alongside the road to Clonakilty. It appeared that he had fallen from his horse and hit his head against a rock. The horse was unharmed and had returned on its own to the paddock and stable built partially from the rocks of the old stone house. O'Bryan wasn't found for almost a day. His eldest son, Kirin O'Bryan, was sure it was foul play; his father was an excellent horseman and would not have been so easily thrown. A few vagrants found in the area were questioned, but none provided an unsatisfactory answer. The magistrate ruled the death an accident.

After his encounter with William O'Bryan after leaving prison, Miles Boyle returned to his mother, now in her dotage, and the small three-room cottage in the hills above Bantry where he and his brothers had grown up. There he stayed, taking care of her and surviving on his own garden and odd jobs. When he was in his early forties, he married a local girl; the union produced five children. Miles stayed near his home and family, except for a few days one summer, ten years after he was released from prison. Miles Boyle died in 1776, ninety years before his great-great-grandson, Amos Boyle, left Ireland for Boston and eventually New York City

Miles Boyle, in the weeks before his death, told his oldest son, Colin, the strangest story the young man had ever heard. Colin passed on the story of the gold-filled chests. A hundred years later, from son to son, the tale had become a family legend.

6c

Summer, 1890
Baile O'Bryan, County Cork, Ireland

For one hundred and fifty years, Baile O'Bryan withstood the ravages of famine, war, and political and religious upheavals. By 1890, Ireland had its share of brutal internal battles between the English, the Anglican Church, forced tithes, the Great Famines of the mid-nineteenth century, and the never-ending skirmishes for independence. The political uprising in America in 1776 would not happen in Ireland if the kings and prime ministers of England could help it.

Ten years before the turn of the century, the house and the lands surrounding Baile O'Bryan were under the care of two brothers, Robert and Michael O'Bryan. A third brother, Clarence, was a priest teaching at Trinity College in Dublin. The loss of the population during the famine put great stress on the estate's operations, and the O'Bryans encouraged people in the area to move onto the property and sharecrop. It was their way to save the property as well as manage it. The stables and paddock area not only provided shelter for the horses and other livestock but home to two families in its rear portions: the O'Rourkes and the Doyles. Their loyalty to the O'Bryans extended back at least one hundred years. Unknown to the local constables and British authorities was the smuggling that continued under their very noses. The tough times of the previous century had affected the three families, and they bonded together to squeeze what few pounds they could from a country bereft of cash. The goods sneaked into the county—wine, tobacco, and eventually weapons and munitions—were traded for cattle and sheep.

Behind the cottage was a pile of old stones remaining from the hut that had collapsed two hundred years earlier. They built a new cottage; its foundation salvaged some of these stones, but for the most part the pile was ignored. A few years before the death of William O'Bryan, and the day after a massive storm had pummeled the southern counties, a two-hundred-foot-long gash appeared in the pasture that overlooked the sea. William O'Bryan discovered the long-lost tunnel that led down through the headland and to the beach. The gash was secretly cleared and rebuilt as a new tunnel that ended under the cottage. Unknown to anyone alive—other than Miles Boyle—the collapse and gash further buried the four chests of gold. Boyle, after murdering William O'Bryan, believed until his dying day that the O'Bryans had found his treasure and used it to become the landed protestant despots he believed them to be.

The legend of the gold hidden in the smugglers' tunnel, albeit passed down through the generations of Boyles, was never heard by the O'Bryans. When Robert O'Bryan, Kevin Bryan's great-grandfather, left for America and San Francisco in 1901, he never knew that under the tumble of boulders he had played on as a child lay buried four chests of gold weighing more than four hundred pounds.

* * *

In the late nineteenth century, Amos Boyle returned to Ireland via Liverpool's crowded docks and then by steamship ferry across the Irish Sea to Cork City. He had left Bantry and Ireland ten years prior, made his home in Boston, and scratched out a living working construction and labor. In time, he moved on to New York and established a small yet profitable construction company serving the immigrant Irish community of New York. The stories his father and grandfather told of the lost family fortune twisted about in his mind. One night, drunk in a bar along the New York waterfront, Amos decided it was time to fulfill his family's destiny by recovering the four chests. In the summer of 1893, he returned to Bantry, visited the graves of his father, mother, and one sister, and took a room in the small hotel on the main street over the pub. The voyage across the Atlantic allowed him time to develop an intricate plan of deception and revenge.

Dressed in his best American business suit and for all the world looking like a successful Irish businessman from the States, he rented a horse and rode the thirty miles of county roads to the O'Bryan estate. His goal was simple, to gain the confidence of the O'Bryans and then find a way to take their lands and the house as retribution for their crimes against his family one hundred and sixty years earlier. Boyle presumed the gold was gone but knew in his black heart that the house and lands were directly related to the Spanish gold, his family's gold.

"Good day, sir," Doyle said to the servant who answered the door.

"And you be?" the servant asked. "Don't know ya, never seen ya before."

"Amos Boyle, my man. I'm a solicitor from New York City in America. I wish to speak to your master, Mr. O'Bryan."

"There be two Mr. O'Bryans. Which one do you wish to speak to?"

Taken aback by the new information, Boyle quickly answered, "Why, it concerns both of the masters of the house."

"And they are by name?"

Again, quickly adjusting, Boyle said, "My good man, I really don't know. I was told that the owners of this house had dealings with important people in New York, and that I would, if needing, find help and support for my cause."

A tall man appeared behind the servant and looked down on the squat figure of Amos Boyle.

"What do we have here, Collins?"

"The gentleman says he's a solicitor from New York City. Personally, I think the man's a—"

"Let the gentleman in, Collins. I think I can handle a lawyer from New York."

"Yes, Mr. O'Bryan." Collins, muttering something under his breath, pulled the front door open and allowed room for Boyle to pass.

"I'm Michael O'Bryan," the landowner said, introducing himself. "And you are?"

"Amos Boyle of New York City. I'm representing clients who, for the moment, wish to remain anonymous. Is there someplace we can talk?"

"Anonymous client? How mysterious. Collins, please take Mr. Boyle's hat and coat. Then find my brother; he should be a part of this."

"Yes, sir," Collins said and then, still muttering, went off to fetch Robert O'Bryan.

"Handsome house you have, sir," Boyle said as they walked through the house to a large room that overlooked the gardens. The day was sunny and bright, and rows of perennials and flowering borders adorned the main window.

"Thank you. It has been in our family for almost two centuries, and we O'Bryans have been a part of this land long before that."

Another man entered the room. He was even taller and more athletic looking than Michael. Boyle studied the men as Michael made introductions. "Mr. Boyle hasn't said a word about why he's here or what his business is with us," the first O'Bryan concluded.

"Mr. Boyle," Robert said and extended his hand. "Welcome. New York City? Now why would someone from America be interested in us and this piece of sod and stone?"

If Amos Boyle had one less-than-endearing quality, it was his ability to lie and to do it so convincingly that even he began to believe his stories. He walked to the window and looked at the gardens, the cottage off to one side, and the woods beyond. He had never questioned the family legend, never for once thought that it might have been a myth, or a classic Irish fairy tale of gold and unfathomable wealth. He knew in his heart that these lands belonged to the Boyles and had been stolen from his family. Further, Boyle had accidentally met a fellow in Boston who knew about the O'Bryans, knew that they were involved in smuggling and moving goods and people into and, when necessary, out of the country. The man had been one of those whom the O'Bryans smuggled out. With this knowledge and the quest for revenge in his pocket, Amos Boyle began to spin a tale.

"Gentlemen, I represent a political consortium in New York. They are interested in acquiring your estate and the others in the county. We believe the troubles that are brewing for independence from Britain may come to a head. These friends of Ireland see your lands as an opportunity to help move the appropriate materials from America to the right people here in Ireland."

The two brothers looked at each other, quizzical expressions on their faces.

"I have no idea what you're talking about," Michael said. "We are farmers, have been and will continue to be."

"This be a mighty fine place for two farmers," Boyle said looking around. "Yes, my people think there's more to the O'Bryans than what's obvious."

"I suggest that you leave," Robert said. "There's nothing to discuss."

"Really? How about the tunnel to the sea?" Boyle blurted, remembering a part of the legend.

Robert looked at Michael, and then said, "You are again mistaken. Tunnel? There's no tunnel. And what would we be needing a tunnel for?"

"For your smuggling, that's what."

"The man's as daft as a mule. Where do people get such ideas?" Michael said. "Lord knows if there was a tunnel, us being born and raised here, we would know. Mr. Boyle, you are one strange duck coming here unannounced and blathering about smuggling. You said you were from around here?"

"Bantry, but I left home ten years ago for the Americas. I put this group together for the future of Ireland. I had it on good authority that you were the men to know."

"Well, your authority was wrong," Robert said. "And I'd keep it to myself if I were you. The local constabulary is keeping an ear to the ground here. What you say about this notion of independence is always on idle tongues. I would be very careful, Mr. Boyle. The British would just love to arrest you and ship you to London and have a personal discussion—if you get our drift. I've even heard there's a reward for such information. Brother, we could use a new plow. What would the English pay to throw this man to them?"

"Might just be enough for a plow but probably not a mule. Mr. Boyle, do you want to continue this conversation with the constable or should we just forget the whole thing?"

Boyle was flummoxed. This was not going the way he'd thought it would. He was positive that after appealing to their loyalty—their Irish loyalty—they would come to his side. Now, they were threatening him with jail.

"I'm sorry to have disturbed you," he said to the brothers. He looked at each of them in turn. "It seems that I misjudged you and your loyalties. I will make sure that my American partners know of your positions. It's a sad day when you can't even trust a fellow Irishman."

"Be very careful there, Mr. Boyle," Michael said. "You are new to these parts. We have been here for hundreds of years. I suggest that you be careful where you walk. The roads can be very dangerous."

Boyle looked at the men. "Is that a threat?"

"Please, my man, no threat," Michael said. "Just the God's

honest truth about the highways around here. There's desperate people about. People who would do anything for a scilling—and I mean anything."

"I can take care of myself, even with your threats."

"I'm sure you can," Robert said. "Why would we threaten you—you walk in making all sorts of accusations about smuggling and a tunnel. How else are we to react? For all we know, you're working with the English. Trying to trick us. That does not sit well in this part of the county. I insist that you leave, Mr. Boyle, before it gets dark."

"Me? With the British? God's honest truth, I hate the sons a bitches maybe more than you."

"Then I believe your stay is over," Robert said. "Collins, bring Mr. Boyle his hat. He's leaving."

Collins was standing in the doorway with Boyle's hat and coat. He handed them to the man as Boyle stormed past him and out the front door to his rented horse.

The warning was a fair one. But it wasn't in County Cork where Boyle was beaten; it was in County Wexford a week later as he headed back to the ferry and England. Three men took everything he had and left him for dead. A local priest nursed him back to health and helped him reconnect to the meager savings he had in a New York bank. The priest also introduced him to someone who heard and believed Boyle's made-up story of his business contacts in New York. The man offered to front Boyle when he returned to the States. With his meager funds, he bought a ticket back to New York City. Within fifteen years, he became one of the largest sources of American-made weapons for the rebels in Southern Ireland. Boyle still believed in the family legend and after his afternoon with the O'Bryans was more than sure they had found the gold.

In time, the political difficulties in Ireland did impact the O'Bryans' household. When Michael returned from service in the Boer War, he married a young girl, ten years his junior, from Cork. She was the daughter of one of his contacts in the Irish Republican Brotherhood. The O'Bryan smuggling intensified, as well as throughout Ireland, as the British tried to find ways to punish the Irish for their attempts to force independence.

Michael's marriage solidified his place in the future of the O'Bryans in County Cork. His brother, Robert, knowing this day would come—along with a thousand-pound price on his head for agitation and sedition—slipped down the tunnel one more time. In the dead of night, he climbed aboard a tramp steamer headed to Charleston, South Carolina. From there he crossed the United States by train and arrived in San Francisco. He was thirty-two years old. His first act was to walk into city hall and request that his name be changed from O'Bryan to Bryan.

Michael kept to himself and his family, leaving the tunnel and its use to others. He had three sons; two were killed during the Easter Uprising. The youngest, Thomas, married, and a month before the truce with England, his only child, Brona O'Bryan, was born.

Chapter 7

There is a great Irish house o'er the sea,
That Kevin did inherit most curiously.
It is a simple tale,
One sure to fail,
Of developers, lawyers, and foul deeds.

7a

In the street-level lobby of O'Shaunnessy, Little, and Lynch, Ltd., Sharon and Kevin confronted the young woman at the reception desk. She looked like a punk poster gal for the Irish tourist industry: bright red spiky hair, cream and peaches complexion, green eyes. If it weren't for the black snake tattoo encircling her left wrist, she would have been perfect.

"One moment," the receptionist replied when Kevin gave his name. She tapped her keyboard and then talked into her headset.

Sharon looked through the glass to the outside plaza; Mr. Grey Jacket had relocated to a new bench. "Got you," she said.

"Pardon, ma'am?" the receptionist said.

"Nothing, nothing at all," Sharon answered.

"Please follow Mr. Reynolds. He will take you to the correct elevator. He will need to enter a key before you can rise."

"Thank you," Kevin said and nudged Sharon. "Before we rise, mind you."

"Shush, the walls have ears," Sharon said.

They followed Mr. Reynolds, who wore a dark grey uniform suit, white shirt, and black tie. He, too, was outfitted with a headset. Sharon, her turn to nudge, nodded to the bulge under the left rear side of the guard's jacket. The shine on the well-worn suit coat perfectly outlined the large upside-down L-shape of a pistol and holster. As they approached the bank of elevators, they passed through an open doorway that was clearly a metal detector. Another guard stood to the side; a yellow light silently flashed as Mr. Reynolds passed through the door.

"Careful, aren't they—for lawyers?" Kevin remarked.

"Solicitors."

"I arrested people for soliciting, back in the day."

"Shush."

Mr. Reynolds pushed the *up* button, and the elevator doors immediately opened. He leaned in and punched in a series of numbers on a keyboard mounted on the panel. He waved Kevin and Sharon in and followed. The doors closed; fifteen seconds later, they opened.

"Please follow me, Mr. Bryan," Mr. Reynolds said. They proceeded across the lobby to a large pair of doors where their armed escort held his key card to a sensor. The view revealed as the double doors slowly opened was impressive: down the Liffey River and out to the Irish Sea. Standing in the glare of the light streaming in through the large windows was a tall, well-formed woman in a business suit. A bright green scarf wrapped her throat; her hair was white and styled in a modern spiked look. Unlike Miss Ireland in the lobby, who spent her money on tattoos, this woman spent a lot of euros on her haircut.

"Good morning, Mr. Bryan. I am Sinead O'Shaunnessy. I was becoming concerned. I hope that you didn't have too much trouble finding us?"

"Ms. O'Shaunnessy, none at all," Kevin said. "This is my friend Sharon O'Mara."

"A pleasure," O'Shaunnessy replied, extending her hand.

"Thank you," Sharon answered.

"Sorry we are late. We were detained and did not realize the distance from the hotel."

"And where are you staying?"

"At the Shelbourne."

"Very nice, I use it for many of my clients when they are in town. If they are not treating you properly, let me know. I may be able to prod them a bit, if you know what I mean. We have much to talk about. Please, follow me."

Sharon and Kevin followed the woman through a rabbit warren of narrow halls and small offices that opened onto the hallway. They would have a difficult time finding their way out if they had to leave unescorted or if there was a fire.

"Impressive," Sharon said. "Are you one of the largest firms in the city?"

"We are actually the largest headquartered here," O'Shaunnessy said as she opened a door to a conference room and ushered them in. "There may be larger international firms here in Dublin, but they are branch offices. We are, by my last count, the largest Irish firm. Coffee, tea?"

"Just some water," Sharon said.

O'Shaunnessy picked up a phone on the conference table and asked that water be brought in.

Sharon walked around the room, looking at the paintings on the walls. All were of historic battles between men armed with axes and swords.

"My family has been connected to the difficult history of Ireland for more than a thousand years," O'Shaunnessy said. "Most of that bloody past dealt with the English. These paintings represent many of those battles. The largest there represents one of the few victories, the battle of Glenmalure in 1580. It was a pyrrhic victory; the English eventually massacred every Irish man, woman, and child they could find, burned their homes and crops—a scorched-earth program at which they excelled. Most of this retribution occurred in and around the city of Cork. Over the next few years, more than a third of the population was starved to death by the English. They took whatever they wanted, and what they didn't take, they killed. Later the English seized the vacant lands and gave them away as favors, or so the story goes."

Sharon walked back and stood next to Kevin. "I knew there was a bloody history, but those paintings lend new depth," she said.

"The history is taught to the Irish children, but today they seem to shrug, ignore the past, and play with their phones. It is very sad."

The water was delivered in crystal carafes and glasses.

"May I guess Waterford?" Sharon said.

"Yes, Waterford. Those particular tumblers have been with the firm for more than half a century. Please sit."

They gathered at the end of the table. Small piles of documents were neatly stacked along the center of the table.

"Mr. Bryan," O'Shaunnessy said, "I suspect that you do not know the history between the O'Bryans and the O'Shaunnessys. Is that a fair guess?"

"I do not," Kevin said. "In fact, when I received your letter, I wasn't aware of much of anything regarding the estate. It had been twenty years since I last had contact with my aunt. That's on me. I should have stayed in communication or at least written a letter or something."

"I understand, and being six thousand miles apart doesn't help, either. But let me give you a little background." O'Shaunnessy then told them about Christopher O'Shaunnessy and his debt of gratitude to Michael O'Bryan for saving his life. The two glaring parts of the story she intentionally left out were the numerous times the firm defended one of the O'Bryan kin when they were suspected of smuggling and how much money she estimated the O'Bryans owed her.

"Seems that your family and the O'Bryans always have been rebels," Sharon said after O'Shaunnessy finished. "Not that I would have expected less."

"It has been a cause we had no choice not to fight against. The English did not discriminate. For centuries, they killed and murdered as necessary, from their imperial point of view. Mr. Bryan, I assume, and from what I know, that is one of the reasons your great-grandfather left Ireland?"

"Yes, he fled the past. That's what I have been told since I was a boy. He changed the family name to Bryan when he arrived in San Francisco—one less connection to his past. He died twenty years before I was born."

"Some of that history I found in my grandfather's memoirs. He did mention Robert O'Bryan, Michael's brother, but little else other than he had gone to America. I have no doubt that you are who you are. After Brona's will was published, we did our own investigations and are certain you are the correct Bryan. It was part of my fiduciary duty to be sure, you understand."

"Of course," Kevin said. "You did a pretty thorough job of it, from what I can see."

"Thank you. But . . ."

"There's always a 'but,' Kevin," Sharon said.

O'Shaunnessy gave Sharon an annoyed look before resuming. "However, before the property rightfully can change hands and the deed be properly registered, all the past-due taxes must be paid. This is something out of my hands."

"I understand. That is why I'm here. I want to take a tour of the property and the estate; I want to know everything before I make a final decision."

"I should hope sooner than later."

"Is the house or the land going anywhere?" Kevin asked. "Seems that these paintings show Irishmen fighting for their lands against someone who wants to steal it from them. So, Ms. O'Shaunnessy, just think of me as someone who has a lot in common with my ancestors. I am expecting friends at the hotel this evening from France and Italy. We are going to the property tomorrow. We are going to make an adventure of the trip, and when I return, I will have a much better idea on how to proceed. I would appreciate a set of keys to the house and any outbuildings."

Sharon smiled at Kevin when he was through. He smiled back. O'Shaunnessy did not return their smiles.

7b

After gathering up the various papers that O'Shaunnessy had neatly stacked, the two Californians placed them in large manila envelopes provided by the attorney, along with one set of keys. They stood, thanked O'Shaunnessy for her assistance, and, after receiving a curt, "I hope you enjoy your visit," returned to the elevator. Back in the ground-floor lobby, Sharon nodded at the dour Mr. Reynolds as they passed through the entry and out into the plaza.

"She is up to something," Sharon said, taking in a breath of fresh air.

"You think? I almost believe she was trying to put me off the property. All the costs, the debts, all that stuff. I got the impression that the keys are to a door with a prize behind it, a prize she doesn't want me to find. All it has done is raise my curiosity. Tomorrow will be fun."

"Mr. Grey Jacket is sitting where we left him. He must be working hourly"—she looked across the sunny plaza to the man on the bench; he was returning a cell phone to his pocket—"and most certainly just a phone call away."

The two strolled through the older parts of Dublin that paralleled the Liffey River, generally taking a circuitous route back to their hotel. They found The Temple Bar and lifted a pint of Guinness while listening to a melancholy singer strumming out an ancient song about the Rising and the victories of the Irish.

"You should come back later," the young bartender said, setting two more pints on the bar. "There's a cover band that does old Clancy Brothers songs. Very good."

"Thank you," Sharon said, looking at the shelves of Irish whiskeys displayed behind the bar. "Kev, I think I've died and gone to heaven."

"Stay here too long and you'd be one drunken angel saying hello to St. Peter."

"Yes, but a very happy angel."

They left the bar and joined the tourists that wandered along both sides of East Essex Street, then turned on Eustace Street and followed it until they reached South Great George's Street. Cutting east, they found King Street, then Grafton Street and St. Stephen's Green. They crossed St. Stephen's Green Road and found a bench near Fusilier's Arch inside the Green.

"This should do just fine," Sharon said. "We'll know in a few minutes."

"Do you think he would have followed us all this way?" Kevin asked.

"As sure as it rains in Ireland, he's a dog on a scent. Thought I caught him when we left the bar, but the crowds swallowed him."

The two friends sat in the warm afternoon sun, watching the tourists and Dubliners crisscrossing the park. They heard a dozen languages, including the annoying announcements from a passing topless two-decker bus stuffed to its gills with tourists.

"We should do that. It would give us an overview of the city," Kevin said.

"Considering the traffic, it would be a very slow overview. Look right."

Mr. Grey Jacket came into view as he walked through the stone arch. The identifying coat now was draped over his arm. He looked nervous, likely concerned that he may have lost his quarry. When he noticed the two, he paused, looked nonchalantly away toward a young woman lying on a blanket. He then turned and walked back out the gate, taking a position just outside, hidden in the shadow of the arch.

"I'd fire him in a minute if he were one of my men," Kevin said.

"You don't have men," Sharon said.

"A blessing and a curse." Kevin looked up the park's walkway and said, "I'll be damned."

"What?"

He stood and walked briskly up to a woman who was strolling the path with a tall handsome man; Kevin stopped directly in their path. Their mutual recognition took only a second. The woman almost jumped into Kevin's open arms.

"When did you two get in?" Kevin asked, squeezing Claudette LeClair. The demure French woman was almost lost in his long arms. A similar welcome happened next to them, as the handsome man held Sharon in his arms. She was giving him a kiss that would have embarrassed anyone.

"An hour ago," Jean-François Voss eventually answered, taking a breath. "We met at the airport. Dumped our bags at the hotel. We decided to take a walk. Damn, it is good to see you two. We are famished, by the way."

Sharon probed the ground with her toes and slid out of Jean-François's arms and dropped lightly to the pavement. "*Moi aussi*," she said.

"I see your French is only slightly better," JF said, not letting go of her hand.

"I need more practice, and lunch would be good. Lots to talk about."

"Believe it or not, we both want fish and chips," Claudette said.

Sharon hugged the tall man around the middle. "You? A pedestrian meal of fish and chips?"

"I have a weakness, forgive me?" JF said to Sharon. His French accent left her no choice but to forgive him all manner of sins; some they had enjoyed together.

"The Duke, just across the street and up a block or two," Claudette said. "We were heading there. It is so good to see you, and happy birthday."

"It is still a few days away, and thank you for coming. I know it's an inconvenience."

"Never," JF said.

"Where's Balanca?" Kevin asked. "I thought he was coming with you."

"Sharon, Fidor extends his regrets. Business and a client demanded his attention in Azerbaijan. Something to do with oil, caviar, and guns. I don't ask anymore."

"Wise choice," Kevin said. "That's too bad. Gina will miss him."

"After her little adventure yesterday and her new friend—who is a Dublin copper taking her to lunch—I'm not that sure she will miss him," Sharon said.

"What's that all about?" Claudette wanted to know.

"We'll tell you at lunch," Sharon promised.

The four friends walked back up Grafton Street. When they passed their stalker—ignoring him—he waited a few seconds before falling into step behind them, staying roughly a block back. They turned onto Duke Street; the pub stood on the corner. It was the after-lunch crowd; the restaurant was half full. They took a table for four in one of the alcoves.

"Now what is this about Gina?" Claudette asked as soon as they sat down.

Sharon told the story of the attempted kidnapping and the miraculous appearance of Officer Liam Donovan.

"My God," JF said. "And she's all right?"

"Yes," Sharon said. "And, of course, there's the added benefit of her Irish champion. I believe she's fallen head over high heels for the fellow."

"Even better that Fidor didn't come. An Irish cop and a man who knows his way around the powers in Russia. I am not sure that's something I'd care to see or get in the middle of."

"Agreed," Kevin said, raising his glass. "A drink to Irish kismet and luck."

"So, you are to be an Irish lord or something? Should I be calling you Sir Bryan?" Claudette asked. "I could really go for a man with a title. France has become so egalitarian it is now almost wishy-washy. Knowing a duke or a lord would be a good thing, something to brag about."

"I was Detective Bryan at one time."

"Yes, but royalty is so much in demand these days in Europe," Claudette continued. "As we've become increasingly secular, it seems that we now elevate those with some moldy old connections to peerage and ancient families. But then again, there's that royal inbreeding and idiocy thing."

"The O'Bryans are just an old Irish name," Kevin said. "Not connected to anything other than the dirt they are buried in. But, if it's royalty you want, I'll see what I can work out."

"And what are you doing these days, Mr. Voss?" Sharon asked as she gently tapped the back of his hand.

"A new line of high-tech sailboats is in production in Marseilles, a big contract with the America's Cup people for navigation controls and, unbelievably, some work with a French carmaker and self-driving cars. That's all I can legally say, but it is very cool stuff. Claudette is doing much of the software for the systems."

"He's being modest," Claudette said. "He's one of the leaders in the field here in Europe. The Europeans are trying to keep up with the tech going on in California—every day something new, something different. And Jean-François is on the leading edge." She grinned playfully. "In fact, a cuter French Elon Musk has been tossed around."

"I'm staying away from all the space technology," JF said amidst the general laughter at Claudette's last remark. "There is more than enough fun stuff on the water and land."

"He's turning red," Claudette said to Sharon.

"Sharon, I understand that you've been visiting Cuba recently?" JF asked when the good-natured amusement at his expense subsided.

"Yes, but the food is not that great. Besides, I wasn't there a week. In and out, a short trip."

"In and out? I understand there is a family that is very happy that you managed to make a visit. I wish I could have been there when the family was reunited. Sorry, I could not leave Marseilles."

"I completely understand, but you are making up for it now. I need my friends here during this most difficult time of my life."

"Oh, dear God. Please stop with the woe-is-me whining," Kevin said. "JF, she is wearing this coming birthday like it's the end of her life. Maybe you can get her out of the dumps."

"I will try to do everything I can."

It was Sharon's turn to blush.

7c

When the four friends returned to the hotel, they found Evelyn Lucca and Gina sitting in the large leather chairs in front of the fireplace in the off-lobby parlor. Evelyn had a glass of red wine; Gina sipped an Irish whiskey. The sextet was a strange mix of nationalities, cultures, and pasts. Friendships were like that, thought Sharon, delighted at the gathering.

"Do you have a schedule?" Gina asked, looking straight at Kevin. "Or are we winging this?"

"In fact, we do have a schedule. Baile O'Bryan is about one hundred and seventy miles south of here. I dropped the minivan off this morning and traded it in for a ten-seat minibus. We leave at nine tomorrow morning. I made it from the airport, I can make it to Clonakilty. We will have lunch at a small seaside resort a few miles from the estate. I also secured rooms for us at the same resort for the next two nights."

"Kevin? You've done this all on your own?" Gina said.

"I can be organized, Ms. Cavelli. Give me a little credit," he said with a smile. "The bus is ours for the three days. I'll make inspections of the house and the grounds. If any of you want to tour County Cork and the surrounding countryside, the bus is at your disposal. We will head back about noon on Wednesday. We have rooms here. After that, we have been invited to Clive Barrington's place in Kent. I assume all of you want to go to Cork?"

The vote was unanimous. Everyone wanted to see the Baile O'Bryan.

* * *

"How was your lunch?" Sharon asked Gina as the two of them later sat in a dark corner of the bar sharing a bottle of French burgundy.

"It was a bit awkward and tentative at first," Gina said. "The man is surprisingly shy. Who would have thought such a good-looking guy like that would be nervous around little old me?"

"I've seen you handle drunks and obnoxious men your whole life—you can be intimidating."

"Thanks, but it was so cute, but I eventually wore him down. Got him to smile and spill a little about himself. He's from a small town north of Dublin called Drogheda. Went to Catholic schools, his folks are still alive, and he has a sister living in Northern Ireland in Ulster, wherever exactly that is. He's been a cop for fifteen years, and when he can, he plays semi-pro rugby."

"You have never dated an athlete. This will be interesting."

"Be quiet. He's a plainclothes detective and can only tell me he's doing some work on the sex trade problem here in Dublin."

"It seems to be epidemic."

"True, but then he changed the subject and wanted to know everything about Kevin's castle and inheritance. He found it all amusing and curious at the same time."

"Curious?"

"Yes. It seems to be that there have been a few swindles during the last ten years that ran a similar scam: target someone with news of an old inheritance. Then lots of stuff about searching for the victim, lots of back taxes, but then an intermediary pops up who is willing to handle the tax thing. Money is exchanged and then, shockingly, no castle, no nothing."

"I can see that happening. However, after our meeting with the attorney this morning, we're fairly certain that this isn't exactly the case. Besides, I would think the scam would be after someone with money, and we certainly know that Kevin is not in that category. And we were tailed the whole time. That's why we need to check out your Irish copper. For all we know, he's part of O'Shaunnessy's little band."

"And how are we going to do that?"

"Kevin is calling Clive Barrington in the morning. Liam may be everything we want to believe he is; then again, he may not."

"Always looking out for me, aren't you?"

"I can't think of how many times you've had my back,"

Sharon said. "It's only fair."

"This attorney, you don't trust her?"

"Not an inch, and neither does Kevin. For once, I'm proud of our boy. He hasn't jumped in with both feet up to his neck. We are on the same page. However, I think he's very excited about seeing the property and wondering, 'what if?'"

"I get that," Gina said. "I'm wondering myself."

Chapter 8

There once was a lad from County Clare,
Who won a great prize at the fair.
'Tis a crock full of gold,
Our charmed boy was told,
But in truth was a Celtic nightmare.

8a

Sinead O'Shaunnessy sat outside Searsons tavern and pointed to a seat at her table. The man she was signaling, wearing a grey jacket, squeezed his way along the brick wall of the pub, lit a cigarette, and settled into the bench seat. He blew smoke upwards; it held in the still air like a thundercloud about to spit lightning.

"Put the cigarette out. You know I don't like the smell," O'Shaunnessy said.

"Too fucken' bad," the man answered. "You pay me to watch; as such, I get to smoke. Only fair."

"They said you were an asshole."

"Yeah, maybe. But today, luv, I'm your fucken' asshole."

"Don't be impertinent. What happened after they left?"

"Nothing. They wandered across town toward their hotel, had a beer at the Temple Bar, and then went to St. Stephen's park. There they met with two others, a man and a woman."

"Met?"

"Maybe ran into. Anyway, they got all lovey-dovey—hugs and shit—and then wandered over to the Duke for lunch. Later they went to the hotel."

"So, Bryan has his group of friends with him?" O'Shaunnessy asked.

"Looks like it. None of them, other than the two you had me follow, looks Irish. Earlier, before he saw you, this guy Bryan drove his rental over to the Avis lot a few blocks away and traded the mini for a small bus. My guess, they are making the trip to Clonakilty."

"Yes, he told me he was. I want you and one of your boys to follow and watch them. Do nothing unless I tell you. Call me when you leave and when you get there. I want reports twice a day."

"Yes, mum. Same rate?" Grey Jacket said.

"Yes, same rate. Just don't screw up. If you do, you won't get a scilling."

"Yes, mum." There wasn't an ounce of respect in his voice.

"And don't mess it up like you did with the girl. You told me it was going to be a simple snatch and now all hell breaks loose. I've heard from my sources that the Garda are asking questions; seems your people got mixed up with a copper. So, don't fuck it up tomorrow, got it?"

The man in the grey jacket crushed his cigarette on the pavement, stood, and, without saying anything, walked away.

O'Shaunnessy watched him turn the corner. *Asshole.* It was getting more and more difficult to find good help these days, people she could trust, even for the outrageous price they demanded. Especially this group—O'Shaunnessy corrected her earlier assessment: *bottom of the barrel asshole.*

The buzzing in her pocket jolted her back to the present as the server placed a glass of wine on the table. The phone's screen read *NYC.*

"Good evening, Sylvia, morning there I expect," O'Shaunnessy said.

"It is, and good morning to you. Did our boy arrive?" Boyle said.

"Yes, and he's brought an entourage with him. There's at least four and possibly more. Bryan is treating this like it is a vacation or something. His attitude worries me, but not enough to make me believe that we can't make this work. They are going to the property tomorrow. I'm having him watched. There should be no problems. He should be discouraged by the condition of the house. I'll stress the rehabilitation costs on top of the past-due taxes as well as the future recurring costs and upkeep."

"Are you going to mention a possible sale?"

"Not yet. I need to get him discouraged. I have quietly contacted someone I know at the Revenue Commission to push for a quick payment to settle the probate and the inheritance. When we have the final numbers, I will offer an alternative and tell him I may have a buyer."

"You won't say who, will you?" Boyle said.

"Of course not. It will be through the shell corporation we put together last year for that hotel you bought here in Dublin. No one will know it's you."

"Excellent. They will learn it's me at some point, but right now I don't want anyone to know. Too much happening over here, and the limited partners might get concerned if they were to think I was not fully engaged in their shitty little deal."

"I will call you as soon as I hear something."

"Good."

Before O'Shaunnessy could say more, Boyle had hung up.

* * * *

Boyle set the phone back in its cradle and thought about the property and all that it meant. The golf course and club would provide a nice addition to the purchase. The course routing plans looked very good, both courses. More than enough of a test to be a championship venue—maybe even a Ryder Cup site someday. The trick would be to get the locals on her side, show them the opportunities and the money that would spin off from the resort and the jobs. The countryside looked desperate and poor. When she and Sinead had driven through the county from Cork, each mile seemed like time was spinning backwards, and when they reached the cliffs, she couldn't figure out how anyone made a decent living. Revolution was spawned in these hills; after the Anglo-Irish Treaty was negotiated, many in IRA units would have none of it. The greatest thorn driven into the heart of Ireland was the establishment of Northern Ireland, a separate country that left the Free State of Ireland and remained aligned with Britain. After the treaty came the yearlong Irish Civil War, which took the lives of many of the brightest and most militant leaders on both sides. The war caused a great social and political rift throughout Ireland. After the assassination of the revolutionary Michael Collins, Sylvia's great-grandfather Amos Boyle—then almost sixty years old—had used his construction company as a conduit for money to buy weapons in the United States and get them to his friends in the IRA. It was a good business to be in; there'd been some competition, which Amos resolved through acquisitions and eliminations. For the next eighty years, in one form or another, the Boyle family had supported the anti-Republican and anti-British IRA. The money the family made in weapons trade provided the capital for the Boyle development business. After World War II, Amos and his young son, Donald, acquired some old naval properties in northern New Jersey and developed housing for returning veterans. They made even more money.

When Sylvia was a child, her great-grandda would tell stories of Ireland and County Cork, and of the family Boyle—stories of leprechauns, gold, smugglers, and Spanish Armadas. At night, young Sylvia would dream of green hills, rainbows, and treasures.

The family's history as gunrunners had contributed to the rift between Sylvia and her children—two of them, that was. Her eldest and middle child spent the requisite holidays together but had physically moved as far away as their trust funds permitted. Only David, the youngest and half-brother to the other two, worked for DBD, Ltd. and embraced his mother's eccentricities. Some said that Sylvia Boyle treated her champion Yorkshire terrier, Lord Smathers, better than her kids and grandkids. Some remarked that she and her dog would be better off in hell.

"Ask David to come to my office," Sylvia said into the intercom on her desk.

"Ms. Boyle, David is in New Jersey this morning at the job

site. Shall I call him?" the assistant replied.

"Yes, tell him I need to talk with him. Have him stop by my office before he goes home tonight."

"Yes, ma'am."

* * *

David Stein, her thirty-three-year-old son by Sylvia's third marriage, had become almost as ruthless as his mother. Tough, opinionated, gregarious, he was known for his no-nonsense negotiation style, no-prisoner attitude, and a string of disappointed and damaged (but well-compensated) women from one end of Manhattan to the other. His only redeeming quality was that he never married and, as far as anyone knew, left no little Davids to dog his footsteps. His one endearing attribute was his loyalty to his mother and DBD, Ltd. He'd even sued his sister and brother over some questionable issues about income and trusts and won. He had not talked to his half-siblings in six years.

Lord Smathers barked once and padded his way across the oak floor of Sylvia Boyle's office and waited near the door. When David entered, the animal harrumphed and padded his way back across the office floor to his small bed. David retrieved a small treat from a dish on the desk and pitched it to the pup, who promptly bit it in two and commenced to eat the parts. Like all the Boyles, the dog did not say thank you.

"What is so important?" David asked after he poured a measure of whiskey and settled into a large leather wingback chair.

"Ireland. I need you to go and see what's happening," Sylvia said. "I trust O'Shaunnessy only as far as it goes. She said this Bryan fellow has brought an entourage to help him with the property. I don't like the sound of it. I want that property, and I can't leave right now. You need to find out what's going on. Do what you need to do. O'Shaunnessy says she has people who will help if you need to have more forceful persuasion."

"You know that we are close to finalizing the New Jersey plans; is this Ireland deal really that important?"

"Yes, it is. New Jersey needs us more than we need them. Let them stew for a week or two; it will be good for them. You shouldn't be gone more than four or five days, maybe less. If needed, you can be very persuasive."

"I'll leave in the morning."

8b

Tommy O'Rourke stood next to his fifteen-year-old Toyota Corolla smoking a cigarette; he nervously flipped the lid of his mobile phone open and closed. They were late, and he needed the deal and he was sure they needed him. The morning fog had begun to thicken in the clearing of the wood. He'd told them seven o'clock—later they might be seen. He heard the SUV before he saw it. The black Range Rover materialized out of the fog and slid to a stop in the mud. O'Rourke had expected two men; four climbed out. Two took wide flanking positions, the other two, both red-haired Irishmen in dark green Barbour field coats, walked directly to O'Rourke and at two paces away stopped and stood their ground.

"Tommy, m'boy, I understand that you have something to say to us," the taller of the two men said.

"Yes, Mr. Dunham, I do. It's a proposition that will have profound value for the both of us."

"Profound value, you say? Now, what could a foolish boy like you have that would have 'profound value' to someone like me and m'brother? Can't you see we have everything?" Dunham waved open his arms and smiled.

"See, I told you, Derek," the shorter redhead said. "All wind, no sail."

"Patience, Cullen. It took a lot of balls for the kid here to make the inquiry. Besides, we owe him and his family a little respect. His granddad fought with ours against the British. That goes a long way here in the hills and valleys of Cork. So, young Tommy, what has got your panties all twisted?"

O'Rourke looked past the two brothers to the men ten paces

away to both his left and right. *Fuck, what have I gotten myself into?* He took a deep breath. "It's common knowledge that if someone wants a little taste of the poppy that you are the men to point the way."

"'Tain't saying we do or don't, so?"

"Well, being in the business myself—supplying things that people need and will pay handsomely for—maybe I can be of help."

"Was guns and now cigarettes—your aunt Molly will have nothing to do with what we sell. I respect her and her choices. We stay to our side of the street; she stays to hers. The profit margins are higher for us, and we put the money to much better use. It can only stay quiet for so long in Belfast."

"I'm told that the Garda are taking what you sell a lot more seriously these days—seems that doors are closing."

"Maybe yes, maybe no," Cullen said. "Why are you concerned?"

Tommy chose his words carefully. "There are other doors in this part of Cork, doors that have been kept as family secrets. For a small, very small percentage, I might be able to unlock one of those doors."

Derek took two steps toward Tommy and, with frightening speed, punched him full in the stomach and then to the side of his head, knocking the younger man to the muddy lane. He stood over Tommy as he heaved and coughed. When he tried to stand, Derek hit him across the back of his head with a blackjack that magically had appeared in his right hand. He turned to the two bodyguards. "Lift him up. Be careful not to get mud on you. I do not want that shit in the car."

The men lifted Tommy upright and leaned him against the Toyota. Tommy's eyes slowly drifted back to reality.

"Tommy boy, listen carefully, we never repeat ourselves. First, I'm embarrassed for you. It is us who make the financial arrangements and decisions, not you. Someone should have told you that. Second, this is all so tawdry meeting like this. Next time, if there is one, we will contact you. Third, we fully understand that you are pissing all over your family name and legacy; we Provisionals are an honorable company. Suppose I was to tell Molly that her nephew was selling her out? What do you think she would do about that? I'm sure old Mac MacLeish would cut out your tongue and feed it to the pigs. Now, clean yourself up and from now on be very careful. If we need something from you, we will find you. Do you understand?"

Blood dripped from the corner of Tommy's mouth and more blood trickled down behind his left ear. He coughed. "Yes, sir," he whispered.

"Louder, so that your honorable ancestors can hear you," Cullen said.

"Yes, sir, I understand."

"Excellent," Derek said. "Now you just stand here and get your wits about you. I do not want you driving in this fog until you have all your faculties. Then, just be glad for what you have. We are not looking for trouble, so go home, and take care of yourself."

He nodded to one of the thugs, who then punched Tommy again in the gut, dropping him to his knees in the mud. From that position, Tommy watched the men climb back into the Range Rover and disappear into the fog.

8c

David Stein waited at the door of the jet, watching as the Cork Airport grounds crew secured the wheels of the Gulfstream. A Jaguar SUV was parked on the tarmac near the base of the deployed stairway. Two men stood nearby. They matched the photos David had been emailed while he crossed the North Atlantic. The man on the right was Fergus Banning; the other was Quinn Thomson, both ex-Irish military. Stein assumed they were O'Shaunnessy's hired guns; their business cards probably said investigators. He had some just like them on retainer in New York. Through their contacts, he imagined, they could raise a small personal army in less than a day.

When Stein stepped onto the tarmac, Thomson took his bag and carried it to the open rear door of the SUV.

"Sir," Banning said, "Customs is this way. After that, we are at your disposal."

"Excellent."

A short ten minutes later, with Thomson driving, they headed out onto N27 and south toward Kinsale.

"Mr. Stein, do you wish to rest for a while before we head to the property?" Banning asked.

"No, I slept on the plane. We can head directly to the coast; did you make arrangements for the next few days?"

"Yes, sir. There's an inn about five kilometers from the property. We have rooms there."

"Good. Do you have everything I noted in my email?"

"Not everything, but we will by noon. One of my men is bringing it all down. The Bryan group is under surveillance in Dublin. I was texted that they left the hotel about twenty minutes ago in a minibus. It will take them at least five hours to reach the property, most probably longer. I assume they will do some of the touristy things on the way."

"Fair assumption. How long for us?"

"Not even an hour. We will have ample time to prepare."

They drove on in silence as the morning fog was lifting. The County Cork landscape rolled by; the green hills and thick groves of dark trees were numbing in their unending parade. Sheep as well as black and white cows dimpled the landscape. Traffic was almost nonexistent. David shook his head and mumbled something to himself about the fucking poor and the reason why his ancestor fled Ireland.

"Excuse me, sir. Did you say something?" Banning asked.

"No, just thinking. My family came from this county ninety years ago."

"I'm from the north myself. It rains too fucken' much here."

"I'm not sure I could tell," Stein offered. He hated the countryside, whether in wet Ireland or the dry pine barrens of New Jersey.

The inn sat on the upper reach of a sandy cove, four two-story buildings spread along the shelf of rock above the sand and waterline. After checking in, Stein and Banning walked to the terrace that overlooked the cove. Courtesy of a wide gap in the cliffs, from the terrace they were afforded a spectacular view of the Irish Sea beyond. The sea was riled; great waves burst over the rocks, throwing foam into the air that floated, cloud-like, above the turmoil. It was obvious that the tide was receding; a line of flotsam marked its way halfway up the beach. No footprint impressions scarred the beach.

"When will they arrive?" Stein asked impatiently.

Banning looked at his phone. "My man says they should be here about two o'clock, assuming they don't stop."

"Then we have time. Your man with the equipment?"

"Twenty minutes out. He will meet us at the property."

The drive to the O'Bryan property took ten minutes. Stein was stunned by the building's condition and the surrounding paddocks and stables. To his eye, it looked derelict and abandoned. He could not understand what his mother saw in the property, but then again, he had more than once been surprised by her vision. As a golfer, he did appreciate the potential of the lands that rolled out to the cliffs. When Thomson drove them up to the house, a white panel van with no identification sat in the cobblestone parking area. One man, wearing a black nylon windbreaker, stood next to the car smoking a cigarette. He crushed it on the stones as the Jaguar arrived.

"Shamus, were you able to get everything?" Banning asked the man as he shook his hand.

"Yes, sir, no problems." He opened the rear panels of the truck, revealing the cardboard boxes secured to shelving on one side.

"Which one?"

"The top left, compact and lightweight. Should I get it?"

"Wait here with Quinn. We are going to look around. Mr. Stein, this way, please."

Banning and Stein walked toward the house. The fog had

begun to roll back in.

"You have been here before?" Stein asked.

"Yes, a few weeks back. Ms. O'Shaunnessy wanted to make sure that I was aware of the property. I assume that you wanted the device for effect?"

"Effect? That's a good word, yes. Intimidation is also a good word. Anything to have this man Bryan think about not going forward. An explosion might just do that, especially if he thinks that the local Provisionals might be involved."

"The equipment matches much of theirs. Some of the C-4 is from a stash of theirs. All the evidence will point the Garda in the right direction."

"The location?"

"There is a spot in the rear of the cottage—that's the building there on the right—that should do the job. I assume that, even though the house is a shamble, you do not want it damaged."

"Personally, I could care less. However, my mother seems to like it. Show me where."

At the rear of the house, eight steps led down to a heavy wooden door. A modern lock had been secured to the door.

"Key?"

Banning produced a key and unlocked the door; a switch on the right illuminated the small room.

"Root cellar, dirt floor, just the two doors. The stair in the corner there leads up to a kitchen area. There's four or five rooms upstairs, nothing remarkable. This is the newest addition to the house, built back during the time before the partition with England. Don't know why it was built—seems to me the main house would have been more than enough."

"Interesting, so where?"

"The far corner, near the stair. As you can see, there are other boxes. The device will be lost amongst them. The detonator is good for a day or a month, digital. Two ways to arm it, by timer and by cell phone through an app."

Stein looked at the man. "An app? Do you mean that there is an app to set off a bomb?"

"Actually, it's the same type of app you use to turn on the lights at your house or open the garage door. Just a little tinkering, and it will turn anything on."

"Or set anything off."

Twenty minutes later, the device had been hidden and all evidence of them being there was wiped away. Shamus headed back to Dublin in the van. After a greasy lunch of fish and chips at a local pub just outside of Clonakilty, Stein and the two Irishmen returned to the inn.

Chapter 9

In tears a lass stood on the beach,
Her love was gone, now out of reach.
Dark thoughts she kept,
She pined and wept,
Of a lost love, none could beseech.

9a

Kevin bluntly told everyone that since he was now a landowner in Ireland it would be best to allow him the chance to gain experience driving the narrow country roads. His real reason was that, after seeing how tight the rear seats of the Mercedes Sprinter van were, the driver's seat seemed to give him the most leg room.

"Fancy ride," Gina said from the rear seat. "You couldn't get one with Wi-Fi or a DVD player?"

"Really," Kevin yelled back. "Look out the windows, enjoy the scenery. You don't want me to turn around and take you back to the hotel?"

"Yes, father," Gina said with a laugh. "Are we there yet?"

"You two stop it," Sharon said. "You're embarrassing me in front of our guests."

Gina gave everyone a big smile. "Yes, mother."

The four females had commandeered the back seats. JF sat in the left front bucket seat next to Kevin. As the women chatted away, JF asked Kevin, "Are you really going to take over this property?"

"Not sure. It will take a lot of money—money I do not have. There's the back taxes, the repairs, all those never-ending costs of maintenance, so there's a lot to think about. Right now, all I want to do is see the old family home. Then, we'll see."

"This attorney, you're not impressed?"

"No. After our meeting yesterday, I'm certain she has something else going on. What it is—not sure. She can't wish away the taxes and is faced with the same costs I am. We think there's a buyer out there. Some kind of a backroom deal—the next few days will be interesting."

"I expect so."

They stopped in Clonakilty and had lunch at a small pub. Waves of lost cultural nostalgia swept over both Sharon and Kevin as they walked down the narrow sidewalks of the colorful village. On either side of the one-way street, the buildings had been painted in one bright color after another, pink, orange, blue, white, turquoise. Baskets of flowers hung from street lampposts and building window ledges.

"Beautiful," Evelyn said. "Reminds me of some of the villages in Tuscany."

"And along the Brittany coast as well," Claudette offered. "But then again, Brittany and Brest can't be more than three hundred miles to the south. Walking those northern French village streets feels more like Ireland and England than France."

"I really need to get out more," Sharon said.

"Me, too," Gina added.

After they climbed back into the van, Gina asked again if they were there yet. Kevin turned and gave her a stern look.

"I can leave you here if you like," he joked. "The house is a few miles to the south. I thought we would stop there first. Sharon and I want to walk the property and look at the house. There's a lot to look at. If you want to walk with us, you are invited. If not, take the van and pick us up in a few hours. Bantry is to the west and Kinsale is to the east. The inn is to the east, not more than a few miles."

"I sadly didn't wear the right shoes to climb over the hills and dales," Evelyn said. "If JF doesn't mind being chauffer, I would prefer the tourist thing instead of the county land surveyor thing. Claudette?"

"Those clouds say rain, so I'll tag along with the two of you," Claudette said. "We will have time over the next few days to see the house. Gina?"

"I'm going with Sharon and Kevin. I've been with them since day one on this adventure, so I need to see my investment through to the end."

Kevin nearly missed the entry road to the property. He stopped and backed up, and then bumped his way down the road to the house. As he pulled the minibus to a stop in the courtyard, the sky miraculously cleared a little and the sun broke through, throwing light on the house and surrounding countryside. To the south and west, out over the sea, dark clouds began to rebuild.

"Better than I thought," Kevin said.

"Better? It looks like it's straight out of *Wuthering Heights*," Gina said. "Yes, from now on I'm calling you Lord Bryan."

They walked around the outside of the main house. JF caught up with Kevin and Sharon as the others strolled behind. "It needs a serious and expensive amount of work and repair," he said. "That's obvious. Rule of thumb: double or triple what you think the costs will be. These old things, while solidly built, still needed maintenance. That is something this old girl has not had for years."

"We can talk more tonight," Kevin said, as JF, Evelyn, and Claudette said their goodbyes. JF and the two women drove out to the main road, leaving the three Americans standing in the courtyard.

"There is a path out to the cliffs," Kevin said. "Let's start there and work our way back before it rains. We can see more of the house and the cottage when we get back."

The stroll through the fields and copse of woods that separated the fields from the cliff took twenty minutes. They were amazed by the views and the spectacular landscape. When they reached the cliff, the panorama up and down the coast astounded them.

"It is alive," Sharon said. "You can feel the sea under your feet, like small earthquake tremors and vibrations. The roar of the ocean rises up these narrow canyons and is magnified. Extraordinary."

"This is a smugglers' coast," Kevin said. "My grandfather told stories of the shipwrecks, the salvage, the small boats run in with contraband from larger ships offshore. That was during the time of the British when they taxed everything. The smugglers brought in and took out goods to avoid the taxman. In the 1800s, if caught, it was either a hanging offense or transport to Australia. The English took their taxes very seriously."

"Reminds me of our IRS," Gina said. "But how the hell could you land anything with waves as massive of those?"

"There were opportunities when the sea calmed," Kevin answered.

"Timing is everything," Gina said.

"It's a long way down to the beach," Sharon said. "Did they haul up everything with ropes?"

"There are inlets up and down the coast. They would slip into these coves and quickly offload. Grandfather said it was a game of cat and mouse. Sometimes the cat would win, more often the mice. A hundred years ago, during the rebellion, thousands of rifles and munitions were slipped into Ireland along this coast by the IRA and others. Many came from the Americas. I understand that smuggling still goes on."

"What could be smuggled now?" Gina asked.

"Cigarettes, drugs, even migrants."

"Migrants from Africa would certainly stick out in this country," Sharon said.

"The world is changing," Kevin said.

"There are those here who would prefer it not change," Sharon added.

They walked slowly back to Baile O'Bryan. The number of broken windows along the backside doubled what they saw in the front. Kevin unlocked the oak front door and pushed it open. They waited in the vestibule to see if ghosts might come floating down the staircase. All they heard was an eerie quiet and the echoes of their own footsteps on the dusty floor.

"Someone has been here recently," Sharon said, pointing to the unswept hardwood floor. Dozens of footprints headed in all directions from the front door.

"O'Shaunnessy is my guess," Kevin said. He looked more closely. "Two different sets, recent, no dust in the cleared spots. Both, from their shapes, appear to be either small men's or women's shoes. I'm going with women. There's others, but dust covers them. So, assuming that the solicitor has been here, I wonder whose prints the others are."

"I'm sure we will find out soon," Sharon said.

They spent the next hour exploring the impressive house. Dark oak paneling lined the walls, the floors were a mixture of tile and wooden flooring, and the rooms were a mixture of wallpaper and paneling. There were empty spots on the walls where paintings once hung. The rooms themselves were mostly empty, although they spooked some pigeons that fled out through the broken windows. Kevin speculated that the furniture and art had been sold.

They found a set of rooms on the upper floor that still had furniture and had been recently occupied. Rumpled bedclothes were piled on the four-poster bed. A tea service, with dirty cups, sat next to the bed.

"My aunt's room, I suspect," Kevin said. "How lonely."

"I'm sorry," Gina said.

"That's okay, I had no idea. I assume that she led a full life," Kevin answered.

"I wonder if we will ever know?" Sharon said.

They visited the adjacent cottage next. They walked through the unremarkable set of rooms, and again there was little furniture; even the cabinets in the kitchen were empty. Gina opened a door in the corner of the old kitchen and peered down the stairs into a gloomy dank room.

"Root cellar," she declared and shut the door.

Back in the entry foyer, they looked at the one remaining painting that hung on the wall.

"That must be a relative," Sharon said. "I always wondered what you would look like in a skirt."

"With that broadsword and dagger in the sock," Kevin said, "I'm quite sure that no one made fun of him." He read the inscription: *Dugan O'Bryan, Chieftain, 1731–1812.* "The man lived in interesting times. That makes him my great-great-great-great-grandfather."

"Good-looking guy. I guess some things are just not inherited," Gina said.

"Really, you still have to bust my chops?"

She pulled him down and kissed him on the cheek. "You are still my favorite Irishman."

As they walked back to the main house, the minibus wound its way down to the courtyard.

"I'm going to do something crazy," Kevin said to Sharon and Gina. "After we check in at the inn and have a decent meal, I'm coming back here and spending the night. That's the least I can do. Get a feel for the house, understand my aunt a little . . ."

"And most probably scare up a few ghosts. These castles always have ghosts," Gina declared.

"No ghosts," Sharon said.

"You sure? Every time we walked into a room, I felt a chill. Ghosts do that."

"So do broken windows. Kev, I understand," Sharon said. "I'm staying with you, if you don't mind."

"There is only one bed."

"I'll take the couch."

"Not me," Gina said. "This Italian girl has no desire to spend the night with a house full of Irish spirits. I'd rather drink mine."

9b

Molly O'Rourke stood in the dark shade of the same tree where she had watched O'Shaunnessy and Boyle only a few weeks earlier, Dergo at her side. Now a Mercedes minibus and six people stood in the courtyard of the O'Bryan house. Three were obviously American, and the tallest had to be the O'Bryan kin. He looked just like Dugan O'Bryan in the cottage painting. This was the second group to visit the farm that day. The first obviously had been men from the solicitor's camp. What they were doing was less than clear. She'd watched them take a box from their van to the rear of the cottage. She hadn't enough time to find out what it was they left in the cottage before the second group arrived. It bothered her, although she felt certain that no one would find the entry to the cave. No one had for a hundred years. Her phone pinged a text.

Need you in Clonakilty, issues at the bakery.

What? Can't you handle it? she typed.

Oven's down, thermostat or something.

Shit, she wanted to check out the cottage after the Americans left. Now she would have to come back. *—OK. Fifteen minutes.*

She walked back through the small woods to her car parked a hundred yards off the road. As she pulled to a stop at a gap in the hedge that lined the road, the white Mercedes Sprinter passed her. She saw that the driver was the tall American; the others were a blur. She guessed that they were staying in the inn a few miles down the coast. As she pulled out onto the two-lane road, she had an idea. She would send Mac down to the bar at the inn and find out what these people had in mind. If there was anyone who could draw out the visitors, it would be Mac. Besides, he loved to drink on an expense account.

"I should have texted you," Sean Doyle said as Molly walked into the bakery. "I fixed it."

"That's okay, I was headed back. Thanks, what was it?"

"A loose wire, took a few minutes. Corrine called me after she texted you, sorry."

"As I said, no problem. Have you seen Mac?"

"Not today. He and Albert were going into Cork this morning. Don't know why."

"Thanks."

O'Rourke punched in a number on her phone. She waited, then said, "Mac, give me a call when you can. There's something

I'd like you to do. And you might include Albert, if you like."

Her phone pinged: *Ten minutes away, see you at An Sugan, famished.*

* * * *

The restaurant had been a staple in Clonakilty for almost forty years. While a bit on the touristy side, it still was one of the best restaurants in this part of the county. When O'Rourke arrived, Mac and Albert were sitting at a table in the back. Tourists were standing outside waiting for a table.

"Nice to have a little pull," Molly said. She tousled Albert's thick hair and gave the boy a kiss on the forehead.

"Me? Never said a thing," Mac said. "Annie just smiled and walked us to this table. When someone said something, she pointed at me and said, 'War vet.' The couple immediately backed away."

"Well, I guess Northern Ireland does make you a veteran of some kind."

"Annie and her boss think so. So, what's up?"

"Lots of activity out at the farm. Many people coming and going." Molly outlined her idea about Mac doing a little surveillance and finding out what he could about the visitors. Mac nodded and thought it was a good idea.

"Laddie, you interested in dinner down at the Smugglers Inn?"

Albert thought a moment, and then smiled. "Fried shrimp?"

"Absolutely."

The server placed a bowl of chowder next to Mac's Guinness and a plate of fried shrimp in front of Albert. Molly knew that Albert would eat, if offered, fried shrimp six times a day.

"Ma'am?" the server asked.

"A cup of the chowder and a glass of Chardonnay," Molly answered.

"What do you make of these Americans?" Mac asked.

"I have no idea. They spent a few hours walking the property and house, but it's the others that worry me. Three Irish who look and act military. I'm guessing they work for O'Shaunnessy.

The other was obviously American, most probably connected to Boyle. I'll see what I can find out. I'm concerned that they left something incriminating or embarrassing at the property. Something to put this American O'Bryan off. I wish Brona had let us know what she had in mind."

"Brona O'Bryan always kept her own council, you know that," Mac said. "I loved her like a mother, but she was a tough woman. She must have had a reason to leave the estate to her only kin. Besides, lass, what the hell would you have done with it? You haven't a scilling to waste on that old ruin."

"I could have helped."

"I think Brona did not want to saddle you with that mausoleum. It would have sucked every flóirín you have. The revenuers would be all over you. She knew that."

"Yes, but whatever happens, our little secret will be gone."

"It's been gone before and then found again. Only God knows the future. We will be fine."

"What were you doing in Cork?"

"Do you remember our conversation about Albert? I introduced him to a school that teaches challenged adults about gardening and landscaping. They provide room and board and training. You liked it, didn't you, Albert?"

Albert held a fried shrimp in his hand. "Yes, Mac, looked like a good place. I liked the flowers and people. Molly, me and Mac talked a lot about it. Got to be on my own someday—Mac has always said that. It will be fun. They even said I might be able to have a dog if I find the right place to work."

"That's excellent, Albert," Molly said as she watched the young man dip the end of the shrimp into the tartar sauce. "You are a good man, Mac MacLeish."

9c

After checking in at the hotel, the six friends agreed to meet in the bar. After dinner, Kevin and Sharon would leave for the house and come back for the group in the morning.

Surprisingly, the inn's bar was crowded when they gathered there. Three men sat in a corner window that controlled the best view of the inlet. An older man with a thick, wiry beard and a young man in his twenties sat at a table near the fireplace. Kevin and his friends managed to arrange a few smaller tables in the central part of the room. Elsewhere, two couples sat along the perimeter of the room and some locals sat at the bar talking with the bartender—her red hair was a tangle of curls and ringlets that defied description.

JF walked to the end of the bar and asked politely if there was a server. The bartender replied, "Only me, luv." The admiring expression on her face, as she gazed at JF, caused the other men at the bar to turn and look at the Frenchman. Three pulled in their bellies, one straightened his shirt, and another harrumphed. JF smiled awkwardly at the men, thanked the woman, and placed the group's order.

"Anything you want, luv, just ask," the bartender said.

A touch of red tinged his face when he returned to the table.

"I can't take you anywhere," Sharon said.

"What?" JF replied with another awkward smile.

"Now, why do you want to stay at the house?" Gina asked.

"Maybe for the memory," Kevin said. "I want to spend at least one night there. If it's as full of ghosts as Gina believes, then the deal is off. O'Shaunnessy can sell it to any fool who wants it. No ghosts? Different matter."

"I never said there were ghosts," Gina protested.

"You certainly acted like it when we entered each room," Sharon said.

"Pays to be cautious."

"And then what are you going to do with it?" Claudette asked. "There are hundreds across France just like it that just sit and rot away. It will bankrupt you."

"It can't bankrupt me more than I am right now, so maybe there's something else," Kevin said.

One of the trio near the window set his beer on the oak table and nodded to the others. They quit their conversation and listened.

"There's a lot of family history in that house," Kevin said. "Too much for me to absorb in just a few days, so if there is anything I can do to prolong the process maybe it will help me make a decision. What's a few days either way?"

"None that will make a difference," Sharon said. "Those buildings have been there for a few centuries. A fortnight, as they say around here, won't hurt."

The man at the window took a sip of his beer and smiled. "Bingo," he whispered to his companions.

The man with the beard looked at the trio by the window and then at Kevin and his friends. He leaned in toward the younger man at his table. "We've got to go, Albert. Molly will be interested."

* * * *

Two hours later, Kevin and Sharon, armed with flashlights lent by the inn, walked down the long hallway of Baile O'Bryan to the stairway that curved its way to the second and third floors. At the foot of the stairs, they found a light switch and were surprised that the electricity still functioned. The stairs and hallway warmed under the chandelier that hung twenty feet from the ceiling on a spiderweb-swathed chain. Their footprints from earlier in the day haphazardly wandered across the dusty floor, some of them blending with those of the previous visitors. The rain, never far from Ireland, began to pound the thick glass windows that flanked the door and the windows high above.

"All I need is a hound and Sherlock Holmes to set the funereal mood," Kevin said as he clicked off the flashlight.

"I miss my pup," Sharon said. "Having Basil here would provide just the right amount of additional security."

"And why do we need that? Even with the locks, this place has been open to anyone who really wanted to break in, and nobody has. So why now?"

"Still spooky." The wind knocked a shutter or something against the house, startling both.

"I'll give you that," Kevin said. "Let's see if we can get a fire going upstairs and settle in. Somehow, I don't think either of us will get much sleep. Besides, I'm exhausted, but my mind is racing."

"Just don't let it start seeing things," Sharon said.

An hour later, a fire burned warmly in the ancient hearth that filled one wall of Brona's bedroom. They rearranged some of the bedclothes and flipped a coin for the bed or couch. Kevin stretched out on the outsized bed.

"She was quite a woman, according to my father," Kevin said. "Single-handedly took care of the place, managed to keep the revenuers away, as I'm finding out, and lived to a ripe old age."

"Where did her money come from?" Sharon said. "Sheep? Not a lot money that I can see there. Farming on this soil? It's thin—unless she had a gold or silver mine under the building. It's all too curious."

"Yes, thinking the same thing. Did you notice the three men by the window at the inn? They seemed out of context. They certainly weren't farmers, too white, no tans. And the one man looked American. His clothes, his haircut—everything screamed New York."

"Damn, they've been nagging me, too." Sharon snapped her fingers. "Mr. Grey Jacket."

"Right! Out of context. Yes, the one in the leather jacket was our Dublin shadow. So, I guess we're the number one attraction here in Cork. The American, maybe O'Shaunnessy's client?"

"Or agent or stooge. Why all this cloak and dagger bullshit? From what I can see, Brona O'Bryan didn't have two euros to rub together at the end. Who would want this particular chunk of Ireland? Lord knows, there has to be hundreds of other—"

The explosion blew in the double window in the bedroom that overlooked the courtyard. Wind and rain instantly followed. Unharmed but shaken, Sharon and Kevin grabbed their flashlights and bolted through the door and into the hallway. When they were halfway to the stairs, the lights went out. Blackness replaced everything except the thin beams of their flashlights. When they reached the entry doors to the courtyard, the orange and white flicker of fire was visible through the windows. One end of the cottage was burning; the shadows of blasted timbers pointed outward at strange angles and directions.

Sharon pulled out her phone. "Shit! What's the number for 911 here?"

"Try 999."

"Right." Sharon waited and punched in speaker.

"What is the emergency?" a voice asked.

Sharon gave the operator all the information she could. Kevin prompted with the address.

"No one is hurt," he said. "The rain is dampening the fire."

"Fire department is on its way," Sharon said.

She clicked off and took Kevin's hand. "What the hell happened?"

"My guess a warning, a warm welcome-home warning."

Two hours later the rain still had not let up, but the fire had been put out. The local fire department had dispatched three engines, but the rain kept the fire confined to the cottage, and only one end of the small structure burned. Twenty minutes after the fire department arrived, a taxi had brought the four inn guests. They all stood in the courtyard watching as the fire was extinguished. A bottle of Irish whiskey—Gina had brought it from the inn—was passed around. Kevin talked with the fire chief, explaining the reasons for their being there as well as the coincidence of the explosion and fire.

"Explosion?" the chief asked.

"Yes, it shook the whole building. When we came outside, the far end of the building was blown apart and burning. Thank goodness for the Irish rain."

"Have to agree with you there." The chief looked at his watch; it was well past one. "I'm leaving one engine and crew here until morning, just in case. I'll stop by later in the morning to take a look around. We don't have arson investigators. Someone from Cork City will have to come down."

"Thank you," Kevin said. "The timing of the explosion is just too coincidental. We are here only for a few days."

"You said your name was Bryan?"

"Yes, sir. From California, but my family name is O'Bryan. Brona O'Bryan was my great-aunt."

"Well, from somewhere in our pasts we are related, Mr. Bryan. Brona was a third or fourth cousin to me, but then again out here most everyone is related. You try and have a quiet night. I see you have company, that's good. Staying here?"

"Yes, for tonight. Tomorrow? We'll see."

One of the chief's men came up to him and quietly said something.

"Someone threw the main switch off at the box. That's curious," the chief said. "He's going to turn the power back on. Goodnight, sir. See you in the morning."

As the six friends turned back to the house, the hallway lights relit the courtyard. They filed back into the house and headed to the main parlor. It was the only downstairs room with chairs and furniture.

"Hanging around you two is always an adventure," Gina said, as she produced another bottle of whiskey and poured one more round of drinks.

They settled in and Kevin found some wood in the kitchen and lit a fire in the huge parlor hearth. It was late in the night when the bottle was emptied as the friends finished their conversations about the past and their speculations for the future. Just as JF started to ask a question, a loud rapping on the door in the entry hall startled them.

"I wonder what the fire department wants," Sharon said and walked out of the parlor to the entry. A few seconds later she returned, preceded by an Irish setter that bounded into the room; a woman and a man stood in the arched doorframe. The man was swarthy, leathery, and his black beard was striated with grey. His dark eyes peered in turn at the faces of everyone in the room. The woman, with raven black hair, green eyes, and a face like alabaster, looked straight at Kevin.

"Mr. Bryan, I am Molly O'Rourke. And I assure you this is not the end of your troubles, only the beginning."

Chapter 10

There be a tunnel far underground,
Two children of Ireland oddly found.
Beyond the oak door,
Which hid a dark shore—
And the briny deep, where they near drowned.

10a

Looking at Mac, JF said, "You were in the tavern at the inn! You and another."

"Yes, sir. Molly asked me to watch over you. Seems that she had an idea something like this would happen."

"Like what? What would happen?" Claudette asked.

"That they would try something to scare you away," Molly said. "Didn't think they would be so . . . stupid and destructive."

"Who are they?" Kevin asked.

"Who are *you*?" Sharon interjected.

"Molly O'Rourke—"

"You said that. But who *are* you?"

"Let's everyone take a breath," Kevin suggested.

The dog had bounded up the stairs and now returned and began sniffing around the room.

"He was Brona's hound," Molly said. "He still misses his mistress. I do, too. She was like my own grandmother, always there, always helpful. She was family to me. As for the people who want the Baile O'Bryan, they're New Yorkers. I believe they are working closely with the O'Bryan family solicitor, Sinead O'Shaunnessy. Frankly, I've never trusted that bitch for one minute. I believe that the buyer is Sylvia Boyle, a high-profile New York developer."

"I know the Boyles," Evelyn said. "They control a lot of the retail square footage in the region around New York City. Sylvia is a tough woman from what I've heard—her fingers are in a lot of the deals. I've never met her."

"I believe her son was at the inn tonight," MacLeish said. "He and O'Shaunnessy's thugs put the bomb in the old cottage."

"Bomb?" Sharon said, looking at Mac. "And who are you, and why do you care? And how would you even know that someone planted a bomb?"

Mac and Molly exchanged glances. Molly shrugged. She introduced Mac.

"There are old customs that go back many, many years, Ms. O'Mara. Ancient traditions that are as much a part of the land and culture of Ireland as the Catholic Church and leprechauns. We have survived the British for eight hundred years, and we will survive the new Irish government. Brona was a part of that tradition. Your family, Mr. Bryan, was an important part of that history."

Sharon turned to her friends and smiled.

"What?" Kevin said.

"I knew it," she said. "The O'Bryans were smugglers."

"Smugglers, criminals?" Gina said, holding up her tumbler of whiskey. "Hot damn. I knew you were just two steps from being in jail."

"More than that, lad," MacLeish said. "Patriots, too. They ran guns and weapons to drive out the British. Then, after the peace, they returned to their old habits—for many it was all they knew."

"You are taking a risk being here," Kevin said thoughtfully.

"The risk is minimal," Molly said. "Everyone in the county generally knows what's going on. What we do is benign, but there are others who are pushing nastier and more deadly stuff. Some of the firefighters out there, watching the building, are friends. That's the way it is here; the trouble comes from the outsiders, people like O'Shaunnessy. They come, they go; we will always remain."

"What's your connection to this property?" JF asked

"As I said, the families around here go back centuries. Hell, you, Kevin, and I, are probably related through some distant bloodlines. Brona was the last of the O'Bryans—that is until you appeared, Mr. Bryan. She told me the story of you, your family, and your great-grandfather and his leaving the county. He was just one of thousands who escaped the famines, the British, the wars—some with a price on their head. America has always been good to the Irish. Anyway, Brona was . . ."

Her voice caught slightly. She looked at Mac.

"Personally, I was in love with the woman," he said. "If she were only fifty years younger—she said the same thing about me. Her experience and connections were the stuff of legends."

"That's exactly right," Molly said. "The farm is a conduit and an excellent lookout. "From the headlands, you can see up and down the coast for almost thirty miles. First it was lamps, then phone lines, now text messages and smartphones."

"I preferred the oil lamps, far less chance of eavesdropping," Mac added with a smile.

"Okay, so are you saying smuggling is still going on?" Gina asked.

"Not saying yes or no to that, lass. We do what we need to do," Mac answered.

"Plausible deniability," Sharon said.

"Ms. O'Mara, this is a country of extreme contrasts, and has been so for more than five hundred years. I mean the rich cities and the poor countryside," Mac said. "The famines of the eighteenth and nineteenth centuries came down on the people in the counties—the cities, not so much. The English hardly lifted a hand. Famine and emigration followed; the English saw it as an opportunity to seize the vacated land. The country starved, and we Irish have long memories."

"The best markets for the goods smuggled in are in the cities of England, so I've been told," Molly added. "Such is the circle of life."

"A cynical remark," Sharon said. The setter returned to the

group and pushed his head against her leg. She scratched the top of his massive skull.

"He likes you. He doesn't often do that with strangers," Molly said. "His name is Dergo, the tenth to hold that name."

"Handsome dog," Sharon said.

"As Irish as the rain. Miss, if there is one commodity the Irish have in great quantity, it is cynicism," Molly said. "That's why our writers and storytellers have such a dark side to their works; many of our songs are about death and war, albeit sometimes with a humorous tone." She looked out the window of the great room. "It's getting light; I've got to get to the bakery."

"Bakery?" Kevin asked.

"It's not all fun and games, and cat and mouse, Mr. Bryan. We do have to work for a living. My bakery is on the west end of Main Street. Stop by, we have excellent goods, if I do say so myself. Mac?"

"Yes, ma'am. I'll get the truck."

Everyone tromped out to the courtyard. The rain had stopped, and the broken overcast allowed the early sun to drive shafts of sunlight across the headland. The fresh air was tinged with the acrid taste of burned wood. They watched the firemen load up their remaining gear. One of the men walked over to the group.

"Mr. Bryan, Lieutenant Timmons." The firefighter put his hand out; Kevin shook it. "And good morning, Molly. We are off. The men are tired and need to get back to the station. Later in the morning, the chief will be back with investigators from Cork. Because it might have been a bomb, there may be some people from Dublin coming down as well—terrorism and all."

"Thank you, and tell your captain for me as well," Kevin said, thinking about the word terrorism. "I'll be here all day. We are returning to Dublin tomorrow."

"Yes, sir. At least the fire didn't spread."

"Yes, there's that," Kevin said.

They watched the fire truck climb the driveway to the road. In the quiet of the countryside, they could hear the vehicle go through its gears long after it had disappeared from view. O'Rourke climbed into the passenger side of the panel van that had *Clonakilty Bakery* painted on its side. MacLeish drove up the drive and followed the fire truck.

"I'll have to say, Kev, that when you throw a party, it's a doozy," Gina said. "I'm famished. But right now, I'm not sure if I'd rather sleep or eat."

"I'm with you," Claudette said. "I lean toward breakfast first, and then sleep."

It was decided that most of the group would head back to the inn. Kevin and Sharon would join them later. There were some canned foods in the pantry of the main house; maybe some coffee could be scrounged. Kevin, his detective antennae up, wanted to look things over in the daylight and get a lay of the destruction before the chief and the inspectors arrived.

"What can you see that they can't?" Evelyn asked.

"It's not really that," Kevin said. "It's just that I'm curious as to why the cottage and not the house."

"I had the same thought," Sharon added. "JF, if you can be back in a few hours, then we can return to the inn."

"You want me to stay?" Gina asked.

"No, get some breakfast and sleep. I suggest that later this afternoon we all come back here. You three haven't had a chance to walk to the cliffs. They are spectacular."

"The place just got bombed, and you want us to take a scenic hike?" Gina asked.

Her half-serious question was met with laughter, breaking the tension that had been in the air the last few hours. After promising to be careful and to call if anything else seemed amiss, Kevin and Sharon watched as their friends piled into the minibus, and with JF at the wheel, he followed after the firetruck. Soon, all that broke the stillness was the calling of a wood pigeon; its haunting *coo-coo* added the soundtrack to a strange morning.

"Why the hell would they blow up that old cottage?" Sharon asked again, as they walked slowly to the blasted end of the building. "Lucky the whole structure didn't go up."

"I think that was the intention, but they didn't count on the rain. You said luck—that was ours."

"If it weren't for the smoky smell, you wouldn't know the fire burned not twenty feet away," Sharon said as they walked into the cottage.

Everything looked almost untouched. The fire crew had pushed in the heavy door. The interior hallway beyond was dark. Kevin tried the light switch near the door; nothing. A hallway table looked to have been pulled away from the wall, and an oil lamp sat on its dusty surface.

Kevin extracted a long match from the bundle of matches he found in a copper canister, and after some adjustment, the light from the oil lamp filled the hallway. It illuminated the room's corners that the sun, washing through the front door, did not reach. They walked down the hall to another heavy wooden door and pulled it open. Sunlight flooded in through the holes in the roof of the burnt-out wing. The backside of the oak door was heavily singed.

"Amazing," Sharon said.

Beyond the door, the floor had been demolished by the blast, and timber and wood had been thrown in a radiating pattern from the far corner of the cellar.

"I would offer that the explosion started there; the pattern certainly supports it," Kevin said. "There's the stair there, the one that Gina opened. It would have provided the access to the cellar. Their plan just seems amazing and reckless—still can't figure out why."

"Amateurs. They think they could intimidate you?"

"Me, how about you? All I am now is pissed. They were stupid."

Sharon went to the corner and looked down into the blasted basement. "It's interesting that the basement under this building is in two sections, the area where the bomb was placed, and here under this portion of the cottage." She crouched down and looked back into the root cellar and then stood and surveyed the room they were in. "Okay, so there's a stone wall that cuts this building in two. I think there were two buildings once, now disguised as one. Maybe each side was built at different times?"

"You're right. This stone wall extends from the basement to the roof. It would have acted like a fire stop. That's probably the reason this side didn't burn." Kevin repeated Sharon's movements, looking into the basement and then crossing the room to look at the stone wall on the main floor. "There's a basement under this portion of the cottage?" he said, his words half a question, half a statement.

"Likely. Ready to explore?"

For the next half hour, they looked in every remaining room and closet, trying to find a door or a stairway. Nothing. They took a turn around the building, looking for windows or some other evidence of a second cellar, again nothing. Back at the entry, Kevin set the lamp on the table. They then pushed the table back against the wall. The canister of matches rocked once, then toppled and rolled off the table. It clanked on the wooden floor as it tumbled around.

Sharon picked up the brass cylinder, noting that it was the shell casing to a small howitzer shell. "Another reminder of the troubles here in Ireland."

"Such a history," Kevin answered. He slid the lamp away from the edge of the table, noticing as he did so that the sunlight from the doorway threw a bright shaft of light across the oak flooring. "What do you see there?" he asked Sharon.

She ran her hand over the wood surface. "I feel a strange wear pattern. There's the usual pattern down the hall, but here there's a secondary pattern, one that turns right into the wall. Hand me that lamp."

She held the oil lamp low to the floor; the flame flickered. She grabbed a few of the long matches, lit one, and held it near where the floor met the oak wall panel. A puff of air put the match out. She lit another match and moved it to a seam in the tight trim of the wall paneling. The flame flared and then sputtered out. She lit another and moved the tiny flame around the panel. There was an obvious breeze along a seam in the trim.

"You've been watching too many old movies," Kevin said. "But I get it; this is a door of some kind."

"There has to be a release or something. Look for a switch."

"Yes, too many movies," Kevin mumbled, as he ran his hand over the edges of the paneling, looking for something that might be a handle or a latch release. He lifted the edge of the painting of his ancestor. It was surprisingly difficult to move. He pushed on the frame's corner. There was a click inside the wall, and the oak panel slid silently to the left and into the wall, revealing a stone landing. The smell of the sea washed up from the darkness. The breeze that it brought with it blew out the oil lamp.

10b

Kevin said, "I'll be damned, a secret doorway."

"Straight out of Sherlock Holmes—relight the lamp. You ready to go exploring?"

"If you mean going down a dark stairway, into a room that is black as a hole in Calcutta, with no idea what's there— absolutely."

"I'll get the flashlights!"

Sharon found a chunk of splintered wood and jammed it into the gap at the base of the sliding door, and then broke off the end.

"That should hold it. I don't like the thought of the door closing and locking us in."

When Sharon returned from the house with the flashlights, Kevin had reignited the lamp and now led the way down the stairway. At the bottom, the dim light illuminated a room built under the undamaged portion of the cottage, as they had guessed. He set the lamp on a table. With their flashlights, they explored the cellar. They found a cot, a stack of empty cardboard boxes against one wall, a table, and four chairs. Another lamp sat unlit next to the one he'd placed on the table. On the opposite side from the stairs stood a massive door built from oak and fitted with thick iron hinges and latches.

"There's some fine craftsmanship evident here," Sharon said as she ran her hand over the old wood. "Same as the hidden door upstairs. They were proud of their work. Shall we go on?"

"JF won't be back for a few more hours," Kevin said. "That should give us time to explore. Me or you first?"

"It's your castle. So please, your lordship." She stood to the side as Kevin pulled up the heavy iron latch and pulled the door inward. It swung easily, even though the door had to weigh hundreds of pounds. The strong aroma of the sea filled the room. On another table, just inside the door, sat three flashlights and two modern high-intensity LED lanterns.

"Obviously, this place is still in use," Kevin said. "I'll bet Molly and Mac were investigating to see what we knew. I'm so shocked they didn't tell us about this secret cellar. I wonder what else they neglected to say?"

A date had been carved into the stone wall. "Sixteen-ninety-five," Sharon read aloud. "This tunnel has been here a long time, probably before the cottage and maybe even the house."

Kevin clicked on one of the LED lanterns and illuminated the landing and a passageway beyond. With Kevin leading the way, they shortly came to the top step of the stairway. The lantern threw light on the first twenty steps that led down. "Ready to descend?"

"Always easier down than up."

Kevin again led the way; Sharon followed. At various spots, they stopped and read hundred-year-old graffiti, dates, and initials carved into the rock: 1745, 1824, 1762, in no particular order. Just a forgotten reminder that men, and probably women, were here centuries earlier. Their names long gone, only a date and their initials left as shadows telling the world that they lived.

They stopped at a landing they guessed to be the midpoint and took a breather. Sharon was having second thoughts about the going-down part of her comment. The back of her calves ached. The smell of the ocean was strong, and the muffled sound of surf rolled up from the blackness below. Soldiering on, they continued down until the steps ended. A narrow stone walkway disappeared around a bend. Fifty feet later, they stood in front of another, even more massive, door. This one opened outward.

"It would be hard as hell to force this door in from the outside," Sharon said. "When it was made, only explosives could open this door."

Kevin circled the lamplight over the door and then pulled the three massive iron bars away from the deep keyholes drilled into the stone frame. Leaning his shoulder into the oak, he pushed. Slowly and silently, the door opened. The sound of the sea filled the corridor. Reflected sunlight illuminated the final length of the stone walkway and the last twenty steps down to a narrow beach.

"Look here," Sharon said pointing her flashlight at the steps. "These have been used for so many years they are cupped from thousands of shoes grinding away at the stone. Amazing."

The two walked to the edge of the sandy shingle and looked out on the waves that slowly surged in and out of the cavern. Natural stone walls climbed upward more than forty feet. Sharon's flashlight barely illuminated the damp roof high over their heads.

"No footprints," Sharon said, washing the light over the sand. "It's a good bet that high tide fills this cavern and it might push its way all the way up the steps. Maybe that's why the steps were wet inside. The tide may push its way over the door."

Kevin looked out the narrow sunlit slot to the sea. "This cavern and beach is completely hidden from the outside. A passing boat would not know it's here, unless they knew where to look—a perfect smugglers' cove."

A wave surged up the narrow cavern and pushed its way up the beach, wiping out their footprints. They backed up a dozen yards; another swell surged up the sand.

"Time and tide wait for no one," Kevin said and took Sharon by the arm. "We've got to go."

At the sound of his words, the heavy door at the top of the stairs slammed shut, echoing throughout the cave. Then the sounds of the iron bars being slammed home into the stone quickly followed. The two friends stood on the first stone step above the sand. Sharon panned the flashlight over the closed door.

"Something tells me we have just been seriously fucked," Kevin said as he took another step up, trying to keep his shoes dry. "Fucked."

They climbed the steps to the landing outside the door. After a couple minutes spent looking over the frame and door, they both came to the obvious conclusion that the original builders had accomplished what they intended. Without some type of explosive, there was no way that this door was going to be breached. Between them, all they had was Kevin's small penknife, a flashlight, the LED lamp, and after a search through Sharon's handbag, a nail file and her phone.

"Well, MacGyver, what are you going to do?" Sharon asked.

"Me? You're the one with the phone. Mine is in my bag in the van."

Sharon clicked on her iPhone and waited. The signal dots were blank—no signal. "Damn. I should have gotten the James Bond special escape app. It came with a laser."

Kevin held up the lamp so the light aimed back toward the beach—except the beach was gone. The swells now slowly surged up over the bottom four steps and then washed over the fifth.

"How high do the tides get here?" Sharon asked.

"How the hell would I know that? But I can tell you it's coming in with an attitude."

Sharon's phone pinged. The sound startled them.

"You're getting some type of signal," Kevin said.

Sharon looked again. "Facebook? You have got to be kidding me."

The message was from Gina; she had posted a photo of a plate of fish and chips. *Here at a delightful inn overlooking the Irish Sea. Having a delicious lunch!*

"Really?" Sharon said. "We are going to be washed out to

sea, and she is posting pictures of her lunch. I'll kill her."

Sharon tried to make a call to Gina—nothing, no service.

"Figures that we get data links but no cell, just great."

"Try and reply to the post. Maybe it will get through," Kevin said.

Sharon tapped "comment" and typed: *Gina, dear, if you can get away from your lunch, Kevin and I are about to drown at the bottom of a tunnel under the cottage. Doors locked, no escape, tide is rising fast—help!* She hit "post," having no idea whether it went through.

The next surge rose over their knees before sliding back out.

"That's cold," Kevin said as he braced for the next surge. It came vigorously, rising past their waists, before receding. They held onto the door's handles.

"Not good—not good at all," Sharon said. "Now I understand why those rings mounted in the walls are so high. If properly secured, a small boat could ride the tide out."

"We can hold onto them if this rises any further. Our other option is to swim for it. And that's not my first choice."

"Damn, it's cold."

The next swell lifted them off their feet; they each grabbed one of the iron rings and held on tight. In the process, Sharon dropped her phone.

"Shit, my phone!" she yelled as the iPhone disappeared into the surge.

The swell pulled back again, dropping them to the stone landing. They waited for the next wave, hoping that the tide had topped out. No such luck. The next swell rose three-quarters up the door and again knocked them off their feet. Holding onto the rings was all that kept them from being dragged out into the sea. This time the sea held, pinning them against the door. They looked at each other, no longer trying to mask their fear. Then again, the flood slowly receded. When it cleared the top step, Kevin, still managing to keep hold of the LED lantern, began to beat it against the door. After three blows, it shattered. The surge began again, this time not as high, but it was a false hope. They knew one of the next onslaughts would fill the cavern well over their heads. As the swell returned to the sea, Kevin banged on the door with his fists.

"Help," he yelled. Sharon joined in the next cry. "Help!"

As Kevin slammed his fists against the door, the sound of scraping iron on iron resonated through the wet oak of the door. First one, then two loud scrapes, were heard.

"Wait, stop!" Sharon yelled. "Don't open the door. The next swell will make it impossible to open. Wait for us to yell."

They heard, from somewhere on the other side of the door, a muffled "Okay."

The next wave of seawater was the highest yet. The pair in the flooded cavern held onto the rings with both hands as they twisted in the frigid water, hoping salvation was just beyond the door. As the wave retreated, it almost tore them off their rings. When the wave cleared the landing, both yelled, "NOW!" and took a step back from the door as it was pushed open. The two Americans flung themselves through the open doorway, turned back to the door, and struggled to pull it tight against the frame. They were exhausted, but another pair of hands reached between them threw the crossbars into the keyholes.

"Goddamn, that was close," Kevin said, breathing hard. Struggling to stay upright, he turned toward the blackness of the tunnel. They could see no one. The beam of a flashlight bounced around on the stone ceiling above them, then across their faces, momentarily blinding them.

"What the hell are you two doing down here?" a voice, somewhat familiar, asked.

"Who is that?" Sharon gasped. "I know that voice."

The flashlight flipped around and panned upward on the face of the man not five feet from them. The eeriness of the uplighting shocked the two survivors

"What the hell are you doing here?" Kevin asked.

"I'll ask you the same thing," Liam Donovan said. "Me, I'm working."

The door rattled against the locking bars as the next surge

rose up the door. Water began to seep in along the frame.

"Will it hold?" Donovan asked as he played the light on the door.

"It will. It holds back the tide and ocean twice a day. Quite a feat of engineering," Sharon said. "But I'm for going up. No reason to test fate. And I'm cold and wet—and I need a minute."

Donovan waited for them to catch their breath, and then they began to climb. As they trudged up the steps, Donovan told them that he'd been assigned to investigate the bombing of a country house in County Cork. It was a part of his job with the Crime & Security Branch of the Garda Síochána. He had experience investigating explosive devices and had been sent down from Dublin to work with the local station. He'd had no idea that he'd been dispatched to Kevin's farm.

"And you don't believe in coincidences," Kevin said to Sharon. He nudged her in the back.

She ignored his remark.

When they reached the midway landing, they again stopped to allow Kevin and Sharon to catch their breath. The climb had warmed them somewhat, but they were shivering in wet clothes.

"You didn't get a message from Gina?" Sharon asked.

"No, why?" Donovan answered.

"There was no cell service, but there was a chance that a Facebook post might have gone through."

"No, nothing from Gina. When I arrived, there was no one about. So, I started to look around and found the door open in the cottage entry to the cellar. I started down the tunnel to investigate, and you know the rest."

"Lucky us," Kevin said.

"Who would have thought there'd be an old smugglers' tunnel under your house, Kev," Sharon said.

"I guessed that's what it was," Donovan told her. "I've been down a few of these over the years. Have to say this is one of the nicest."

"And dangerous, especially if you don't know the tides,"

Sharon said. "Thanks for being here."

"Just one of the services we provide," Liam said.

The sun was high when they walked out of the cottage and into the courtyard. Barreling down the driveway, the Mercedes minibus slipped and slid in the mud. It pulled to a stop ten feet from the trio, and the doors flew open and Gina, Claudette, Evelyn, and JF ran to them.

"Nice bit of driving," Kevin said to JF.

"Years of practice coming to rescues," JF said.

"Are you two okay?" Gina said as she wrapped her arms around Sharon. "I got your Facebook post. Oh, my God. We dropped everything and took off. And you are wet!"

"You left your fish and chips?" Kevin asked.

"Seeing that you are now alive, you owe me for lunch, your lordship." She gave him a huge smile and hugged him as well. It was then that she noticed Liam. "What are you doing here?"

"Rescuing these two—it is a coincidence, as Kevin put it."

"Now more like a miracle," Kevin said.

Donovan repeated his story for the would-be, but late, rescuers. They retired to the house and Evelyn found some blankets in the upstairs bedroom and covered the two soaked tunnel rats.

"That will teach you for going down into strange places that you know nothing about. Curiosity and a cat come to mind," Claudette said. "You said the door closed behind you? Was it an accident?"

"I doubt that," Sharon said. "When it slammed, we could hear someone sliding the iron bars across the door, locking it from inside. Whoever it was then must have run up the steps and escaped before Liam arrived. About twenty to thirty minutes went by between the door closing and us almost washing out to sea. You didn't see anyone when you arrived?" Sharon turned to Liam.

"No, but I did pass a black Jaguar SUV that was heading north, two people in the front seat," Donovan said. "Could have been them. Not sure, and no way to know now."

"Well, it sure wasn't a ghost that slammed and locked that door," Kevin said.

10c

An hour later, the County Cork fire inspector arrived with the fire chief. Donovan sequestered himself with the team and together they walked through the damaged cottage. The six friends stood off to one side and watched.

"There's not much more we can do here," Kevin said, still wrapped in a blanket. "Donovan said that he would meet us later at the inn, bring us up to speed. I was hungry three hours ago. Now I'm famished. All Gina's picture of fish and chips did was make me hungrier. JF, would you drive?"

"No problem. Ladies, your carriage awaits," JF said.

"My butt's getting a little tired of that 'carriage,'" Gina said.

JF maneuvered the Mercedes out to the two-lane road and headed north toward the inn. The women gave the passenger seat over to Kevin, and he gratefully stretched out his long legs.

"It was close?" JF asked him.

"Too close. Not sure what would have happened if Donovan hadn't shown up. Treading water in the surges or finding a way to make it to a beach was impossible. All we could do was hang on."

"Lucky."

"I'm not a big fan of luck, but that's what it was."

JF glanced in the rearview mirror. "Now what's this fool's problem?"

Kevin, sitting in the left passenger seat, leaned in and looked at the large rearview mirror to his left. The oval grill of a black SUV filled the glass as it rushed toward them. JF slammed on the accelerator and the Mercedes jumped forward, just feet ahead of the charging vehicle. The SUV tried to match their speed; everyone in the van could hear the roar of its engine. JF continued to accelerate, and the vehicle stayed tight to their bumper.

Twisting around in her seat, Sharon yelled, "It's a Jaguar."

The narrowness of the road made it difficult to put distance between them. Every time JF gained some distance, he had to decelerate into a curve. A stop sign ahead alerted him to an approaching intersection where a tractor, towing a trailer, was slowly making the turn. The large tractor and its cargo nearly filled the intersection. JF slammed on the brakes and swerved, just missing the rear corner of the trailer. The SUV gained the advantage and rammed the rear of the van just as JF accelerated. Only the increase in the van's speed saved them from being driven off the road. The SUV caught the rear corner of the trailer. The impact broke the trailer from its hitch, upending both trailer and tractor. As the tractor began to pitch over, the driver, a young man, leaped from the open seat and narrowly missed being crushed by the tumbling tractor. The Jaguar continued on after the Mercedes, the driver seemingly unfazed by the accident he caused.

"Damn, I wish I had a pistol," Sharon yelled from the back.

Everyone cinched their seat belts tighter and held on to anything they could. As JF swerved from one side of the road to the other, he again looked in the rearview mirror and was met by the taut expressions on his friends' faces.

"He's coming again," Kevin yelled, looking at the side mirror. "Brace yourselves!"

The vehicle's front bumper crushed the rear of the van, breaking out the lights and cracking the windows on the rear double doors. The impact shoved them ahead a few feet. They braced for the next attack.

"What the hell?" Kevin shouted, still looking in the side mirror.

Behind them, the Jaguar had started to swerve back and forth across the road. Its left front tire caught the edge of the swale alongside the road; the vehicle almost flipped over. It slammed back on its right-side tires only to bounce back up on its left. Then the rear tires caught the edge of the ditch. A split-second later, the black beast was tumbling down the center of the road, taking huge divots from the asphalt paving. Its inertia spent, it tumbled into the ditch, the passenger's-side door twisted open. A hundred feet behind the overturned SUV, a body lay in the middle of the road. Beyond the body, another vehicle had stopped, blue police lights flashing from its roof; across the hood, the word GARDA was printed. JF slowed and pulled the van to the side of the road.

"Do you think it's wise?" Claudette asked, looking back through the cracked windows. "They could be together."

Liam Donovan climbed out of the police vehicle. He walked slowly toward the body, a pistol in his hand. He glanced at the overturned vehicle and then back at the body before speaking into his walkie-talkie. He knelt and placed his fingers against the neck of the twisted body. As JF and the others exited the Mercedes, Liam stood and motioned them to stay where they were. He then approached the SUV. Through the open door, he looked into the cab. Ten seconds later, he was back on the road walking toward them.

"What is this all about?" Liam asked when he reached the van.

"We haven't any idea, Officer Donovan," Kevin said. "He came out of nowhere and plowed into the rear end of the van. He tried to force us off the road. Then he lost control and began swerving. Then he flipped."

"I may have helped. I tried to get close. When he saw me, he started to swerve and momentum just took over."

"The man in the street, is he . . ." Gina said, looking down the narrow lane.

"Dead? Yes, he's dead. Obviously thrown out and busted up when he hit the pavement. The driver is also dead. Do you recognize him?" Donovan held up his cell phone. The image was of a man bent over the steering wheel, his face oddly twisted toward the camera.

"Jesus," Kevin said. "Sharon?"

Sharon looked at the photo and nodded affirmatively. "It's the guy who was tailing us in Dublin, O'Shaunnessy's man. He was at the inn when we arrived."

Liam nodded. "I know him. He's a hoodlum and thug from Dublin. Fergus Banning—fancied himself a private investigator." He told the group to remain where they were, that the local police would arrive shortly to take their statements. "I need to check something," he said.

They watched him walk back to the body lying on the asphalt. He delicately reached into the jacket of the deceased man and extracted a wallet and other documents. He was back on his walkie-talkie and had begun taking pictures of the scene as the sound of a klaxon echoed across the lush green hills surrounding the roadway. Behind Donovan's police cruiser, three civilian cars had stopped. People stood next to their vehicles watching.

Liam walked back to the van. "His passport says David Stein, New York City. Do you know him?"

"No," Sharon said. "However, we were told that a possible buyer of Kevin's farm was a developer from New York. I don't think this is a coincidence."

Liam opened the man's wallet and took out a business card. "This says Donald Boyle Development, LLC., New York."

"Good God, that's Sylvia Boyle's company," Evelyn said. "She has a son who works for the company. His name is David, not sure about the last name. I assume it was Boyle, but it might be Stein."

"From what I saw," Donovan continued, "Banning was trying to run you off the road and kill you."

"Why were you there? Why were you following us?" Sharon asked.

"Just after you left, I saw this SUV pass the farm. I'm pretty sure it was the same one from earlier; there's not too many Jaguars in this part of Ireland. I followed."

"Lucky for us," Evelyn said.

"Do you think they were the ones who closed the door of the tunnel?" Gina asked.

"I would not be surprised," Donovan answered, "but we may never know."

The interviews took an hour; the local police authorities were professional and thorough, especially when Donovan's report reinforced that of Kevin and his friends. A preliminary vehicle check reported that the Jaguar belonged to a car rental service in Cork. The Mercedes van was drivable. Twenty minutes later, they arrived at the inn more thirsty than hungry—except for Gina and Kevin.

Sharon and Kevin changed into dry clothes and returned to the bar. They ordered beers and drinks and headed out to the terrace. Orders were placed for sandwiches and fish and chips. A fire burned in the fire pit; the sun was setting. Kevin left the group and walked to the front desk.

"Gina said something this morning about never a dull moment around you two," JF said. "I thought our little adventure in San Francisco and Venice was exciting, but this tops it." He raised his pint of Guinness and saluted Sharon.

"Excitement just seems to follow us," Sharon said with a smile. "Personally, this is a lot more than any of us bargained for. Now there's going to be one very upset New York developer when she hears about her son. All for a piece of land . . ."

"The two men, Banning and Stein, were staying here. A third man, according to the front desk, left early this morning," Kevin said when he returned. "I'll let Donovan know. You were saying . . ."

". . . a very pretty piece of Ireland, and with what now seems to be an exciting story to go along with it," Evelyn said, turning to Kevin. "This morning, before we rode out to your rescue, the three of us were talking—JF, Claudette, and me. Kevin, we want to help. I've found in my business dealings that if you have time to consider your options, the chances are that a better decision will be made. Right now, this Dublin attorney is pushing you hard to make a final decision. There's too much in play right now, and with the unfortunate accident this morning, I think it is going to get even more dangerous. What we would like to offer you is a partnership. We would form a corporation to support you financially. This would allow you to close the deal on the property and take some time to explore your options. This would remove the attorney and whoever she's fronting from whatever deal they're cooking up."

Kevin looked at his three friends and took a sip of his Jameson. "I can't let you do that. There are too many unknowns, too much to consider."

"The investment is minimal," Claudette said. "Enough to clear the tax debt, that's it. Sure, there's a long list of other things that need to be done, but they can wait. Once the taxes are paid, we can explore the hundreds of other options. I even bet my attorneys can work out a settlement with the tax people. Hard cash money speaks loudly."

"This could become a resort, or a school, or fill some other need that the county may have," JF said. "These take time to study, to market, to develop the process. But without control of the property, they mean nothing. We have the money to make it happen and get started; we'll get paid back when a deal is done. Kevin, this isn't charity. We all expect to make a profit."

Stunned by their offer and the fact that, for some strange reason, he was beginning to be attached to the farm, Kevin hesitated. His imagination spun in a whir of thoughts and ideas. "I need to think about this. Your offer is beyond amazing, and I appreciate it. However, there are a lot of other things to consider—a little time?"

"Kev, I don't think that time is the issue. Right now, there's the issue of attempted murder," Sharon said and looked up at Liam, who had just walked out onto the terrace.

"You may be right, Ms. O'Mara," Liam said as he pulled up a chair. "The incident with the Jaguar obviously was premeditated. The preliminary report is in from the investigators at the cottage and, yes, it was a bomb—C-4 explosive, probably. We estimate about two pounds. The explosive is a favorite of the IRA; Banning had some connections in his past to the more radical cells in Ireland. We are checking the chemical composition to see what it matches. We can only guess about the lockout in the tunnel, but it fits."

"This is just a pretty piece of land, like a hundred others here in County Cork," Kevin said. "To kill me or injure my friends just to acquire it is, well, beyond disturbing. I don't get it. And besides, it will cost a fortune to make anything on the property happen."

"I've seen drug dealers kill each other over a thousand euros' worth of heroin," Liam said. "Nothing surprises me anymore."

Chapter 11

There stood three smugglers from County Kinsale,
Shackled, before the judge, hoping for bail.
Two pleaded for mercy,
The other leniency,
Calling them pirates, he sent them to jail.

11a

Sylvia Boyle stood looking out her office window high over the Hudson River. The rising sun washed over New Jersey; the tears coursing down her cheeks were reflected in the glass. She still had two children, she said to herself—two that hated her. David, her treasure, her heir, was dead. A police officer had called from Ireland early that morning, offering his condolences and sympathies. *What the hell did he know? He didn't care.* The man asked a few questions about David's business in Ireland—why he was there. Stunned, she ignored his questions.

"Ms. Boyle," Liam Donovan said, "your son was killed in what seems to be an accident in the southern part of County Cork. There's a lot of unanswered questions. When would it be convenient to contact you?"

"More answers or more questions? You tell me my son is dead, and you want convenience," Boyle demanded.

There was a pause. "Answers, hopefully. Nonetheless, do you know why your son was here in Ireland?"

"Business, family business. He went on the company jet; it returned to Newark. It was to return to bring him home when his business was done."

"There was another man with him. He was also killed in the accident. Do you know a Fergus Banning?"

"No, I don't. Why?"

"They were traveling together when the vehicle they were driving lost control and flipped over. Your son was thrown from the car; he died instantly. The other man died from head injuries sustained in the crash."

Still in shock, Boyle could only look out over the river.

"Ms. Boyle, are you still there?"

"Yes, but this conversation is over. Who should I contact regarding my son's remains?"

Donovan gave her the number of the county coroner and the funeral home where David and Fergus Banning's bodies would be released. Boyle told him that she would arrive at Cork Airport that evening to arrange for the return of David to New York. She would have ended the conversation, but Donovan said, "We have opened an investigation about some activities, illegal activities, that may have involved your son."

"Illegal?"

"Yes. However, if you are coming here, I would like to discuss those activities with you then. Can you make the time?"

Sylvia paused. "I will contact you when I arrive."

He gave her his phone number. "Thank you, Ms. Boyle, and I am sorry for your loss."

Bullshit. Boyle set the receiver back on the cradle. *Just fucking bullshit.*

She walked away from the window and, even though it was early in the morning, poured herself a whiskey. As the liquid warmed her throat, she looked at the clock on the bureau and then punched the speaker button on the phone and speed-dialed O'Shaunnessy.

Before the solicitor could answer, she demanded, "O'Shaunnessy, what the hell happened? Banning was your man—why did my son die?"

"We are not sure. David called when he was en route from New York and asked for help on the ground. I gave him Banning's number. All I know is that Banning, and one of his men, met David at Cork Airport and then they went to the property. The first I heard of the accident was when Banning's man called and told me what happened. Sylvia, why the hell was your son here? Why did he go to the property? There was no reason. I have it handled."

"Really? I understand from someone at another firm there in Dublin that an inquiry is being made about the property and the back taxes. Why would that be happening if you have it handled?"

"That's the first I've heard of this."

"Well, find out what the hell's going on. I'll be in Cork late this evening. Meet me at Cork Airport. Make arrangements at a decent hotel. I want to meet with the police and find out what happened. It seems clear to me that this whole deal is falling apart due to your incompetence. I also want to meet with the heir, the American. Can you at least make that happen, O'Shaunnessy?"

O'Shaunnessy also knew that the whole deal was crumbling, and not through her fault. "Yes, I'll set up a meeting for tomorrow," she told Boyle. "I will see you tonight." She waited until she heard the line go dead, knowing better than to expect a thank you or goodbye.

* * * *

Kevin's phone rang three times before he swung his legs out of bed and picked up. Rain splattered the room's window. Light was just breaking over the headland.

"Mr. Bryan, I hope to God that you are all right," a voice said. "I just heard about the explosion and the possible connection to an accident. Unbelievable. Do they know what happened? Who the driver was?"

Kevin, still groggy from sleep, pulled the phone from his ear. The screen read *O'Shaunnessy*. He put the phone back to his ear. "Yes, Ms. O'Shaunnessy, we are fine."

"I'm shocked. Is there anything I can do?"

Kevin had expected the call. He wished it wasn't so early. "I need a few minutes to collect myself—yesterday was a long and difficult day. Can I call you back in thirty minutes?"

O'Shaunnessy paused, and then said, "Of course, I

understand. Thirty minutes. Thank you."

Kevin clicked off the phone and tossed it on the bed. He stood and stretched his torso, and then headed into the tiny bathroom and turned on the shower. After the usual morning rituals, he felt better. He dressed, grabbed his phone, and headed down to the lobby lounge, where he found Sharon and Gina eating breakfast. Except for a woman cleaning glasses at the bar, they were the only ones in the room.

"Good morning, sunshine," Sharon said. "Coffee?"

"Intravenously, please."

Sharon signaled to the petite bartender. She pointed to her coffee, then to Kevin. The girl smiled and nodded. Kevin dropped his long frame into a chair opposite Sharon, sitting so that his legs stuck straight out, heels to the carpet.

"God, I'm stiff. Too much of a crazy day yesterday."

"Better than being a stiff in the morgue, like that Boyle guy," Gina said.

"Yes. There's that. And how are you doing?" Kevin asked Sharon.

"I found sand in my underwear, but I guess it's better than sleeping with the fishes."

"Where is the rest of our merry band?" Kevin asked.

"JF called the rental people. They have a small office in Clonakilty and asked him to bring the van in so they could look it over. Claudette and Evelyn went with him and are walking the town. Donovan gave JF a copy of the police report, so maybe it will help soften the rental agency's concerns."

"Somehow, I think this is going to cost me a fortune," Kevin said. "And Donovan?" He looked directly at Gina.

She smiled and cleared her throat. "Officer Donovan said that he would be back here later this afternoon. He'll tell us all he knows then."

"Kev, like you've been saying, there's something really stupid-crazy about all this," Sharon said. "Here's what we know: O'Shaunnessy's people—assuming they're her people—blew up the cottage, tried to kill us twice yesterday, and most probably tried to abduct Gina. It still doesn't make sense."

"I need to call O'Shaunnessy in ten minutes," Kevin said. "She called earlier, acting all naïve and concerned."

"Since it was her guy who blew up your property and was driving the SUV, the nerve," Sharon added.

"I want you two listening. Maybe you'll hear something I'll miss. But I agree, there's something else going on here."

"That smugglers' tunnel worries me," Sharon said. "Not just that it's there, but something is nagging me about the history."

"So far, we have a lot more questions than answers," Kevin agreed.

They still were unsure of Molly O'Rourke's connection. "Is that why she and that Mac guy came to visit?" Gina asked, reiterating what Kevin and Sharon had earlier discussed. "To find out if you'd discovered the tunnel?"

"I think so," Kevin said.

"Maybe they are the current operators of the tunnel; maybe they are still bringing in contraband. For all we know, they could be drug smugglers, gunrunners, or worse. Claudette said last night that they've got the same problem on France's coast: terrorists, drugs, and refugees from the Middle East and Africa."

"All distinct possibilities," Kevin said. "Outside of some graffiti and modern lamps, there's nothing to tie anyone specifically to the tunnel. And the graffiti's most recent scratchings were from the 1940s. We found the initials B.O. carved in the stone, possibly Brona O'Bryan . . ."

"Your great-aunt? You *are* a family of criminals," Gina said matter-of-factly.

"Thanks for that," Kevin said with a smile. "I prefer pirate."

"Okay, so the plan is to keep the lawyer in the dark about what went on, feel her out. I won't say anything about the tunnel." He took out his phone and punched in O'Shaunnessy's number.

"Mr. Bryan, I hope everything is all right."

"Yes, I'm fine. My friends are shaken though. How did you know to call me?" Kevin switched the phone speaker on so that

Sharon and Gina could listen in.

"The fire department informed me about the explosion," O'Shaunnessy said. "Our firm is on some of the property records. I'm so sorry."

"We are okay. Lucky, I guess," Kevin said. "There was also an accident though; someone tried to run us off the road."

They almost could hear O'Shaunnessy trying to think this out. They knew that she knew what had happened, or at least they were pretty sure she knew about David Stein and his connection to what was unfolding. They also knew O'Shaunnessy may have been involved in the explosion, or at least her henchman and Boyle had been involved.

"Run you off the road? Someone tried to kill you?"

"Not just me, but all of us. The police have been guarded. They won't tell us anything. Have you heard something?"

"I'm just the solicitor for the estate, Mr. Bryan. Other than the explosion, I have no idea as to why the police would contact me."

Donovan already had told them that he had contacted Sylvia Boyle. She would have called O'Shaunnessy.

"I understand. It's all so confusing. That's why I'm trying to get more time," Kevin continued. "My friends are worried and want to help. They have contacted another law firm to assist me in clearing the tax debt and to move forward with the final acquisition of the property. They feel that it is better for me to go this route, and I concur. Of course, you will be reimbursed appropriately for your time and expenses to date."

Silence. Then, "Is that necessary, Mr. Bryan? My firm can handle all the work; there's no need—"

"It's better for everyone. We're going to spend another few days down here. I need to find out if some of the stories I've heard about the property are true."

"What stories? What have you heard?"

"Things about smuggling, drugs, the IRA. I want to be sure that what I'm inheriting is free of complications, especially local problems."

"Smuggling?" O'Shaunnessy stuttered. "I don't know anything about smuggling."

Kevin looked at his friends; both women tilted their heads in surprise.

"I didn't say that you did, Ms. O'Shaunnessy. Nonetheless, I've made up my mind. We will be back in Dublin in a few days. I will contact you then to finish our business. Good day, Ms. O'Shaunnessy." Kevin clicked off.

11b

Later that morning, after the rain had passed, Molly stood in the tall grass behind the stone wall that separated the pasture above the O'Bryan house from the dark copse of woods. Looking down, she could see the Mercedes van parked in front of the half-burnt cottage. She shook her head in both disgust and wonderment. Did this Bryan know about the tunnel and the access to the beach? Had he told the authorities? How quickly a centuries-old secret could be unexpectedly discovered. Maybe this was what she needed to get out of the game, leave all this shit, move on, she thought. The bakery was doing well, though not as profitable as she hoped. Over the next ten years, through the business, she could launder the bales of euros that were hidden in the safe. She and her team hadn't been caught, so there would be little to alert or spook the revenuers. There was maybe two million euros, all twenties, fifties, and hundreds tucked away. Moving a few thousand here and there would allow it to be safely liquidated, all eventually to be rolled into a nice account in Geneva.

She watched the van leave the courtyard and pull up the hill and out onto the road. She gave them twenty minutes before she and Dergo walked through the pasture on the old sheep trail, around the pile of stone behind the cottage, and surveyed the ruins. Inside the cottage, the sliding door to the cellar was closed. When she checked, the latch attached to the painting still functioned. She surveyed the cellar and its meager contents; the door to the tunnel had been left undamaged as well. At least they respected history, she thought.

It was a conundrum. What to do? What to save? Was there anything left to save?

"Why didn't you tell me about the tunnel? It might have prevented all this," a voice said. When Molly whirled around, the tall American, Kevin Bryan, stood above her on the stair landing. His friend Sharon O'Mara stood next to him.

"We're a secret lot, we Irish," Molly said, looking up at the two. "Years of oppression and war—we'd suspect our own brothers."

"This is your tunnel?" Sharon asked.

"Hardly. I'm just this generation's caretaker. The stories and tales go back centuries. It was once hidden under a sheep's shed, then a small cottage, and then grew to what you see now. How long it has been in use, no one knows; the carvings on the walls say more than three hundred years." She looked at Kevin. "I'm sorry that I was not forthcoming. You O'Bryans have always been a part of this land. In fact, on the hill above the road, there was a great Irish oak that four hundred years ago dominated the view. The British used it to hang a half dozen of your ancestors after the Battle of Kinsale. We citizens of County Cork and the English have a long and very nasty history."

"You said that this Boyle woman may be the buyer," Kevin said.

"I think so, and now that those men died in that unfortunate accident . . ."

"One of the men killed was her son," Sharon said.

"Yes, the younger man, the one tossed to the road," Molly said. "His name was David Stein. He is also supposed to be Sylvia Boyle's right arm and successor."

"And you know this how?" Kevin asked.

"The Internet is a powerful tool."

"It wasn't an accident," Sharon said. "They tried to kill us, but their SUV flipped. Yes, it was unfortunate—for them."

"Molly, ancient smugglers' tunnel aside, what's so important about this piece of property?" Kevin asked. "Why would this woman from New York want or even care about this piece of Ireland?"

"The Boyles are from Bantry," Molly said. "A local historian told me this." She walked up to join them on the landing. "We might as well get comfortable," she suggested. "This is a long story."

Molly continued her story as the three of them left the cottage and strolled the grounds.

"The family is from west of here, about fifty kilometers, near Banteer. After Amos Boyle—he's the great-grandfather of Sylvia Boyle—left Cork in the late 1880s, he went first to Boston, then moved to New York, and then came back to Ireland. He made connections, and then returned to New York. He married and had a son, Donald Boyle. That man had a son; Donald the second was Sylvia Boyle's father and founder of Boyle Development. Sylvia's father died in Africa, killed by a wild animal, I'm told. There is a centuries-old rumor that the Boyles held an old vendetta against the O'Bryans. During Amos's return to Ireland, he tried to involve the O'Bryans in his support of the IRA. The historian said that Amos ran guns to the IRA for more than thirty years. They came out of the United States, mostly New York. Donald the first continued the tradition. The guns he sent here went north to Belfast. It was quite lucrative. My man says that the Boyles may have kept fifty percent of the money raised as a fee for their services. What's curious is that no one knows where Amos got the initial money to start his business in New York. Rumors abound, but one minute he's as poor as a church mouse, the next he has a penthouse on Park Avenue. Then again, the stories about your clan aren't much different."

"What do you mean, my clan?" Kevin asked.

"Auntie Brona's father, Thomas O'Bryan, also ran guns. He brought them up that tunnel there." She pointed toward the cottage. "My family and a few others here in the county worked for them, some for hundreds of years. Whatever the people needed and were willing to pay for came up that tunnel."

"What did Amos Boyle do here in Ireland before he returned to New York?" Sharon asked.

"Hard to say. The general story was that he was a petty thief and was loosely connected to the smuggling of liquor to the States. When the local constabulary got after him, he fled to Boston. That is hard to pin down; smugglers usually don't leave a paper trail, as we would call it today. In this part of Ireland, it seems everyone is a cousin of everyone. My historian, a lovely old man in his nineties, by the way, said that somewhere or somehow Amos Boyle found money. The oldest story is gold, and he used it as his bankroll—possibly Spanish gold from the early seventeenth century if believing that oldest version of the story. We Irish always believe in luck and leprechauns and pots of gold. That treasure gets woven into the fabric of our stories, so I pretty much discount them."

Molly lit a cigarette. Sharon begged one and then stuck her tongue out at Kevin when he attempted to remind her that she had quit.

"Old habits are hard to break," Molly said. "I know that all so well."

"So, the Boyles are not just some New York land developers who happened to have an opportunity fall in their lap?" Kevin asked.

"Doesn't look like it. They have a history with the area, a long history and one that may be linked to your family. Brona told me the story of two men who came up through this tunnel during the last years of World War II. They were locals. In fact, one of the men's great-grandson and great-granddaughter work for me. The men were IRA soldiers named Rian Doyle and Colm Casey. They were trained as spies by the Nazis and were sent here to find out when the invasion of France was to happen. From here in Ireland they entered England."

"What happened?" Sharon asked.

"They never made it off the dock in Wales. They were found out and attempted to escape. Both men were shot down like dogs. Colm Casey was my grandmother's father. So, the battles with the English continued long after independence. Even today, the hatreds in the north are real and palpable."

"Amos Boyle may have been financed locally?" Kevin asked.

"Yes, by a man in Cork City. He acted as the intermediary. He would send money to Amos in America for farm equipment; it would return as guns and munitions. That is one of the rumors, and it gets even stranger. That's when we come back to the gold. Soon after the failure of the Spanish Armada's attempt to invade England in the late 1500s, the new king of Spain, Phillip III, sent troops and landed near Kinsale—about twenty miles up the coast. They were to join forces with the local Irish militias and push the English out of Ireland and create a Spanish base to invade England. Eventually they were defeated along with the Irish who supported them. In retribution, the English unmercifully starved this part of Ireland; it lasted for centuries."

"I'd heard of that from my grandfather," Kevin said. "The so-called Great Famine in Ireland was more like intentional genocide encouraged by the Brits. A blight started it, but the British could have helped feed the countryside. Tens of thousands died."

Molly nodded. "Maybe millions. The English then moved their own people into the abandoned farms."

"And the gold?"

"A rumor. There's always another rumor or tall tale in this country. This one says that the Spanish arrived with chests full of gold that were to be used to buy the loyalty of the Irish. We've always been a mercenary sort here. After the Spanish defeat, the chests were never found. It's been assumed that when the English permitted what was left of the Spanish invaders to escape, the English seized the gold. Others, my historian included, think otherwise."

"Do you mean that the Boyles might have had access or control of this treasure?" Sharon asked.

"Possibly—who knows?" Molly said. "Maybe Sylvia Boyle believes the gold is still here, hidden somewhere. Her interest has focused on these headlands and the area around it. I also believe she wants this land more than anything. I don't get it, though. She's a billionaire; the gold can't be worth all that much to her. However, there are old family grudges and vendettas behind this, like I said, hatreds that go way back between the Boyles and the O'Bryans."

"I had no idea, incredible. Sharon, I can't believe that we are involved in another treasure hunt," Kevin said.

"Spanish treasure, revenge . . . just great. Let the fun and the games begin," Sharon answered with a flourish. "*Olè!*"

11c

The sun hung low in the sky, seeming to float just above the ocean's horizon. Sharon walked down to the sandy shingle of beach that extended to the cliffs that enclosed the inn. She'd almost forgotten how good the taste of a cigarette could be. The Dunhills that Molly had weren't too bad. To Kevin's disproval, Molly had given her the half-empty pack. Puffing smoke out into the crisp breeze blowing in from the sea, she reflected on the reality that, if not for Donovan, she and her best friend would be fish food. Her birthday was two days away, and everything seemed to be in shambles. Putting aside the minor point of possibly not reaching her fortieth birthday, she and her friends were now caught in a swirl of castles and kings, war and peace, smugglers and bakers—what a mess. A foolish and bizarre mess. O'Mara smiled.

"Penny for your thoughts?" Gina said as she walked up to her friend, a tumbler in her hand.

Taking the glass, Sharon smiled again. "Thanks. What a crazy, screwed-up few days, and not to mention, vacation."

"I think it's good we're here for Kevin. If he'd come alone, I'm not sure what would be happening," Gina said. "Whenever I travel with you two, it's never dull."

"Dull would be good right now."

"But boring. How is our boy doing?"

"He's confused as much as I am, and all over some Irish

fairy tale about treasure?" She ticked off the list on her fingers: "Your attempted kidnapping, the cottage bomb, two attempts to kill us, and now two dead men—it doesn't even come close to making sense."

"Greed can do that."

"True, but there seems to be something else going on. This Boyle woman is rich, rich in the terms of really filthy, stinking rich. Treasure? What could it be worth today? Hell, a ton of gold is only worth about thirty-seven million dollars." Sharon paused. "Quite a lot, I guess."

"You guess? That is a lot of money."

"Yes, but for a billionaire? Is it worth it? And I'm not sure that it's even a ton. Maybe it was only a few hundred pounds. A fortune back in the days of Queen Elizabeth, but now, hell, it may not even exist."

"People have done very strange things over treasure, like that Nazi woman from Argentina. She wanted that SS gold so much she'd try anything to find it. She's now in prison for life for murder. You put her there. And that was all about a strange treasure map, something that we don't have."

"Not all treasure comes with a map."

"True, but it's fun when it does. So, now what?"

"Your Dublin copper says that the Boyle woman is coming to Ireland. She may even be here now."

Gina smiled. "First of all, he's not my copper—he is cute, though. Second, I'll ask him if he's heard anything about Boyle landing. She must go through Customs somewhere. And third, we need to be ready when she shows up."

"You're becoming quite a detective, if not a bit horny."

"It's been a while, and I lean toward guys who save my life. The rest of the madness comes from hanging around with the two of you. I'm suspicious of the Budweiser guy when he delivers beer at the bar now—it's all your fault."

"Thirsty?" a voice called from behind them. Claudette and Evelyn stood on the dry sand beyond the surf line. Evelyn held up another tumbler, and then smiled. "I didn't know you had one."

"I think you girls are trying to get me drunk," Sharon said. "Takes more than two glasses."

Sharon and Gina climbed up the beach to join their friends. The sun was half-drowned; the red-orange glow of its setting lit up the sky. A chill wind blew up from the sea and across the four women; they all shivered.

"An ill wind, a portent," Claudette said.

"Are you French always so superstitious?" Evelyn asked.

"Hardly, but the last few days have been exciting. I think we are all on edge."

They walked back up the hill to the inn. Kevin and JF were sitting in the bar, a soccer game on the TV. The women took a table near the window; the men dragged chairs over and sat.

"I was thinking of moving up the schedule and tomorrow we head back to Dublin," Kevin said. "There's too many bizarre things going on here, and we can resolve the issues of the property more easily there."

"We came to somewhat the same conclusion," Sharon said. "The treasure?"

"There's no treasure," Kevin said. "As Molly said, it's all just a four-hundred-year-old tale. A good one, I'll agree, but still just an Irish fairy tale."

"What treasure, what story?" Liam asked as he walked into the bar.

"An old tale of Spanish treasure and revolution," Gina said as she made room so the cop could sit next to her. Liam obliged.

"Not the Kinsale hoard?" Donovan asked.

"It has a name?" JF asked.

"Yes, and it goes back hundreds of years. Why?"

Kevin relayed to Donovan what Molly had said, though he did leave her name out of the conversation. All the cop did was grin and shake his head.

"I'm not saying there is or there isn't a treasure of gold and silver, just that after all this time, no one's come forth with it. Occasionally a few coins show up from that sad part of Irish history. The coins from that era are well known; there's dozens in museums in Spain, and even a few in London scavenged from the wrecks and survivors of the Armada. In Ulster, there's a display of the gold recovered from the Armada ship *La Girona* that sunk off Antrim County. Dozens of other Armada ships floundered on the rugged Irish western coast, but none, that are known, along the south side. All that was fifteen years before the Kinsale invasion by the Spanish."

"There's a chance that it might be true? That there is a fortune?" Sharon asked.

"There's always a chance, most probably none," Donovan said.

"Liam, you have to forgive Sharon," Kevin said. "She's always been a romantic, and a chaser of treasure and dreams."

"I am not," Sharon answered.

"Yes, you are," her five friends said in unison.

"There's a lot of people out there who are better off because of you," Gina said. "I've always believed you're the last of an idealistic era of do-gooders."

"That and three bucks will get you a latte," Sharon said.

"Cynical as well."

"I'll take that as a compliment," Sharon said with pride.

"Stop it, you two," Kevin said. "See what I have to put up with?"

"Poor baby," Sharon added as she blew Kevin a kiss. "Liam, we were going back to Dublin to finish some legal issues regarding the property as well as celebrate my birthday. Are you finished here?"

"A day or two more, then I'm done. The deaths of the two men who were chasing you has put more paperwork on my plate. That will take a day or two to resolve. I understand that Sylvia Boyle, the mother of David Stein, is on her way here to Ireland. Cork Airport passed on her itinerary and flight plans. She's supposed to be here tonight."

"Oh great, let the fun and games begin," Sharon repeated.

11d

Sinead O'Shaunnessy glanced at her phone. In the cold gloom of the clear damp night, the glow of the screen lit up her face like a flare. It was 12:35 PM. From the far end of the County Cork runway, the sharp whine of the engines of Boyle's Gulfstream filled the air. Nothing else moved on the tarmac. One lone attendant stood fifty feet away holding two flashlights; the foot-long tips glowed red. He waited for the aircraft to approach.

Boyle had called her twice during her transatlantic journey, wanting updates on her son and the latest about this California heir, especially where he was. O'Shaunnessy knew little more than what the police had told her. Boyle's son died after an accident during what appeared to be a high-speed chase of another vehicle. Nothing more about the incident had been released. David had not been the driver. The driver, who had a police record, was found still buckled into his seat. Though it seemed obvious, the cause of their deaths was to be officially determined by autopsies. That said, Boyle had let O'Shaunnessy know that she would forbid an autopsy; nothing would be done to desecrate the remains of her son. The police told O'Shaunnessy that it was a matter of procedure. That was when Boyle hung up on her the first time.

The second time was after O'Shaunnessy told her that Kevin Bryan was moving forward with the inheritance, and had the financial resources to complete the necessary government tax liens and processes. The line went dead as soon as O'Shaunnessy finished delivering that news.

O'Shaunnessy stood in the shadow of the hangar that Boyle had reserved, waiting. With the attendant's arms upright in an X, the jet rolled to a stop, and the engines began to spin down. From the port side of the aircraft, the door popped free and unfolded to the tarmac. Two men emerged from the aircraft. One quickly and athletically bounded down the steps to the tarmac; the other took the arm of a tall woman wearing outdoor clothing. He preceded her down the steps. The two men were scary. O'Shaunnessy had seen their type before. In fact, her man Banning looked cut from the same mold that said military, professional soldier, mercenary. *What the hell have I gotten myself into?* she thought.

Boyle walked directly to the solicitor.

"Thank you for meeting me," Boyle said. "I apologize for my abrupt reactions to our conversations. There has been a lot to process and comprehend."

"I completely understand," O'Shaunnessy said as she looked at the two hard men.

"These are my security team; you do not need to know their names. However, I have complete trust in them. Do you understand? They are not your concern. Customs?"

Since Boyle had succeeded in wrecking his quiet evening, the one lone Customs official, who doubled as the gate attendant, took his time. O'Shaunnessy was surprised that Boyle stood passively in front of the agent while their paperwork was processed. She'd expected fireworks. When asked about the purpose of her visit, Boyle simply said, "To collect and then return to the United States the remains of my dead son."

This seemed to soften the agent's mood, and he quickly finished. Then he said, "Sorry for your loss." The men took the bags and carried them to O'Shaunnessy's Land Rover.

"I assume the additional equipment I requested is in the vehicle?" Boyle asked as they neared the car.

"I hate guns. They are nothing but trouble," O'Shaunnessy said. "But Fergus's people supplied what you requested. They are in the back." She remotely clicked open the rear hatch; it slowly rose.

"Stop, not here," one of the men said sharply.

"That's okay," Boyle said, seeing the Customs agent crossing the tarmac to his car. "Take a quick look, then we'll go."

Inside was a large metal case. O'Shaunnessy handed a set of keys to the man who'd spoken. Since Boyle had not introduced her two companions, O'Shaunnessy mentally dubbed them Red and Brown, due to their tight, yet thick, beards. Red took the keys and unlocked the case and then removed two Glock 17s, hip holsters, and additional magazines. Brown cleared the magazine and inspected one of the weapons; he did it with the second gun as well. He then reloaded both pistols. Red then removed the two long rifles, Canadian C7s.

O'Shaunnessy watched, but she knew nothing about guns and pistols. If she had known these were military weapons stolen from a British barracks outside of Ulster during the Troubles, she'd have been even more afraid of Boyle and these men.

"Why do you need those things?" she asked Boyle.

"My contacts turned up a few more issues that you neglected to tell me. The first is that Kevin Bryan isn't just any ex-cop; he is a well-trained and experienced police detective. The second is that his American friend traveling with him is Sharon O'Mara."

"So?"

"Well, she has quite a reputation. She's ex-military and fancies herself as someone who comes to the aid of the downtrodden—probably all bullshit, but I never go unprepared. Her name popped up in some news articles I found. One of my California sources says that both she and Bryan have connections to the British police and the American military. Obviously, they are not the simpletons you thought they were, especially this Bryan fellow. This complicates things."

"I didn't know," O'Shaunnessy nearly whined. "How was I supposed to know?"

"I'll take care of it from now on. You just handle any of the legal repercussions. No one kills anyone in my family without paying for it." Boyle removed a folder from a small case she carried. "This folder has additional information I want you to investigate. It's about the Boyle family here in County Cork. I want to know where my grandfather Amos Boyle lived, as well as the Boyle family. I know it was somewhere near Bantry. I want everything you can find—and I want it by the end of the day. I've made arrangements to stay near Kinsale. I will call you when I need to talk with you." She turned to the two men who had armed up. "Time to go."

Brown took the driver's seat, after helping Boyle into the rear seat. Red took the front passenger seat.

"I'm not going with you?" O'Shaunnessy asked, looking at Boyle as she lowered the window. "How will I get home?"

"Take the bus."

Brown pulled away from the hangar, leaving O'Shaunnessy standing on the tarmac wondering what just happened.

Chapter 12

In New York there once lived a bitch,
Who, to many, resembled a witch.
She stormed and she fumed,
And her hatred did bloom,
And in time became quite unhitched.

12a

One hundred feet above the smugglers' tunnel and its hidden cove, Sharon gazed into the maelstrom churning amongst the rocks. The wind off the Celtic Sea pulled at her red hair and buffeted her face. She inhaled the rich salty taste and wiped a tear from her eye. *So, this is my island, the land where my family came from.* She turned and looked up at the green hills that rose from the headlands and disappeared into the mist beyond. *I now understand this tenaciousness. To be a part of this country with its history of music, culture, and oppression would turn most anyone to drink.* The thought made her laugh out loud.

She watched a lone figure walk toward her along the single path from the house. It was the O'Rourke woman, a tartan woolen cloak wrapped about her shoulders and neck, the ever-present hound pacing her stride for stride. Sharon waved; Molly waved back.

"Lonely out here," Sharon said, extending her hand as Molly drew closer.

"Not if you know the little people are about," Molly said, taking her hand.

"Really, leprechauns, fairies, ghosts?"

"Sharon, luv, all these mystical creatures are about—and if you believe in them, they are real. My grandpappy would go on for hours talking about the fairies and the spirits that lived in the roots of great trees, under rough hills, and in dark caves. He would talk about the tapping of their cobbler's hammers under the earth, the screams of the banshees during a storm, and the ever-presence of treasure—especially those gold coins in great pots. Catching a leprechaun was what young children and old fools tried to do—a way to find instant wealth. But the little people are tricky. The land and its creatures can't be that easily fooled."

"The stories of the Spanish gold are just that, stories and legends?"

"Maybe and maybe not. The landings in this area by the Spanish were real. Thousands of Spanish sailors and soldiers that escaped their sinking Armada ships and made it to shore were captured. All along the west of Ireland, when caught, the English summarily executed them. Any Irish that gave them comfort also were killed. The wars between Irish patriots and the English go back a thousand years. People turn to mysticism and fables when the times get rough, and our Holy Catholic Church doesn't help with all its supernatural beliefs. You look to have a little of the Irish in you, luv."

"My parents were both of Irish decent, so I've been told. I was very young when they died. I was raised in Colorado, in the middle of the United States. After high school, I went into a local college and took Army officer training. When I graduated, I served for eight years as an officer in the military police. I saw a lot of the world I would like to forget." She looked back at the hills. "Where I was, there was not enough green to fill a bucket."

"A lass of the old sod; I knew it. One can tell," Molly said. "Are you going to marry that Bryan fellow? You make a nice team."

"If I had a dollar for every time someone mentioned that . . ." Sharon answered with a smile. "Right now, and for the immediate future, no. We are close friends and have been through a lot together. But both of us are set in our ways, and it would require a considerable shift on both our parts to move from friends to lovers."

"I take it he's available?" Molly said with a laugh.

"The boy is so available it hurts, but he also has friends that would take apart anyone who hurt him. Ms. O'Rourke, be very careful. That slope can be a slippery one."

"Just wondering."

"Don't wonder a lot." Sharon turned and looked across the pastures that sloped away from Baile O'Bryan. "Do you think there's Spanish gold under this land?"

"It may be one of the reasons that Boyle is interested. My research has turned up that she's more into the development game for the fight and the win than she is for the money. For someone like her, money can be made a hundred different ways, and a lot more easily. With my bakery, some months it's good, some months not so much. I fight to survive. Boyle is well beyond that. If my historian is correct, she's here to reclaim this land as her family's. Her need is as twisted as the stories of evil goblins and fairies, and our stories go back a thousand years. I know what Brona O'Bryan would do."

"Brona was a tough woman?"

"One of the sweetest and toughest Irish women you would ever know or wish to meet. Like that Kevin fellow, she was tall; all the O'Bryan clan were tall—the women over six feet, the men half a head more. All were dark and imposing, full voiced, even a few could sing. I only knew Brona; she was the last as far as I knew. She would talk and tell stories about her uncles and aunts, but the O'Bryan line burned out, as can happen. Your Kevin Bryan does seem to be the last. Brona never married and never had children. This land and the house were her children. When I was a wee lass, she scared the bejesus out of me. Always wore a tartan cloak like this one. The wildest red hair, sharp green eyes. I believed that she could look through me and see my soul. Later, I learned that she could."

Sharon was fascinated in what O'Rourke had to say about Brona, but for the moment only to the degree that it affected Kevin.

"Do you have any ideas for what to do about Boyle?" she asked the baker-smuggler. "According to Donovan, she's here to finish what her son tried to do—scare us off or at least force Kevin to sell the land."

"Can you and your friends help him?" Molly asked.

"Yes, we've pledged to help Kevin acquire the land; that will give him some time to figure what is to be done."

"Good," Molly said.

Kevin was headed their way. They watched him walk up the path toward them.

"Sharon, there may be another way that might work. When his lordship gets here, I'll make you an offer that might astound you."

12b

Sylvia Boyle's first stop was at the only funeral home in the town of Clonakilty. Red stayed with the Range Rover; Brown accompanied Boyle into the home. A small, bald, green-eyed elfin-looking man met them in the small vestibule.

"Are you Mr. Brennan?" Boyle asked the man.

"Yes, mum, I'm he. Are you Ms. Boyle?"

"Yes. My son?"

"I am very sorry for your loss. Please follow me."

While she crossed the Atlantic, Boyle had spoken with Inspector Liam Donovan and learned that her son had been moved to a funeral home in Clonakilty where they had the proper facilities to take care of the body. The only other place would have been the county morgue in Cork. Boyle preferred the lower profile. She called the funeral home and discussed her requirements.

"I understand that you wish to take your son home with you," the director said. "You do realize that to transport the body it will have to be embalmed."

"Thank you, I understand the complications. I will let you know what I want done."

"I've had this situation before. I suggest that you check and make sure you can place the remains in the plane's cargo hold, if it has one. Again, I'm sorry for your loss."

The list of complications had piled up quickly. She could not take the body until the Garda had cleared the accident report and the county issued a death certificate. Donovan wasn't sure how long that might take. And U.S. Customs would not allow the body to enter unless it was embalmed. And she would have to have the U.S. State Department involved. All a bother.

Mr. Brennan led her through the hallways of the funeral home until they came to a set of double doors. Brown stood off to one side.

"I have placed him in a temporary casket for the moment. I thought it would be more appropriate. I hope you don't mind. I also applied some makeup. His face was slightly damaged during the accident."

Before she entered, Boyle asked, "The other man, what happened to him?"

"An ambulance arrived early this morning from Dublin. They took Mr. Banning's remains. I do not know where they were taking him."

Boyle was certain that O'Shaunnessy was involved.

Brennan opened the door. Boyle thought she was prepared, but seeing her son in the casket was almost more than she could take. Brown quickly moved to her side and supported her as she began to collapse. She took a few deep breaths and regained her composure.

"Thank you, Mr. Brennan. I appreciate what you have done."

He nodded and left quietly as she stood looking at her son, her heir, hers and the company's future. Now it was gone. Centuries ago, according to the Boyle family legend, one of the O'Bryans had killed one of her ancestors and that murder led directly to the deaths of other Boyles. Now another Boyle, her favored son, was dead—all because of the O'Bryans.

After about ten minutes, Mr. Brennan returned.

"Mr. Brennan, please prepare my son as required. I will

give you further directions later in the day. Would you, though, investigate transportation to New York City?"

"Of course, ma'am."

Sylvia Boyle offered a rare comment of appreciation: "Thank you for your efforts and what you did for David."

"You're most welcome, Ms. Boyle. If there is anything else I can do, just let me know."

Boyle walked back to the SUV; her broken heart beat heavily in her breast.

"I will put an end to this charade tonight," she said to the two security men. She looked back at the funeral home. "Tonight."

As Boyle reached for the handle of the door of the Range Rover, a muscular-looking young man walked across the narrow street directly toward the three. Red instantly pulled his Glock and held it at his side. If the man approaching made the wrong move, if necessary, Red would put him down. Brown placed himself between the intruder and Boyle. Tommy O'Rourke put his hands up and stopped.

"I just wish to talk to Ms. Boyle, gentlemen."

"Who the hell are you, and how do you know who I am?" Boyle asked.

"Tommy O'Rourke, ma'am. My aunt's been looking into you—Molly O'Rourke is her name. So's I knows about you and your connection to the O'Bryan place. Not much goes on around here that I don't know about," lied Tommy. "My condolences about your son. Damn shame."

"What do you know about it?" Boyle demanded.

"Damn shame, as I said, him being forced off the road and all."

Boyle moved forward so that she stood next to Brown. "What do you mean?"

"Ms. Boyle, there's a lot about the O'Bryan house and grounds that you may not know about. I could help, as they say, fill in the pieces."

"What do you know about the death of my son?"

"I have a friend in the local constable's office, and he tells me that the vehicle they were driving was forced off the road. It was the American who was driving the van."

"That's not what the police said."

"I don't know what they told you, I only know what I was told. And it didn't sound like no accident."

"And what do you want?"

"To help, that's all. And if you think I've helped, maybe a few euros for the help."

"Ms. Boyle, we should go. There's no need to deal with this hustler," Red said. He opened the door of the SUV.

"No, ma'am, no hustle. Just want to help."

"Young man, what's your beef with the O'Bryans? My experience says that no one offers anything without a reason and a price." Boyle stepped toward the SUV but didn't move to get in.

"Them O'Bryans have been all too high and mighty around here for years. I did some things for them. Never paid me for what I was worth. So, your being here may be a chance to balance the ledger, as you might say."

"Please, ma'am, the kid's a punk. We should get to the hotel," Red insisted. "Just ignore him."

Brown's eyes never left Tommy.

"I's understand, me being such a punk. Hell, I would tell me to get lost, too, but if you need any help, just give me a call." Tommy handed a piece of paper to Brown, who glanced at the number.

"Why would you turn on your aunt?" Boyle asked.

"We're not all that close, and I've a score to settle with her, too."

Tommy stood in the road and watched as the Range Rover pulled away and drove down the narrow street. He was reasonably pleased with his performance, just enough bullshit and bravado to spark Boyle's interest. Maybe he'd get a few dollars out of this. If the local IRA didn't want to deal with him, he'd find another way to make his fortune.

12c

From a block up the street, Mac MacLeish sat in the front seat of his car watching the conversation. *What are you doing, Tommy boy—what the hell are you up to?*

Three days earlier MacLeish had received a call from Derek Dunham, head of the local cell of the Real IRA, telling him that Tommy O'Rourke was trying to sell out his aunt. Dunham told him about the beating he'd given Tommy as well as how he viewed the impropriety of the young man turning on his own kin and clan. MacLeish thanked the gangster and wondered where he'd be if he'd stayed in the business of radical politics. Twenty years earlier, soon after the Good Friday Agreement, Mac had left the organization and returned to County Cork. The local factions allowed him his own peace, just as long as he didn't cross paths with their current drug operations. Politics was one thing, drugs was another. MacLeish hated what the local gangs were doing, but he also valued his own life and the lives of his friends. The call from Dunham was both an acknowledgment of their history and a note of caution. *Watch this boy—do not let him step out of line.*

MacLeish slowly pulled into the street as Tommy made a U-turn and then followed the youth. The two men and the woman Tommy met up with had looked American; maybe the woman was the one that Molly had talked about, the one who had walked the land above the tunnel with the lawyer. Molly had said something about a son dying in the car crash near Baile O'Bryan; that was why the American woman stopped at Brennan's Funeral Home. Her son had to be one of the two victims from the crash.

On the east side of Clonakilty, Tommy pulled to the curb in front of a tavern he'd been known to frequent. MacLeish didn't bother to get out; he knew Tommy would be there until closing. Instead MacLeish drove west through the village and turned into a neighborhood of residential homes. In the driveway of one of the more comfortable-looking houses sat the van for the bakery. After a sharp rap of the door knocker, Molly opened the door and let him in. She quickly closed the door behind him. Dergo pushed himself against Mac's legs and nuzzled him.

"You were right," Mac said, as he and Molly sat down at her small kitchen table. "Tommy is in for a pile of trouble; first Dunham and now this Boyle woman. What did you do to set him off?"

"Mac, I did nothing. In fact, I've probably indulged him. The kid's been headstrong and a little off balance since the day he was born. Maybe it was the drugs my sister took before she died. You know that more than anyone."

"Yeah," he said, agreeing, "but for him to think he could play Derek Dunham and his brother, that's just stupid. I don't know what he's trying to do with the Boyles, either, but he hasn't a chance. That woman will spit him out when she's done."

Molly fetched them each a beer. "This morning I met with the Bryan fellow and that friend of his, Sharon O'Mara," she told Mac as she set the beers on the table. "He's lucky to have friends like that. I suggested that we become partners and then he could sell me the house."

"What the hell are you going to do with Brona's old house? It will take every euro you have to fix it."

"It's not just the house; it's the house and the tunnel. Mac, we've put away enough to buy the house and fix it up. Would make a great B&B."

"A fucken' B&B? You don't know how to run a B&B, lass. And I can't imagine you making beds and cooking breakfast for a bunch of noisy tourists every morning. Hell, even I don't want to be that ambitious at my age."

She smiled at her old friend. "They declined. They appreciated what I was offering but said they weren't sure about my financial connections and what that might mean down the road. Bryan used to be a cop, and the O'Mara woman is ex-military. Between them, they figured out what our second careers are. I said I understood and respected what they said."

"And I thought Americans were opportunists."

"I guess not all of them."

"There goes your chance at County Cork businesswoman of the year."

"The trophy would have been nice. Something like this would be my chance to get us out of this racket once and for all."

"We can wish. This Boyle woman complicates everything. This all goes way back. She's not going to let it go. She has two bodyguard types with her that reinforced that, ex-military by their looks."

"This is really not our fight."

"I know that, but it's one that we owe Brona."

"You would have to say that," Molly said.

"Brona was the last of the Irish O'Bryans. I loved that woman, and I'll do everything to protect her name. The gold, that's a pipe dream if there ever was one. If there be truth to it, she'd have told me. So, for the next few days, I'll keep my eyes and ears open. That's the least I can do."

"You are a good man, Mac MacLeish."

"'Tis me cross to bear."

Chapter 13

Here is our lad Kevin Bryan,
Who with five friends went to Ireland.
To see his inheritance,
Without any assurance,
Of where his adventure would end.

13a

Kevin explained the offer from Molly O'Rourke to the group over dinner.

"You believe that she has that kind of money?" JF asked.

"Yes, I believe her. It seems the bakery business is quite lucrative," Kevin said with a laugh. "Our guess, it's the smuggling game that's a wee bit more profitable."

"Smuggling?" Evelyn asked. "Here?"

"I think it's cigarettes. We'll ask Liam what he thinks," Kevin said.

"I suggest that we leave Liam out of this, for now," Gina said. "You told her no, that's good. Our concern should be this Boyle woman. From what you and Liam have said, she will be a witch to deal with."

"She has to be the one behind this," Sharon said. "Molly thinks she's been watching this land for years and, after Brona's death, decided to take it. According to Molly, there's a long and messy feud between the families."

"A one-sided feud if there can be such a thing," Kevin said. "Molly was certain that Brona didn't know anything about it, but from the Boyle point of view it went back hundreds of years. For a family to hold a grudge that long is surprising. Maybe it's the gold that's driving it. Treasure can do that."

"You and your damn treasures," Claudette said. "First my grandfather and his Nazi treasure, now this. But Alain's was a treasure worth hunting, and it's still lost in the German countryside. What could be here? Kevin, you could be sitting on one of the greatest hoards of gold and silver ever lost in Ireland. I can't believe that you'd toss it away to someone like this Boyle woman."

"Are you believing her cockamamie story?" Kevin said.

"Stories like this, this crazy, almost always have a basis in fact," Claudette said. "So, why not? It's fun to think about. Somewhere buried under all that lush green grass and stones are chests full of gold doubloons and pieces of eight. Enough to make a woman dream of almost anything."

"Now you are making fun," Kevin answered.

"Not really, but it is exciting to think about. However, short of bringing in an excavator and plowing up all this lovely land, I sincerely don't know how you could find it."

"That's probably what Sylvia Boyle would do," Sharon added. "Build a resort, rip up the land and construct a golf course, and in the process, find boxes of Spanish Armada gold. All neat and pretty."

"I like it, good cover," JF said.

"You would," Sharon said with a laugh.

"Isn't tomorrow your birthday, Miss Sharon O'Mara?" JF said, grinning at her. "So, I suggest that we spend the day looking for buried treasure. This all reminds me of that old movie *It's A Mad, Mad, Mad, Mad World*. All we have to do is look for the crossed palm trees. What a glorious birthday present."

"You're all certifiably crazy," Sharon said. "I mean it, certifiable. But I would like to do something special for my birthday."

The server walked over to their table. "Ms. O'Mara, there's a phone call for you at the desk. You will have to take it there."

Sharon stood and looked at the group, a quizzical expression on her face. She followed the server out of the room.

"Sharon O'Mara," she said and listened for a minute. "Interesting. Does Inspector Donovan know? . . . Thank you, Molly . . . I'll let Kevin know."

She walked back into the room. "Fascinating. That was Molly O'Rourke; she says that Sylvia Boyle is now in town with a couple of New York goons. Boyle visited her son at the funeral home and returned to a hotel near Kinsale. Molly talked with the funeral director, and he was ordered to prepare the body for shipment to New York. He told her that Boyle seemed extremely upset."

"Who wouldn't be?" Evelyn said. "Her son just died. But do you think she's planning something?"

"That's a woman who always gets what she wants," Sharon said. "Your guess is as good as mine. But I suggest that we be prepared."

Kevin had walked to the window looking out over the sea while Sharon took the call. He turned back to the group. "This is all such bullshit. I get you all caught up in this inheritance silliness and almost get you hurt, and now these thugs. This has to stop, now."

"Kevin, it's becoming obvious that Boyle and O'Shaunnessy are conspiring to get this property of yours," Sharon said. "And O'Shaunnessy doesn't know that we know it's this woman Boyle."

"It's not mine, yet."

"Yes, but you told her you were going forward without her. That will drive O'Shaunnessy crazy. I'll bet she's in for a piece of the deal; this could cut her out. And the death of Boyle's son will make this even more personal. Boyle may even blame O'Shaunnessy for her son's death."

"Or me," Kevin said.

"Everything you know is what O'Shaunnessy has told you," JF said. "Right now, I wouldn't trust her with my pet poodle."

"You have a poodle?" Gina asked.

"Don't change the subject," Sharon said.

"Really, I'm trying to imagine that man holding a poodle."

"Gina, he's a standard black poodle," JF said. "Duke weighs in at almost thirty kilos, and is the love of my life. Of course, he's . . ."

"Look, you two, we're talking about the estate and the house, not the AKC—focus," Sharon said and looked at Kevin. "What are you thinking?"

"Find out what Boyle wants," Kevin said. "Maybe we can work something out."

"How do we get a hold of her?" Evelyn said.

"Inspector Donovan has her phone number," Gina said. "We can ask him to set up a meeting, talk this through."

"She will learn that we know who and what she is," Kevin said.

"And there's a downside to this?" Sharon asked.

"I can't think of a reason not to bring this all to a head."

"It's worth a try. Can you call him, Gina?" JF asked.

"Of course." Gina walked out the door to the terrace with her phone.

"Kevin, you know we are all a hundred percent behind you in this," JF said. "Whatever you need."

Claudette hadn't said a word during the conversation; she only stared out the window to the sea.

"Claudette?" Kevin asked.

She turned to him. "You were right when you said this was all bullshit. It *is* all bullshit. Why do you want this property? It really means little to you; you have a life halfway around the world. This land will be a millstone, dragging you down. If this Molly O'Rourke wants the property, sell it to her. And to be brutally honest, if Boyle wants it, set a high price and let her have it. I've run into people like her, single focus, egocentric, and damn anyone who gets in her way. Kevin, it's not worth all the bullshit and now, death. And besides, unless you have forgotten, one of the reasons we are here is Sharon. Tomorrow is her birthday. And I for one am not going to spend it talking about some broken-down house and property, no matter how pretty it is." She raised her glass of wine and saluted Sharon.

"Thanks, Claudette," Sharon answered, and then looked at Kevin.

He sipped his Jameson and looked around at his friends. "You're right, Claudette. It is all bullshit. The sooner I can rid myself of this, the better."

"Good for you," Sharon said.

Gina walked back in, waving her phone. "It's all set. While I was on hold, Liam talked to Boyle, and they will meet us at the house tomorrow morning, ten o'clock. She was stunned that we knew it was her. Liam said he covered by connecting her son through the driver and O'Shaunnessy. He's not sure she believed him, he said." She looked at the faces of her friends. "What? What happened?"

"A change in the ship's course," JF said. "Kevin?"

"Thanks, Gina, for talking to Liam," Kevin said. "If Sharon doesn't mind my messing up her plans just a little, I'll meet with Boyle tomorrow morning and settle this once and for all."

"The meeting at the house was really Liam's idea," Gina said. "But it is your birthday."

"I really had no plans," Sharon said.

"Phooey, we will still have a party," Gina said. "After the meeting, let's have a celebration right here. I'll get the hotel to help. Maybe Molly can bake us a cake. Claudette, will you be my sous chef?"

"Absolutely," Claudette answered.

"If you ladies don't mind," JF said, "and if Kevin doesn't, either, I'll tag along with them. Maybe having someone with a little financial clout will even out the conversation."

"Thanks, JF. I appreciate that," Kevin said. "What time did Liam say?"

"Ten o'clock."

13b

The call from Inspector Donovan came as Sylvia Boyle was sitting in the bar of the hotel finishing a glass of bourbon.

She hadn't realized how tired she was until she let slide her surprise that Bryan knew her connection to O'Shaunnessy. So, the American ex-cop knew it was her and wanted a meeting? O'Shaunnessy must have said something to Bryan—*the bitch*. She should have dealt with this directly from the beginning, Boyle realized. She'd never trusted anyone in her business dealings. However, this could all be dealt with at one time. And the Irish policeman . . . she wondered what his angle was. Why had he been the one to call and say that Bryan wanted to meet and discuss the future of the house and property—would she be interested? Of course, was her answer . . . *No one kills my son and gets away with it. This man will pay, and then I will destroy everyone else he cares for.*

Chapter 2

Sylvia's grandfather, even at a great age, told stories—tales of Ireland and the little people, tales of the war for independence, of bombs, and of guns, and tales of the clan Boyle. Some evenings, when a young girl, she would sit wide-eyed and listen to the stories he would weave: . . . *We never were a powerful clan like many who licked the shoes of the English. However, we are a proud family, and we can trace our roots back more than ten generations to three Boyle brothers. It is Miles Boyle that we owe our line to; he was the last of the three brothers to survive the murders by the English. Conal and Kyran were the other two, strong and brave they were. It was through their efforts that some of the Spanish sailors were sheltered after the failure of the Armada. With their help, these sailors returned home safely while the English were butchering those that they could find. It was at great risk to themselves, for if they were caught, they would have suffered the same fate as the Spanish sailors.*

One grateful officer told the brothers that there was a treasure of four chests filled with Spanish gold hidden in the Cork countryside, and for their help in saving the officer and his men, it was theirs. All they had to do was find it. A clan of dark leprechauns—who through their cunning and magic—transformed themselves into the protestant family called O'Bryan. It was they and their dark arts that guarded the four chests. All the land to the edge of the sea, from Kinsale to

Skibbereen, was under their power and control. It was a cursed land where the English had hanged patriotic Irishmen from a great oak, and Spanish soldiers were put to the spear and rope when found. The O'Bryans conspired with the English to ensure that no honest and true Irishman would ever be able to control this magical land. It was the gold, and black magic, that secured the O'Bryans to the land. But, if found by true Irishmen, the curse would be thrown and the gold would be theirs.

Later, it also was whispered that the O'Bryans controlled a secret passage through the bowels of the earth that allowed the English to sneak into the south of Ireland and listen through keyholes and open windows. The Spanish treasure was hidden in this passage, but it was discovered and then stolen by the brothers Boyle. They were, now that the curse was lifted, to use the gold to run the English out of Ireland. They secreted the gold out of this tunnel and hid it. But within a few days, they were discovered as the three brothers prayed in a small church. During the fight—where the townspeople of Clonakilty helped the brothers—the middle brother, Conal, died. A sham trial was held where the head of the O'Bryan clan, William, perjured himself, and this ensured that the two remaining brothers went to prison. There Kyran died, while defending his brother, Miles, from an attack by the other protestant prisoners.

Years later, after Miles was released, he crossed Ireland to Bantry and returned to his mother. He told her the sad story of her sons and his brothers. It was her oath and curse that was to forever set our clan against the O'Bryans. When the time was right, Miles Boyle returned to the cursed land and looked for the treasure. He was discovered by William O'Bryan on the road, and a mighty fight ensued, fist on fist and knife on knife. Miles was triumphant and revenged the deaths of his brothers. Miles never found the treasure. But as sure as the O'Bryan land is cursed, if that treasure is ever recovered by a Boyle, it and the whole of the surrounding country will become once again the land of the Boyle clan, and we will rise up strong and mighty amongst the clans of Ireland.

* * *

"I suggest we meet at the house, Inspector Donovan," Sylvia had said. "I will meet you in the courtyard . . . yes, I've been to the property courtesy of the solicitor, Ms. O'Shaunnessy . . . how about nine thirty, we will have a few minutes to talk . . . I'll ask Ms. O'Shaunnessy to come down as well . . . excellent, see you then."

Boyle then called O'Shaunnessy. "I want you there at nine o'clock; there is much to discuss . . . I really don't care. If you want to be a part of this, you will be there . . . Sinead, shut up and listen; be there at nine."

13c

After the six friends finished breakfast, they stood in the sea mist that drifted through the courtyard of the hotel. They had a replacement van to drive; it was parked in the courtyard with its doors open, but no one wanted to get in yet.

"Not a good omen, creepy," Gina said, tightening her coat around her. "I'd have preferred a sunny day, myself."

"What was it that Liam said?" Sharon asked.

"When I talked to him an hour ago, he said that he would meet you there. Boyle asked him to be there at nine thirty. She said she had a few things she wanted to discuss about her son and complications that have arisen about returning the body to the States. Since he was an American who died here in Ireland, the American embassy is involved. Liam told her he would see what he could do."

"Strange. Did you contact O'Shaunnessy this morning?" Sharon said to Kevin.

"I left a message. Her assistant said that she hadn't arrived yet but was due in soon."

"Why did you want to talk to the lawyer?" JF asked.

"To tell her we were talking directly with Boyle. That's the least I could do. She's caught up in all this, but for different motives, I think. Since we know that Banning worked for her, the connection could be dangerous as well. When we get back to Dublin, I'll find out."

"The party starts at three o'clock, so don't get distracted and be late, Sharon," Claudette admonished. "Gina talked with Molly and told her that you would be at the house and then back here this afternoon. She said the cake would be delivered by two thirty."

"We will not be late," Kevin promised.

As Sharon, Kevin, and JF climbed into the van, Evelyn said, "There's not much I can do here. Gina and Claudette have it covered. Can I tag along?"

"Climb in," Sharon said.

Their route was along the same road where Boyle's son had tried to run them off the road. There were still remnants of flares on the macadam and drag marks in the grassy swale where the Jaguar had been loaded onto the car carrier. No one said anything.

When Kevin pulled the van into the Baile O'Bryan driveway, they saw three vehicles parked in the courtyard: a black Range Rover, a Jaguar sedan, and a small Ford Fiesta with its bold yellow stripe and GARDA printed on its door panel and hood.

"I'm guessing the Rover is Boyle's and that the Ford is Liam's," Sharon said. "The Jaguar, not sure. Kevin, you said that O'Shaunnessy wasn't in her office. Maybe she's here."

"A possibility. I can see Boyle calling her."

There were no sounds other than the cooing of a wood pigeon in the massive cypress tree that overhung the courtyard. The mist was as thick in the courtyard as it had been at the inn, but above the sky was clear. The charred remains of the cottage were visible through the tangle of shrubs that hugged the foundation of the ancient family home. The odor of burnt wood drifted in the damp air.

"Sorry, Kevin, right now this place gives me the creeps," Evelyn said.

The four walked to the front door; it was cracked open an inch.

"Kevin, in your American horror movies, this is where we are supposed to turn around and run," JF said with a laugh. "But, *non*—we push open the door, charge in, and unleash the hounds of hell."

"Dramatic are we this morning?" Sharon said. "But then again, you might be just a little right."

"How's that?" Kevin said.

Sharon crooked her head to the courtyard behind them. Standing on the cobblestones directly behind them, a man with a prominent red beard held a weapon. The C7 was aimed directly at Kevin.

"Inside," the man said. "Now."

JF pushed the substantial oak door open and led their quartet into the entry. Standing inside was a second man with an equally unruly brown beard. He also held one of the Canadian C7 automatic weapons.

"What the hell is this all about?" Sharon asked.

Neither man said anything. They simply pointed the muzzles of their guns toward the far side of the large entry foyer.

From above, halfway up the stairs, a woman stood looking down on the group.

"You must be Sharon O'Mara. I'm glad we finally meet. And you two, which of you gentleman is Kevin Bryan?"

Both Kevin and JF remained silent.

"Please, a simple question, though I do think it's you on the left. You do bear a strong resemblance to the men in the few paintings that remain and adorn the walls of this mausoleum. It's good that you brought along your friends. It's always good to have loyal friends around."

"And who the hell are you?" JF demanded and started to move toward the stairs. Brown beard adjusted his stance and leveled his C7 at the Frenchman.

"My, my, such a sweet accent and so handsome. I have forgotten my manners. I am Sylvia Boyle. The others work for me."

"I thought you wanted to talk," Kevin said. "This does not

look like talking."

"And your friends? Names, please."

"None of your business," Evelyn said.

"Two are missing. Where are they?"

"As she said, none of your business," Sharon echoed. "Where is Inspector Donovan?"

"He's indisposed for the moment."

"And I assume that O'Shaunnessy is also here," Sharon said. "Is she guarding Liam?"

"Ms. O'Shaunnessy and I have professionally parted our ways. She is with the policeman."

"What the hell is going on, Boyle?" Kevin demanded. "This is all such bullshit over a chunk of wet Irish farmland. If you want it, I'll sell it. It's no big deal to me. Two months ago, I barely remembered my great-aunt, and now, I've dragged my friends into this mess. So, if you want this, name your price."

"There is no price that will return my son to me, none. You killed him. It is your fault that my son is dead"—her voice rose— "and he was just one more death in the long list of dead Boyles that your family has been responsible for over the centuries. I know all about you and your clan."

"What? What the hell do you mean, my clan? My family has been in California for more than a hundred years. Until yesterday, I didn't even know what or who the Boyles were. And in fact, I still don't. You've got money and I assume some power, so why do you want this piece of old smelly timber and dirt?"

"Don't play this game with me, Mr. Bryan. The only reason you are here is to make sure this land stays in the O'Bryan family, why else? There are riches here, to be sure, but it is my duty to my family to make sure the O'Bryan lineage stops here. I am my family's sword of vengeance."

"Did she really say that?" Evelyn whispered. "Really?"

"*Elle est folle*," JF said.

"What did he say?" Boyle demanded, taking two steps down.

"He said you're fucking crazy," Evelyn said. "And I totally agree."

"Bryan, throw your keys next to the others on the bureau," Boyle said.

A scream echoed through the upstairs. Everyone jerked around and looked up.

"What was that?" Kevin demanded.

"I guess that O'Shaunnessy's gagged slipped," Boyle said. "Mr. Bruno, would you go see to our guests?"

The man with the red beard closed the front door behind them and then climbed the stairs. He disappeared down the hall. A few seconds later, there was another scream, and then silence.

"Good, lawyers always talk too much," Boyle said. "Now, all of you, up the stairs." She raised her arm and revealed the pistol she was holding, until now masked by the railing and balusters of the stairs. She pointed the gun at Kevin. "Now."

As Boyle backed up the stairs, the man with the brown beard herded the four up. At the second-floor landing, he said, "Follow her."

Boyle led the way down the hall to an open door and then stood back and waved the pistol to direct them into the room. Sharon was the first through, followed by Evelyn, JF, and Kevin. To one side of the room stood red beard, the C7 up and ready. In the center of the room, secured with duct tape to an old Windsor chair, was Inspector Liam Donovan, a strip of tape over his mouth. On the four-posted bed lay Sinead O'Shaunnessy, her legs and arms bound with tape. Her eyes were closed.

"You didn't kill her?" Evelyn asked, looking at the first man.

He smiled, and then shook his head, no.

"There's a time and place for everything," Boyle said. "Right now, Mr. Bryan, I have some paperwork that needs your signature."

"What? Paperwork?"

"I think she wants you to sign over the property to her," Sharon said.

"Good guess," Boyle added.

"Do you think that this will have any legality in court?" Kevin said.

"Not your problem. My lawyers will make it work. O'Mara, there is a roll of tape on the table. Please secure Frenchie's hands and ankles, then do the same to the woman. I'm sorry, but I didn't hear your name."

"Fuck you, bitch," Evelyn said, surprising Sharon, who smiled.

"Whatever," Boyle said. "The tape, now."

Sharon spent the next few minutes securing her friends, leaving the tape as loose as possible. They sat on a small settee beneath the window facing Boyle.

"Now, Mr. Bryan, your turn. Please bind Ms. O'Mara."

"And if I don't?"

Boyle raised her pistol and casually aimed it at JF's thigh, and fired. Evelyn screamed. JF howled from the pain. Sharon lunged toward Boyle. Brown beard swung his weapon and slammed it against the back of her head. She fell to the floor.

Boyle turned to Kevin. "Are we done screwing around? I said, tie her up."

Kevin looked at JF; the pain was obvious on his face. Reluctantly, he knelt and bound Sharon with tape. She remained on the floor, unconscious.

"The documents are on the desk. You have one minute to sign the ten pages, that's all. Then I will leave you. The clock is ticking."

Kevin crossed the room to the desk. A short stack of papers were arranged under a ballpoint pen. He quickly looked at the first sheet; it was a transfer of a deed of trust. Neat little *Sign Here* stickers were attached to the other pages.

"Just where the stickers are, and I suggest you hurry," Boyle said. "We have limited time."

"Why, what's your hurry?"

"That is not your worry. Please sign."

Kevin quickly signed the pages, and then palmed the pen.

"Please drop the pen," Boyle said. "Mr. Bruno, will you now

truss up Bryan like the others?"

Red beard took the tape and pushed Bryan to the wall. "Turn around."

Kevin stood looking at the man, who was much shorter. Alone, he'd have taken down the thug.

"Do as he says, or I will shoot Frenchie in the other leg," Boyle said.

Kevin faced the wall and was quickly bound in grey tape. Red beard pushed him to his knees and taped his ankles. Boyle crossed the room and retrieved the stack of papers.

"Mr. Bruno?" she said.

The red-bearded man clocked Kevin across the back of his head with a blackjack he'd retrieved from his jacket pocket. Evelyn screamed again as Kevin collapsed to the floor.

"Yell again, and I'll shoot you next," Boyle said to her. "Gentlemen?"

She led the two henchmen out the door, slamming it behind them. Those still conscious in the room heard the door lock.

After a five-second beat, Sharon rolled over and slowly worked her way into a sitting position. "Are you okay, JF?"

"What do you think? The fucking thing hurts like it's on fire."

"We'll be out of here in just a—"

"Fire!" Evelyn yelled. "The door."

Smoke pushed its way around the doorframe. Some type of flammable liquid had been poured under the door and across the carpet. The liquid spread out from the door's sill and was now burning. Three-foot-high flames rose from the threadbare oriental carpet, making it impossible to reach the locked door even if they had been free of their bindings.

Chapter 14

What would you do in this spot?
The castle on fire, everything hot,
Locked in a room,
Faced with fiery doom,
Your hands secured with stout knots.

14a

The smoke from the burning carpet quickly filled the room. It curled and twisted up to the high ceiling.

"Evelyn, twist your wrists back and forth," Sharon yelled. "You should be able to tear the tape. JF, if you can, you try it, too." Sharon, now in a seated position, scooted away from the flames that were just five feet away. "Is it working?"

Evelyn was the first to free her hands. She instantly reached down to the tape that wrapped her ankles. She gave the fabric a twist at the slight tear at its edge, and it tore free. JF was seconds behind.

"Get the others free," Sharon said. "We need to get out of here. Evelyn, see if Kevin is okay."

JF limped across the floor to Sharon's side. He tried to break the tape's edge, but it resisted. He moved to the desk and started pulling out drawers, soon returning with a small dagger used for letter opening. In seconds, he had freed Sharon, Liam, and was removing the tape from O'Shaunnessy. Sharon took the blade and cut away the tape from Kevin. He started coughing.

"Evelyn, help me," Sharon said. She grabbed a corner of the heavy carpet, Evelyn grabbed the other, and they folded it over the burning section. They managed to smother the flames inside the room, but thick smoke still poured in under the door and through the overhead transom above the frame. It was getting harder to see or breathe.

Sharon looked out the window. They were easily forty feet above the ground on this side of the building. It was a straight drop. She went to the door, balling her fist in her shirt as she tried the knob. It was locked. She put her hand on the door's oak surface and yanked it away. Even with the protection of fabric, she could feel the intense heat.

"They've set fire to the house; we can't get out this way," she said. "And the drop is too much from the window."

"We can try and knot together the bedspread," Donovan said as he helped the semi-conscious O'Shaunnessy into the Windsor chair he had just left.

"Might work. Get started, it will take some time," Sharon said. She picked up the roll of duct tape the thugs had left on the desk. "Evelyn, I want you to put a half dozen wraps over that wound on JF's leg. It should help to stop the bleeding." She pitched the roll to Evelyn. "Good catch," she said with small smile.

Kevin slowly got to his feet, steadying himself with one hand on the wall.

Liam stripped off the brocade bed cover and pointed. Sharon's heart sank; there were no sheets or blankets underneath. It was then she noticed there were no curtains or blankets, either. The room was empty except for old pieces of furniture—and smoke. She looked at Kevin who was rubbing the back of his head. Evelyn was busy with JF.

"How's JF?"

"Not good. He's lost a lot of blood, but it has stopped bleeding," Evelyn answered. JF's eyes were fixed on Sharon. He offered a thin smile.

"Liam, please push that bed cover against the door. We can try and keep some of the smoke out."

Even with the carpet blocking the sill, smoke pushed in from every crack. They were all coughing. The varnish on the door was beginning to craze and darken. The door itself also was beginning to smoke.

"We only have a few minutes. Any ideas?" Sharon asked.

They looked at each other, each believing that this was the end.

"I'd rather die in a fall than burn alive," O'Shaunnessy mumbled and pointed to the window.

"That's our last option. Anything else?" Sharon scanned the room and the ceiling. The smoke filled the room, rising and swirling above them. She could still see the picture rail that ran the perimeter of the room nine feet off the oak floor. At the far side, to the left of the fireplace, the smoke was thinner. She squinted to see, her eyes stinging and tearing. A massive painting of one of Kevin's ancestors holding the severed head of a fallen enemy took up most of the wall.

"What do you see?" JF moaned from the couch.

"Not sure," she answered. "Evelyn and Liam, look for a seam that might be allowing the smoke to escape. I swear that's what's happening along the molding." She pointed.

Everyone was coughing, the smoke was lowering, and a large black spot was now visible on the upper and lower panels of the door. The wood door was smoking.

"Is there a door or something here?" Sharon asked urgently. "These old castles had escape routes or secret passages."

"You've watched too many old movies," JF said.

"I mean it, look."

Liam was running his hand along the wall. "It's remarkably cool; there is something different here. But I don't see a handle or another way to open it."

"The cottage," Kevin said. His voice was weak, but Sharon heard him.

"In the cottage, there's a painting that, if you rotate it, a door opens," she yelled at Liam.

He grabbed the edge of the painting and gave it a jerk. Instantly, the wall along the edge of the fireplace opened about three inches. Not waiting, Sharon pushed hard and the wall swung into the black void behind it.

"I don't know where it goes, but here we're dead," Sharon yelled. "Kevin, buck up and help JF. Liam, you help O'Shaunnessy. Evelyn, you lead."

"And get out of this imminent hell? You bet I will."

To Sharon's shock, Evelyn pulled out one of the candles in the candlesticks on the fireplace mantle, walked to the now burning face of the door, and lit it. She returned to the opening in the wall, but the gap created by the secret door had generated a draft. Evelyn's candle went out.

"I've got me lighter, lass," Liam said. "I suggest we get out of this room now and light it when we can shut the door behind us."

Everyone went into the narrow gap behind the wall. Kevin and Liam pushed the panel shut and tight and heard it latch. Their last view was the room burning. Liam lit the candle and three others the group had grabbed before they fled through the opening. In the empty, as-yet smoke-free, space between the walls, a steep brick stairway headed down. There was no time to debate; Evelyn led the way, followed by Kevin and JF, and then Liam and the solicitor. Sharon brought up the rear. She held her candle high; the walls on either side of the narrow stair were red brick. She imagined that this corridor and the fireplace stacks would be all that remained when the house burned. They came to another panel on the ground floor. Evelyn put her hand near the wall; it was too hot to touch. "The fire is on the ground floor. Keep going down," their leader said without hesitation.

They went down another forty steps. Sharon guessed they were more than twenty feet below the house. She had no idea whether there was a cellar.

"The steps end," Evelyn said to those behind her. "There's a passage ahead."

"Keep going," Kevin said. "We might as well see what's left of my inheritance."

When Evelyn stopped again, Sharon had counted sixty-two paces from the bottom of the stair. The smoke had begun to follow them—not yet heavy or thick—but they could taste its acrid odor.

"What do you see?" Sharon called out.

"Nothing, there's nothing—only a stone wall."

14b

From their tomb under the burning house, the uninjured searched the tunnel's walls looking for anything that might be a lever or a handle that would give them freedom. Sharon slipped past the others and faced the wall. "Look for a latch or something. There has to be some kind of device to get out of here."

"We don't have much time," Evelyn said, her voice laced with fear. "This tunnel will fill with smoke until we can't breathe."

"What hell must be going on directly over our heads," O'Shaunnessy said. "And to think it's my fault all this is happening. I'm so sorry, Mr. Bryan . . . for all of this."

"We'll deal with that later—if we get out of here," Kevin answered. "Right now, keep looking. This tunnel can't just dead end."

Sharon watched as JF slowly slid down the wall and silently landed on the dirt floor. The pain from his leg had to be nauseating. Despite the makeshift tourniquet, each beat of his heart pushed more blood toward the hole in his leg; at least the bitch had missed the bone and artery.

Lying prone on his back, JF felt himself sliding toward unconsciousness. His fingers dug into the dirt as the next wave of pain washed over him. "Sharon," he managed to say, "I feel something under me. Smooth and hard. Down an inch or so."

Sharon crouched and dug with her own fingers and found the metal surface. "Everyone, dig around here. See if you can find a handle or a latch."

With multiple sets of hands frantically digging and pushing dirt away, it was only seconds until they found a recessed ring large enough so that two hands could lift a hinged trap door. It slammed open against the stone face of the tunnel.

"Shit, more steps," Kevin said as he held one of the candles over the black hole.

"My turn," Liam said and started down the rungs mounted in the wall of the hole, and disappeared. "Bottom!" he shouted up. "About fifteen feet down, there's another tunnel—I'll wait."

"Room for all of us?" Kevin yelled.

"Only two or three at a time. I'll check out the tunnel."

Evelyn went next, followed by O'Shaunnessy, who was shaky on her legs but managing to walk. Sharon and Kevin helped JF to his feet and half carried him down the steps. When they reached the bottom, they saw Liam's candle flickering in the distance. They followed his light. After about forty feet, they faced an oak-paneled wall and another door.

"This is a good sign," Kevin said. "Please tell me there's a handle or something."

"It's a heavy latch, forged iron from the looks of it," Liam said. "Doesn't it remind you of the latch of the door to the tunnel to the sea?"

"Absolutely," Sharon answered.

"What tunnel to the sea?" O'Shaunnessy asked. She stood behind Evelyn. Behind her, JF gripped the wall.

"I'll tell you later," Kevin said. "Liam, would you give it a try?"

"Gladly."

The Irish constable took hold of the heavy latch and pulled it upward; it moved easily and quietly. Kevin and Sharon then pushed. The door initially stuck, but with the sound of an old seal being cracked, the door slowly moved outward about two feet. Thick, choking smoke engulfed them again. The fire burned in the rafters of the room beyond.

"Good God, from the frying pan into the fire, literally," Evelyn said. "We're back in the house."

Kevin and Sharon simultaneously stuck their heads through the door again, took another look, and then slowly pulled the door almost shut.

"Okay," Sharon said calmly. "We are in the cellar under the cottage, the half that wasn't burned in the explosion. Unfortunately, it's now on fire, like the house. We can't stay here. We need to get moving; the stair above this door is burning."

"But where can we go?" O'Shaunnessy whined. "We can't go back."

"We have a way out," Sharon said. "Sorry, JF, there will be more steps. But I assure you, every step down will make us safer. Liam, if I remember, there were a couple of lamps on the table; they are still there. Grab them as Kevin and I pull open the door to the smugglers' tunnel. Evelyn and"—Sharon turned to the attorney—"what the hell is your first name?"

"Sinead."

Sharon smiled. "Evelyn, you and Sinead are in charge of JF. On the far side of the room is another door. Kevin and I will unlatch it and pull it open. Liam, you go first and get light into the tunnel. You girls and JF will follow, and then we'll pull the door shut. There is another lantern on a ledge just inside the door. Sinead, you—"

There was a crash on the far side of the door in front of them. The door vibrated; smoke surged around the doorframe. "We need to move now, before we are blocked in!" Sharon yelled.

They pushed open the door; more flaming debris fell from above. Liam ran to the table and grabbed the two lamps. Following Sharon and Kevin across the burning room, Evelyn and Sinead helped JF limp to the heavy oak door. In one swing of the latch, Sharon released the door and, with a pull, swung it inward. Liam and Kevin, and then the trio with JF limping between them, rushed past Sharon. They waited a few feet inside for her.

Sharon turned back to the inferno and watched an enormous beam, entirely on fire, break away from its wall supports and crash onto the stone floor of the cellar. One end of the beam drove into the far stone wall. Rock and debris exploded from the impact. Her eyes burning yet unable to look away, she stood in awe. Hundreds of brilliant shards and disks of gold tumbled from the breach in the wall to the floor; they cascaded, handful after handful, from the hole in the wall. Then another beam broke free and fell, obscuring everything in smoke and fire. She pulled the oak door closed, threw the latch, turned to Kevin, and smiled.

"You lucky son of a bitch," she said.

"What? What did you say?"

"We've got to go. I'm not sure how long this door can withstand that hell."

Liam was already leading the others down the stone steps. They stopped four times to rest, once at mid-level with its historic graffiti on the walls. They did what they could for JF. By this time, Liam and Kevin were carrying the Frenchman. O'Shaunnessy asked Sharon how they knew about this smugglers' tunnel. "Later," came the answer. "I have questions for you as well. We'll trade."

After twenty tortuous minutes, they reached the door at the base of the stair. It was as Sharon and Kevin remembered. The tunnel was now dry, but sand had filled in the cracks and crevices along the floor.

"I sure as hell hope, after all this, the sea isn't at the door," Liam said.

They had no other option.

"Here goes," Sharon said. She threw the latch and pushed, and the door easily swung open. The sound of the surf and the smell of the ocean blew in from the narrow sunlit beach. It was still morning. Sharon checked her watch. What had seemed like hours had been less than sixty minutes. It was 10:56 AM. Sunlight reflected off the water and lit up the rock ceiling. A rhythmic surge of waves slipped into the natural cavern, up the beach, and then retreated.

They all more or less collapsed on the sand, breathing in the fresh salt air in great gulps. Sharon examined JF's leg.

"Not good," she said quietly. "I saw too many of these types of wounds in Iraq. He is in total shock now. We were lucky to get him this far. He needs a doctor, and the only way is that way." She pointed to the water.

"I'm a fair swimmer," Liam said. "It can't be too far to a beach and people."

"That's crazy," Kevin said. "It's my bullshit that got us into all this. I'll give it a try."

"That water is cold," Sharon said. "And neither of you are in condition to swim a hundred yards, let alone what's probably more than a mile. If I remember from our hike, the cliffs aren't too steep. So, I'll swim out and climb the cliff face. The fire has to have brought the fire department. I'll get them to send a boat and—"

Her voice was drowned out by the guttural sound of a motor slowly making its way into the cavern. Each second it got louder and louder until they saw the prow of a motorboat slide through the sunlit opening and up onto the strip of beach. A man jumped from the boat into the shallows and waded up to the company.

"Someone need a ride?" Mac MacLeish asked as the red setter leapt from the bow to the sand of the beach.

14c

Molly was at the boat's controls. She raised the engine's prop from the water and then threw a line to Sharon, who secured the line to an iron ring embedded in a boulder next to where they were sitting. With Mac's help, JF was lifted into the boat. Evelyn climbed over the gunnel and slipped a life preserver under his head. She wrapped him in a blanket Molly handed to her. After O'Shaunnessy found a place to sit, Kevin and Liam took their seats. Mac and Dergo waited on the beach as Sharon climbed in, then he released the line and pushed the bow away as Molly lowered the idling engine's prop back into the water. Mac expertly climbed into the craft. The big dog took a running leap and landed on the forward deck, a move he obviously had done often. Molly engaged the propeller and slowly backed the boat out of the cavern and into the sunlight. Once free of the wash from the surf, she slowly rotated the boat and headed out to the relatively softer sea. There she opened up the motor and roared east away from the cliffs and the massive pillar of smoke that rose vertically into the brilliant blue morning sky.

Sharon, holding tightly to the rails next to Molly, yelled into her ear, "How did you know?"

"I'll tell you later," Molly shouted over the motor and wind. "Right now, we need to get that Frenchman to the hospital. Mac is calling the emergency people in Clonakilty; they will meet us in the cove. It seems the only good luck we have is the tide; right now, it's high enough for us to reach the pier. If not, I'd have to beach her. Not something I want to do to this boat."

Sharon stumbled back to JF. "How's he doing?" she asked Kevin.

"Not good. His pulse is weak."

"When I find that woman, I'm going to kill her. I swear it."

"Get in line."

Sharon turned to Liam, who was looking out at the sea. "I'm sorry. I hope you didn't hear that."

"Hear what?" he answered with an Irish grin on his face.

The natural tidal bay that extends south from the village of Clonakilty drains to the Celtic Sea. As Molly said, the high tide allowed her to pilot the boat to one of the old stone piers that hooked out from the mainland into the main channel. The local Irish Red Cross were waiting for JF as they tied up. Standing on the pier were Claudette and Gina. Within minutes, JF was transferred to a gurney and into the back of an ambulance.

"I'm going with him," Evelyn said.

"I'm going, too," Claudette added. "I think you three have enough to deal with." She pointed to the two Garda police cars parked next to the ambulance. Four police officers stood next to the cars. Liam already was talking with who looked like the senior officer.

"Take care of him, Claudette," Sharon said. "He means a lot to all of us. When he comes to, tell him we will be there as soon as we can."

Gina stood with Sharon and Kevin as the ambulance headed

up the steep gravel road to the highway above. O'Shaunnessy, in shock, sat on a bench looking out to sea. Molly wrapped JF's bloodstained blanket around her. The big setter placed his shaggy jaw on the solicitor's arm. She meekly stroked his head.

"What the fuck happened?" Gina demanded, turning to her two best friends. "Molly called us at the hotel and said that the house was on fire."

"You called the fire department?" Sharon asked Molly as she walked up to the group.

"I was on my way to deliver your birthday cake and some of the food for the party," Molly answered. "You couldn't miss the smoke. I called the police and the fire departments. When I drove into the courtyard, there were three vehicles parked, and both buildings were burning. I tried to get through the doorway; that was impossible. I guessed that if you were trapped or couldn't leave the house, you were either dead or you might find one of the hidden passages. Brona told me years ago that the house had two or three secret passages in the walls. She hadn't been in them in years, but it was comforting to know that if the taxman ever showed, she had a secret way out. They all lead — or they did — to the cellar under the cottage. When I couldn't find anyone outside, I called Mac to meet me at the boat."

"The cottage is gone, too," Kevin said. "We were lucky to escape before it collapsed."

"Sad, there were wonderful treasures of your family in those buildings," Mac added, having come up to stand beside Molly. "Three hundred years of history, gone."

"If it weren't for this lass's keen eyes and thinking, we'd all be dead right now," Liam said, walking up to the group. "Spotting that crack in the wall made all the difference. I must say hanging around with you three makes for a fun and entertaining week."

Sharon bummed a cigarette from Mac. Gina gave her a disapproving look.

"What happened, Liam?" Sharon asked. "Before we got there?"

"Boyle wanted to talk about some issues regarding her son's

body and its return to America. At least that's the story she told me; it was a ruse to get me there. When I came through the door, that redheaded bastard pushed a pistol in my face, disarmed me, and took my phone. They took me up the stairs to the room where you found me. That woman, whoever she is, was tied up on the bed."

"Strange," Kevin said. "She's the attorney that was working for Boyle. Name's O'Shaunnessy."

"Boyle wanted to know why you, Kevin, wanted her son dead and why you ran him off the road. I told her that's not what happened. She said that she had a witness and information claiming what I said wasn't true. Her informer said it was you, Kevin, who killed him, and that your reasons go back hundreds of years."

"Tommy! It was that fool nephew of yours, Tommy O'Rourke," Mac said to Molly, interrupting. "The boy ain't right in the head. I saw him talking to Boyle yesterday after she left the funeral home. He has to be the one who made up the story."

"And what's this bit about going back hundreds of years?" Sharon asked. "Kevin's only been here a few times. What does he have to do with all this?"

"We Irish hold grudges a long time," Mac said. "And are notorious for passing them on for generations, I should know."

"But about what? What the hell is this all about?" Kevin asked.

"Well, there is the old story about the Spanish gold and treasure," Molly said with a laugh. "Seems to go with the O'Bryans and the land."

"And smugglers and secret tunnels, and the little people living under the hills," Sharon teased. Gina gave her a look. She knew her friend too well to miss the smile she quickly hid.

"Yes, there's all that, too. Is there anything else you need from me, Inspector?" Molly asked Liam. "There's a cake and a keg of Guinness in my van that needs to be delivered. I assume that the guest of honor won't be too long?"

"No, but if I think of anything, I know where to find you,"

Liam said.

"No party until Jean-François is okay," Sharon said. "Kevin, we need to get to the hospital."

"Will you be coming later to the inn, Inspector Donovan?" Gina said. "I'm sure there's more than enough."

"If asked by a lass like you, most certainly. By the way, I have an APB out for Boyle and her men. Her plane has been seized, and her passport is flagged. She won't get far."

"Gina, how did you get here?" Sharon asked.

"When Molly called and told us what she was going to do, she told us where she would land here in the harbor. I borrowed one of the hotel's cars; we need to get it back before we go to the hospital. And to let you know, driving on the wrong side isn't that easy. I'm impressed that our lordship could handle it."

"What wrong side?" Liam asked with a smile. "We each have a vehicle at the estate. Unfortunately, Boyle threw my keys on the bureau in the hallway next to another set. Ms. O'Shaunnessy is going to have a tough time getting home. I'll contact the rental people and help you with the van. Two vans in two days; they are not going to be happy."

Sharon, Kevin, and Gina watched as Molly turned the motor launch back into the channel and headed away. Dergo stood in the stern, looking back at the group on the pier. Liam took O'Shaunnessy with him; she hadn't said a word since they landed. He said she would be taken care of, and besides, he had questions for her.

Shortly, it was just the three of them standing on the end of the pier, looking out over the sea under the warm late-afternoon sun. The column of smoke on the western horizon had changed from black to white.

"As we were heading down the tunnel, you called me a son of a bitch," Kevin said.

"She's called you that before," Gina said.

"The tone was different, almost reverential."

"Yeah, right. Sharon calling you a son of a bitch in a reverential tone, I sincerely doubt that."

They both looked at Sharon. This time she did not hide the huge grin on her face.

"Actually, what I said was: you *lucky* son of a bitch."

"With all this today—a lucky son of a bitch?" Kevin questioned.

"Yes, you are one lucky, Irish, son of a bitch," she said and kissed him on the lips.

Chapter 15

A leprechaun did hide his gold,
Under a great oak, in dirt most cold.
"Under this great mound,
Me riches will not be found,
'Til an O'Bryan appears, it's foretold."

There once were three friends from the States,
Who pursued a castle in probate.
Seeking Irish land and gold,
They found a fable, most old,
Of a treasure that was mostly fake.

15a

The next day was a blur for the gang of five; they joined their sixth member recovering in Cork University Hospital. After Sharon told her friends about the gold, it was all she could do to stop Kevin and Gina from driving directly there and seeing it for themselves. JF was lucky—that is if having a crazy person shoot you in the leg was lucky. The EMTs had done a professional job as they transported him the thirty miles to the hospital; it was the best facility in the county for bullet wounds. The wound was a through and through. The bullet, guessed to be a 9mm, probably was lodged in the seat of the now overcooked settee sitting in the basement of the carbonized skeleton of Baile O'Bryan.

"In three hours, it will be dark," Sharon said. "We will go in the morning. I suggest that we talk to Liam and get his help. We will need to secure the site, check on Irish law about finding treasure, maybe get a university archeologist on board. We also have to make sure that Molly's friends don't find out about it."

"Molly? Why her?" Gina asked.

"Even though she's a smuggler—and I like her—this might be too much for her and some of her associates. They might jump at the chance to loot the site, especially that nephew of hers. Molly's the one with the curiosity in the history of the region; she could be a great resource if we use her carefully."

"I still can't believe Boyle. What was she thinking?" Kevin said. "In fact, what is she thinking now? She's dangerous—we know that—she thought nothing of killing all of us. For what? I never will understand the psychotic mind."

"She's a total wacko-psycho, and that's the most scientific of medical terms I can think of," Gina added. "Right now, she's laying low. We have not seen the last of that bitch."

"You're right," Sharon said. "When she finds out we survived, it will ratchet up her hate. She will try again."

"Great," Kevin said. "That's it. I'm done—and so are all of you. As soon as JF can go home, we're packing up, going back to Dublin, and catching the next flight back to San Francisco. Let all these crazy Irish fight this thing out. The spoils to the victors, last man standing sort of thing—I want none of my friends hurt. JF was one too many."

"You have a responsibility, and besides, that gold is yours," Sharon told him. "It is on your property . . ."

"Responsibility? What responsibility? Technically, it's not even mine—yet."

"Certainly more than anyone else's."

"That's a matter of history and geography," Kevin said. "I do not want any of you hurt beyond what has already happened. That woman is capable of anything."

Liam, after a long conversation with the group, insisted that they stay in the county for the next few days in case there were more questions. He gave them the name of a professor of antiquities at Trinity College.

"The guy is very good," Liam said. "I worked with him on some artifact arrests we made involving old Viking jewelry that was being smuggled out of the country. He can help you through the new laws about historic artifacts and found treasure. They're complicated. There's been a lot of theft and illegal searching of old estates and ruins. Ireland has put a clamp on everything to make sure that potential sites aren't looted. I've also put a twenty-four guard on the Baile O'Bryan ruin to keep people away. However, I can only keep the news of the gold out of the press for a limited time. It will get out."

Just as Sharon had imagined during their escape, all that remained of the house were four massive brick chimney stacks and an ancient system of parallel brick walls that zigged and zagged through the ruin. The cottage—what had remained after Banning's explosion a few days earlier—also burned and had collapsed into the cellar. The professor was eager to come to the property. Driving down from Dublin, he arrived late that afternoon. Kevin, Sharon, and Gina were waiting for him. Claudette and Evelyn remained with JF in Cork.

The professor looked like one of the leprechauns that were believed to be living under the hills that surrounded the burnt carcass of the building. He tumbled out of an old mustard-colored Vauxhall. He was dressed in tweeds, a Sherlock Holmes–style deerstalker hat, and rubber boots that went to his knees. A leather satchel was slung over his shoulder, and he smoked a crooked pipe. Gina burst out laughing when she caught sight of him.

"Dr. Cornelius Laird, at your service," the professor said, extending his hand to Kevin, who then introduced the rest of his gang. "A pleasure to meet you," said Laird. He looked toward the ruins. "Holy Mother of God, what a fine place this was. I remember being here almost thirty years ago. I came down to look for something at the request of the woman of the manor. I have been wracking my brain, trying to remember her name."

"Brona O'Bryan?" Kevin said.

The professor smiled. "That be her, and she was near a foot taller than me. What a striking woman."

"Why were you here?" Sharon asked the professor, as they

walked across the parking court and gingerly wove their way through the debris of the main house.

"For the same reason I'm here now—treasure. Back then, the lady said that there's an old legend about Spanish gold buried on the property. Now, lassie, if I had a doubloon for every call like that I get, I could finally retire. We talked. I looked around, even dug a little, but nothing. She understood, thanked me, and I understand she sent a small financial gift to the department for their use in research. So, what have you discovered? You were circumspect on the phone."

"It's in the far side of the cellar," Kevin said, taking the lead toward the cottage. It was early evening, and the sun was lost in the thick clouds and marine layer that had started to move in from the sea. They walked by the two police officers standing guard in the parking lot; they were the only police presence. The gutted roof structure of the cottage stood above the burned and collapsed floor. Most of the floor had tumbled into the cellar. As they approached, the opening to the cellar glowed dimly from floodlights that had been placed in a rough circle at the top of what remained of the walls. The effect was eerie and, like the sky, ominous.

"Police?" Laird said. "All this over a fire?"

"It's also a crime site, the attempted murder of six people, one a police officer," Sharon added.

"Good Lord."

Sharon, Kevin, Gina, and the professor climbed down an aluminum ladder to the stone floor of the cellar. They could see reasonably well thanks to the lights, but Kevin clicked on a flashlight beam and led the way through the debris to a spot on the far wall. A blue tarp was secured to a crossbeam that sat at a forty-five-degree angle. The tarp was draped across debris that extended out from a pile of charred beams lying against the stone foundation.

"I never knew about this cellar," Laird said, relighting his pipe. "Miss O'Bryan never mentioned it. Interesting."

"I think she played a close hand," Kevin said. He looked at

the burnt face of the door to the tunnel; it was black from smoke, but it had held. Earlier they'd tried the latch and it still worked, a testament to craftsmanship and to luck.

"This is why the police called you," Kevin said, grabbing an edge of the tarp and pulling it back.

"Sweet Jesus," the professor exclaimed as he looked at the hole in the wall and the golden waterfall that had spilled out. Coins lay in the soot and burnt debris, some were scattered on the timbers, and others were wedged in the cracks of the massive stones used to build the walls. Inside the hole, the dark shape of another chest was visible. "May I?"

"Certainly," Kevin answered.

Professor Laird reached down and selected a coin, spit on the surface, and then rubbed it with the corner of his tweed jacket. He extracted a magnifying glass from his pocket and stared at the surface of the coin. Gina snickered again.

"Shush," Sharon admonished.

"I swear he's the dwarf Irish version of Sherlock Holmes," she said softly.

Gina's friends gasped at the seemingly rude remark.

"No problems, my dear. This garb is intentionally concocted to achieve that purpose. People believe I'm smarter and brighter if I look like this. I can assure you that it works every time. And besides, a lassie like you will always get this man's heart a-fluttering."

"Stop it, you two," Sharon said. "And, Miss Cavelli, if you don't stop bothering the professor, I'm going to send you topside."

"Spoilsport."

Laird turned the coin over and over, inspecting every edge.

"Fascinating," he said

Laird picked up another coin and inspected it carefully. The three watched as the professor became even more excited. He looked at another coin, then another. He took a small toolkit from his pocket and carefully scratched the surface of one of the coins, and then he scratched another coin.

"Unbelievable, dumbfounding. You said there are other chests?"

"We can see at least one more chest," Kevin said, peering into the hole. "There's the corner of another chest behind it, but until we excavate, it's hard to tell."

"The legend says there were four chests," the professor said.

"There's a legend?" Gina asked.

"Oh, yes, my dear, yes! And they have been verified through records found in the archives of King Philip's court in Madrid, Spain. Around 1600, a few years after the failed Spanish Armada, the Spanish again tried to attack England, this time through Ireland, specifically through Kinsale to the east of here a wee bit. A ship was sent, with what was essentially a bribe, with four chests of gold to be paid to the rebel Earl of Tyrone, Hugh O'Neill, to enlist his support in attacking the English. The chests were landed here in Ireland and were under the control of a Spanish officer named Juan Flores de Mendoza. The ship's captain wrote in his log that Mendoza and the chests were delivered to the Irish rebels through a hidden cove under the coastal cliffs. His sailors then returned to the ship, but the officer and the gold were never heard from again. Cross-referencing military reports from that period, it was found that a platoon of English red coats encountered a rebel group about this same time. As was the standing order, the rebels were summarily executed. There was a vague note about a Spanish officer traveling with them, or he was encountered soon after. It's hard to determine the sequence; the report was badly written and had deteriorated."

"And this is that gold?" Kevin asked.

"Quite probably. No other chests such as this have been discovered in this region, and certainly not in this quantity. There were family legends rumored to involve the gold and its location. However, unlike leprechauns and banshees and other traditional folk, I tend to look for facts, not ghosts. So, to see this hoard, it just gets me all a-twitter and excited." A tear formed in the corner of the professor's eye and held there just above his muttonchop sideburns.

"Good God," Gina said, turning to Kevin. "Unbelievable. You see, your lordship, not only do you inherit a burned-down, ruined castle but chests of gold as well. As Sharon said—you are one lucky son of a bitch."

"You are the heir to all this? Well, Mr. O'Bryan, congratulations," Laird said.

"It's actually Bryan, Professor."

"However, as we say in Ireland, every sunny day will be followed by three days of rain. So, I need to tell you—"

Two pistol shots echoed in the sea mist and rising wind that had moved in over the ruined cellar. From above and beyond the quartet's view, harsh voices yelled; then three more gunshots silenced the voices.

15b

Gina yelled, "What the hell is going on up there?"

"Quiet, don't say anything," Sharon said. "Hide behind these timbers."

More silence. The only sound was the storm blowing through the trees.

"Officers, what's going . . . ?" Kevin began.

Before he could finish, a figure stepped into the arena of floodlights that washed the cellar. In the glare, they couldn't make out who it was.

"Mr. Bryan, you really know how to royally fuck things up," a familiar woman's voice called down from the top of the ladder.

As they watched, Sylvia Boyle took a position next to the ladder. A man with a dark beard moved in and stood next to her, the unmistakable shape of an automatic weapon in his hands.

"You didn't have to shoot them," Sharon shouted back.

"They are fine. It was a little noise to help persuade them to lay down their weapons," Boyle said as she started down the ladder. "Now, what have you found there?" She reached the last rung and stepped out onto the stone floor. When she turned to the group, they saw the unmistakable silhouette of a pistol in her hand. She made her way over the debris and looked at the gold scattered across the floor.

"Mr. Bryan, who is this . . . person?" Laird asked.

"Miss Sylvia Boyle," he answered. "She's the one who tried to kill us when she set fire to the house and this building."

"I obviously failed," Boyle answered. "It seems, though, that my reward is my ancestor's gold."

"Your ancestor?" Sharon said.

"Yes, my great-great—God knows how many greats—grandfather Miles Boyle found this gold. But your ancestor, Mr. Bryan, who after murdering his brothers, had Miles jailed and then stole the gold."

"That's what you are after, this gold?" Kevin said. "Boyle, you are fucking crazy! If my family had known about this gold, why did it remain buried in the wall of this cellar? Why didn't they cash it in or do something with it?"

"That's your family's problem. All this land is rightfully mine. The gold is mine, and my family's. You killed my son, and you will pay for that."

"Your son was trying to run us off the road. It was his own fault," Sharon said. "None of that would have happened if he'd just left us alone. Kevin would have made you a deal, but no, you wouldn't listen. O'Shaunnessy has told the police everything that led up to you kidnapping us and setting fire to the building—everything. It's over, Boyle. There is nothing here. The only certainty I know is that you will be spending the rest of your life in a cozy Irish prison."

From above the rim of the cellar, gunfire began again. Boyle's man at the top of the ladder turned and began to shoot into the darkness. A second later, he spun around, staggered, lost his footing, and fell into the cellar. Another man took his place at the top of the ladder.

"Put your weapon down, Miss Boyle. It's over." It was the unmistakable Irish lilt of Liam Donovan. "Drop the pistol, now! Your men have been arrested. You are alone. Let them go and stand away."

Boyle looked at the gold, then at Kevin. "They will never take this land away, and if I can't have it, you can't have it, either." Her face twisted with years of pent-up rage, Boyle elevated the pistol and started to take aim at Kevin. Gina grabbed a chunk of wood, the size of a baseball bat, and threw it at Boyle. The wood spun in the lights and smashed into Boyle's arm. The gun fired; the round zipped past Kevin's ear and struck the stone wall of the cellar. As Boyle tried to re-aim, Sharon threw her shoulder into the woman's side and drove her into the wall, knocking over the professor in the process. The pistol fired again. The three slid through the gold coins, scattering them everywhere. Their impact against the wall let loose an additional torrent of coins that fell onto them as they lay tangled in a heap. Boyle, pistol still in her hand, was the first to gain her feet. She swung wildly with the weapon, trying to club Sharon. Her actions surprised Sharon; she hadn't expected Boyle to have the skills of a street fighter. Sharon tried to grab her legs but missed.

Out of the corner of her eye, Sharon saw Liam climbing down the ladder. Kevin pulled Gina away, trying to shield her. Boyle turned, looked, saw Donovan, and her only way out blocked. Shoving the pistol into her pocket, she bolted through the burnt debris to the door to the tunnel, threw the latch over, and pulled it open. Standing in the open door, she raised the pistol and took a shot at Liam just as he reached the floor. She missed. A split second later, the door slammed shut.

Sharon, Kevin, and Liam ran to the door. With Liam covering him, Kevin pulled open the door. Sharon stared into the blackness.

"What the hell is she thinking? She can't see a thing," Sharon said. "One mistake and she'll tumble down a hundred steps."

"We'll stay here," Liam said. "Trying to follow will set us up like sitting ducks at every step. She must come back up; we can arrest her then. She's not going anywhere."

They clustered around the pile of gold. Gina helped the professor to his feet; he was bleeding from a nick on his forehead where a piece of the second bullet had ricocheted off the stone.

The rain now started in earnest.

"What the hell was she thinking?" Kevin asked, repeating Sharon's earlier question.

"Who knows," Liam answered. "Does she know anything about the tunnel?"

"What tunnel?" Professor Laird, his voice shaky, asked as he looked at the door across the cellar.

"An old smugglers' tunnel. She can't get out," Donovan said.

"Only if she swims—and this storm is really kicking up," Sharon said. "We know what that means. The tide and the surge will fill the cove, and she may not be able to open the door. And if she does open it, she will be sucked out into the sea."

Two more police officers joined Donovan in the cellar.

"Anyone hurt?" Liam asked the men.

"Just the bloke who took a shot at us. He's got a bullet wound in the shoulder and what looks like a broken leg. Lucky guy. The fall should have killed him. There were two others; they've been arrested. One is somebody we know, name's O'Rourke."

"O'Rourke?" Sharon asked.

"Yes, ma'am, local tough guy, Tommy O'Rourke. He was carrying a pistol. He's not going anywhere, sir."

"Hold them until I get there, then you can take them into town. I will be up in a few minutes," Liam said.

"How did you know?" Kevin asked.

"That Boyle would try and make a play or something? I didn't know—it was an educated guess. I had a few additional men hiding around the perimeter, waiting. She and her men parked up the road and walked in."

"How did she know we were here?"

"I don't know," Liam said. His eyes traveled over the gold. "Jesus, Mary, and Joseph, I can't believe what I'm looking at. They told me about it, but seeing is believing." Liam picked up one of the coins and turned it over in his hand. It glowed in the lights. He turned to one of his men. "Post someone on that door for the night. Arrest anyone who comes through it."

"Treasure makes people do strange things," Sharon said. "I know that well. I'm soaked. I suggest we get out of here. Professor?"

Professor Laird adjusted the brim of his checkered deerstalker cap. Rain dripped from its brim. The bleeding on his forehead had stopped but a wet crimson trail coursed down his cheek. He said, "I was going to tell you something that is very important before we were interrupted by that terrible woman."

"And what is that, Professor?" Kevin asked, tightening his raincoat.

Laird held up one of the coins and it flashed in the lights. "From what I can see, these are Spanish escudos from the late sixteenth century—some are dated from about 1570 to the 1590s. From my first look at this handful, they have the marks of King Philip II. Others were minted in South America—Lima, Peru, to be exact. But I need more time to further explore the others. This is quite a find, more for their historical value than their real value."

"It's gold, Professor, hundreds of pounds," Kevin said. "Worth millions."

"Maybe. But from my first look at these"—he held out his hand; rain brightened the coins' appearance—"the king of Spain was going to have the last laugh."

"What? What do you mean?" Sharon said.

"Well, if the story is true that this was to be used as a bribe to have the Irish rebels join the new Spanish invasion, the Irish would have been duped. You see, Mr. Bryan, these coins are fakes, counterfeits. They are lead alloy with a thin gold coating. It seems that Philip II foisted a fraud on the Irish. The coins have amazing historical value, but as gold, almost nothing."

"Well, I'll be damned," Gina said.

15c

As the rain increased its intensity, Kevin started to laugh. He continued until everyone, except the professor, was laughing. Sharon pointed to the gold strewn about the floor—coins still tumbled from the hole—and laughed. Gina pointed to the burnt rafters and the ruins overhead and said, "Your lordship," bowed, and laughed. Kevin returned the bow to his two close friends and then raised his arms. "To my kingdom," he said and laughed and danced around. Even Donovan saw the absurdity of everything that had happened, and he joined in. Eventually, as they stood soaking in the rain, the professor began to chuckle, then laugh outright.

"Let's get out of this miserable hole," Kevin said. "I can do with a drink of Irish anything."

"I completely agree," Sharon added, and they started toward the ladder.

From above, the sound of a dog's deep growling startled them. They looked up and saw the red setter Dergo standing poised and stiff; next to him were Molly and Mac. The dog glowered at the burnt face of the tunnel door. The door moved and began to open; then without an order, the dog leapt from the edge of the cellar's foundation and in three long strides met Boyle as she burst through the doorway. Just as the red hound reached the woman, she fired four shots into the five standing over the gold. As she re-aimed the weapon, Dergo bit hard into her arm and with his momentum dragged the screaming woman to the burned debris strewn across the floor.

Kevin yelled and fell to one knee. Sharon grabbed him under one arm and held him up. The others looked back at the door to the tunnel. Boyle shrieked again as the dog savagely bit down on her arm and twisted and dragged her through the ruin. The pistol flew from her hand and skidded through the rubble. Mac took hold of a burnt timber and swung himself down into the cellar.

"Molly, tell the hound to stop," Mac yelled.

"*Dergo, stad, stad*," Molly yelled from above.

Mac ran to the dog and Boyle, grabbed Dergo's collar, and as the dog released his prize, pulled him away from the New Yorker. Her dreadful cries and whimpering filled the cellar.

Liam, pistol drawn, stood over Boyle as Mac gave additional commands to the dog.

A loud slam startled everyone. The door to the tunnel banged hard against its frame. With each breath of wind up the tunnel, it slammed again and again, like an ancient drum conjuring up its sordid past.

Sharon settled Kevin on the stones and ripped open his shirt. A hole was visible high above his right nipple and below the shoulder bone; blood oozed from the finger-sized wound. His eyes were open; rain fell on his face.

"Gina, get me something to stop the bleeding. It's bad—we need to get him to the hospital."

Gina wore a thin cotton sweater over her blouse; she pulled off her raincoat and then the sweater and handed it to Sharon, who held the fabric against the wound. They heard Liam on his police radio ordering paramedics to return to the cellar. He yelled up to his men for a medical kit.

"We have an ambulance nearby, standard with these operations," Donovan said. "They were already taking care of the man who fell." He was now handcuffing Boyle, who continued to cry from the pain of her lacerated arm.

The EMTs quickly climbed down the ladder. When they reached Kevin, Sharon leaned in and whispered, "Fight, I want you to fight with all you have. There will be no dying on me. Do you hear me, Kevin Bryan, no dying."

He looked at her and tried to smile. "Don't leave me." The EMTs then took over.

The medical techs stabilized Kevin, started IVs, and stopped the bleeding with an anticoagulant dressing. In ten minutes, they were on their way across County Cork to the hospital. Sharon never left his side; she held his hand the whole way.

* * *

The next morning, at the hospital, Kevin lay in the bed next to JF. The four women hovered over the two, bugging the nursing staff, questioning the doctors, and asking repeatedly if the two invalids needed anything. Claudette and Evelyn were the most attentive. They also wanted to know everything that had happened. Sharon and Gina filled them in.

Unknown to them beforehand, Liam had laid a trap; Sharon was still pissed at the copper for that. He'd assigned his men to watch the ruin and the hoard of gold. After the professor had given the all clear, they were to systematically remove the gold from the wall and secure it at Clonakilty police headquarters. Someone in the police department intentionally let a few of the locals know about the gold. Tommy O'Rourke took the bait.

Liam believed that Boyle had been waiting for the right moment when there was the least activity at the site. Eventually she ran out of patience. During his interrogation, Tommy O'Rourke bragged it was he who pressed the issue and convinced Boyle to move forward. Tommy said that Boyle had called him after the fire. She needed his local knowledge to help her. Tommy sneaked onto the property and saw the gold, but he couldn't get close due to the police standing guard. He'd reported back to Boyle, who told him to meet her in front of the funeral home. He was given a pistol and went with Boyle and her henchmen to Kevin's farm; only after his arrest did Tommy learn his pistol was empty. He was being charged with the attempted murder of a police officer, assault, and, if Liam could make the charge stick, gross stupidity.

After Boyle arrived, Liam had waited until she went down into the cellar to confront Sharon and her friends. He then moved in with his people, arrested one of Boyle's men and Tommy O'Rourke, and shot the other thug when he turned his weapon toward the police.

"They tell me Boyle's man will be all right," Liam said when he arrived at the hospital. "Boyle's in the local jail. Her arm is severely lacerated but it's wrapped, and she's still in pain. It was stupid and crazy on Boyle's part. I still don't fully get it. I've been told that there are a dozen corporate lawyers from New York landing in Dublin tomorrow to add to the circus that this is becoming. Now that will be fun. And Molly wants to know how all of you are doing."

"Her dog saved all of us. Is Dergo okay?" Sharon asked.

"He's fine. It was his sharp hearing that saved you. Molly said that the ghost of Brona O'Bryan was there with her dog, helping him to know to wait and then attack."

"I told you there are ghosts," Gina said.

Later, as they gathered at a nearby local pub over pints of Guinness, Molly and Mac joined them. Sharon asked Liam about O'Shaunnessy.

"The government prosecutor's trying to find something to pin on her, but not surprisingly, O'Shaunnessy has lawyered up. She tells an interesting story of her family's relationship to the O'Bryans that goes back to the Boer War. She claims that she and her firm have been loyal friends of the O'Bryans and that she was very close to Kevin's late aunt Brona."

"I find that hard to believe after what Kevin and I saw in Dublin," Sharon said. "Personally, I think she was in this conspiracy up to her bad haircut, and Boyle duped her. In time, Boyle would have probably shut her out of everything."

"Most likely," Liam agreed.

"Thank you for not shooting my nephew," Molly said. "Maybe some time in jail will do him some good."

"The kid is really mixed up," Liam said. "He started to say things about you that I have a hard time believing."

"Like what?" Molly asked.

"Smuggling and other illegal operations with the IRA."

"I run a bakery. It takes up all my time," Molly said matter-of-factly.

"How much do we owe you for the cake?" Gina asked.

"Don't worry about that," Molly said. "I gave it to the senior center in town. They were thrilled and want to thank Sharon O'Mara, whoever the lass is whose name is on the cake."

"You got me a cake?" Sharon asked.

Epilogue

Below Barrington House, the lawn extended to the River Ouse that wound its way through this verdant part of the Kent countryside. Sharon and Kevin, his arm in a sling, strolled along a stone path. To their left were the perennial gardens complete with vibrant summer blooms, and to their right extended the cherry orchard, rich with ripening fruit. Their host, Clive Barrington, pointed out the various trees, when they were planted, and by whom.

"That White Oak, American, I'll have you, was planted in 1796," Clive said. "It was grown from an acorn that my ancestor brought back from a business trip to Philadelphia. He also brought back other exotic trees from the Americas, maples, ash, and beech. Some are still alive and prospering; others have lived out their lives and are gone."

Kevin looked up the massive tree from root to crown—three men, standing hand in hand, could not have enclosed the tree's trunk.

"Handsome. Your gardens are magnificent, Clive," he said.

"Thank you, but I'm just a caretaker. Some days I'm not sure who owns whom. Do we own the land, or does the land own us? My family has occupied this plot of England since it was granted to us by King Henry VIII in 1545. The Americas, such as they are, were discovered only fifty-two years earlier. We've been here a long time."

"It's beautiful," Sharon added. "And thank you for the invitation. The last few weeks in Ireland have been, I could add, less than relaxing."

"I should say," Clive said. "I'm sorry about the house, Kevin. It sounded quite nice, even though these places, at times, can be millstones around your neck. Maybe it was all for the better."

"I'm beginning to believe that myself," Kevin said. "If it hadn't burned down, I don't know what I could have done to repair it. Our friends, especially Jean-François, have been helpful and, according to the lawyers, the past taxes have been paid. There was even some insurance that might cover some of the loss from the fire damage. So, I own it now."

"You have weathered the shooting well. The shoulder?"

"Mending, but sore as hell. This is the fourth time I've been shot. Besides being lucky, I guess I'm not easy to kill."

"Stop that," Sharon said. "I'll take lucky every day."

She looked back up the great lawn to where their friends were talking on the terrace that overlooked the estate and the river. JF was sitting in a wicker chaise lounge with his leg propped up on a footstool. Kevin's inheritance and her birthday adventure had put all of their lives at risk. She didn't know how she would be able to make it up to them.

"And the long-term prognosis?" Clive asked.

"He should heal well," Sharon said.

"I meant the estate. What will you do with that millstone?"

"There's an intriguing woman in the village who has access to some money—how she earned it is questionable," Kevin answered. "Considering your position in the constabulary here, I shouldn't tell you more. However, she's offered to cover the debt I owe to JF for the taxes—if she would be allowed to take ownership. I'm thinking it over."

"That's good. You are not the landed-gentry type, Kevin. That takes either being born into, like me, and thus to have no say in the matter, or be willing to take it on. Financially, there's no plus side. But it is nice to be able to enjoy it. In today's world, owning a small piece of heaven has its benefits."

Kevin nodded thoughtfully. Each in their own thoughts, they reached the riverbank and a small dock that extended out into the river; an ancient wood dory was tied to one of the piers. Their mutual reverie was broken by the rhythmic slaps of two rowers in their sleek skulls as they coursed past; both rowers waved.

"Good morning, John, and you, too, Ned," Clive called out.

"Beautiful morning," drifted back to the trio.

"Idyllic," Sharon said.

"It is that," Barrington said. "It can lull you into a sense of shameless lethargy."

"And there's something wrong with that?" Sharon asked.

Barrington sighed, stopped, and turned to the two. "What are you two going to do with your lives? I've known you long enough to see that you're smart, creative, and have extraordinary skills. Sharon, where are you going with this? Are you going to keep this facilitator venture of yours moving forward? If so, for how long? It's demanding and physically takes a lot out of you; do you have an exit strategy? And you, Kevin Bryan—you have great detective skills and you do nothing with them. You are young. I ask you, where will you be in ten years?"

The questions hit the friends like a gentle slap, a slap of reality.

"I'm not sure, Clive," Sharon answered. "It's hard to look at your life and make those kinds of decisions."

"No, it isn't; people do it every day. You have the resources to look across the wide world of opportunities, so don't use that lame excuse. I'm serious, and I don't expect an answer, but you need to start thinking of one. That's the father in me speaking. My generation fought in the post–World War II wars of the 1960s and '70s. Sharon, when we met in Iraq, I was at the end of that career. I changed, adapted, and now use that experience to fight the new wars of terrorism, drugs, and the horror spread by so-called self-radicalized independent contractors. That is a fancy and antiseptic term for terrorists. I also learned things then that have no substance in today's world. Yet, I also know things that do have value. And so do the both of you."

"I understand," Kevin said. "*Carpe diem.*"

"No, not *carpe diem*. In fact, that's the worst maxim for today's world—live for today for tomorrow we may die, or some other god-awful rot. No, both of you have twenty or thirty good years left to you to carry on the fight. What are those years going to mean to you, to your families, and to your country?" Clive pointed to their friends on the terrace. "They all have self-driven purposes: software, high-end technology, fashion, business. I've learned that with purpose comes responsibility and accountability. So, what is your purpose?"

Sharon and Kevin watched Clive walk up the hill and mingle with his other guests; he needed to be in London the next morning. He had offered the estate to them for a few days—*carte blanche*. In the morning, Claudette was returning to Paris on the Ashford train. JF was tagging along and would transfer in Paris to Marseilles. Both of their businesses were growing, and Sharon had noticed that there was a budding affection between them as well. She was happy for them both—there was a touch of jealousy over Jean-François—but the man was also an impossible dream for her. Evelyn was off to Dubai; her family's newest STIA store was opening in a week. She needed to be there with her brother. Sharon remembered that at one time Evelyn had been her boss at her leather goods store in San Francisco's Union Square neighborhood—how things had changed. She smiled as she looked at Gina, her best friend. Gina was going back to Dublin to spend a week with Liam Donovan; he had offered to show her the finer points of Ireland. Sharon wondered if he knew what he was getting into.

"He's right, you know," Kevin said. "We've been just drifting along, going with the flow."

"I know, it's just embarrassing to be called on it," Sharon answered. "We know better. Maybe it's our way of avoiding the truth."

"And what truth is that?"

"That we need to grow up. We have, as Clive said, thirty more years ahead of us. You have always been there for me and for others. You make a difference; there's a bunch of kids that keep in touch with you, kids whose lives you saved. They have futures because of you."

"It was my job."

"That's not true, at least not entirely, and you know it. This security gig you are into may help pay the bills, but it's the front line you like—in fact, you need it. I've seen it. I know that San Francisco and Oakland police departments have both called.

They want you to rethink the forced retirement that Lafayette put you on. You can make a difference."

"It's all too crazy."

"My guess is that you can pick your position. It's hard to find anyone today with your skills and experience. I'd bet that some of the smaller Bay Area cities would see you in a much better position than detective, maybe assistant chief or higher."

"I hate management."

"Think about it."

"Me? What about you? You have a few bucks in the bank and no pension. But the future never goes in a straight line— things can and will happen; you need to be prepared. How is Basil going to get his bones? You like this facilitator business; it fits you, and you seem to fit it. God knows, there isn't a lack of clients out there. I know that you've had at least five calls."

"Gina? She can't keep her mouth shut. But then again, she keeps me up to date on you and your disreputable life."

"With such friends . . ."

"Good friends," Sharon said.

"She is that."

"Hey, you two! Are you coming back up to the house?" Gina said as she walked toward them. "Clive's found some old scotch that needs testing and a couple of bottles of Pétrus. JF and Claudette already have poured, and there's a cake with a bonfire of candles ready to be ignited. We are waiting for the birthday girl."

Gina slipped her arms around the waists of her friends and steered them back up the lawn toward Clive's Gothic pile. She began telling them about her upcoming week with Liam and how she was going to expand the number of Irish and British beers at Geno's.

"With such friends . . . " Sharon pulled the two of them close.

The End . . . for now.

A Note from the Author
The Flyer

I have tried to pare these stories into a manageable length that you can read in less than eight hours. At about 60–75,000 words, the idea is that you can read about half the book on a four-hour flight and the rest on the way home. I call them *Flyers*. But if you aren't flying, settle back, pour a good drink, and enjoy.

Gregory C. Randall was born in Traverse City, Michigan. He grew up in Chicago. Greg has never forgotten his roots. Mr. Randall makes his home in California.

Mr. Randall is the author of fiction and nonfiction works available through Amazon.com.

For more information about the other Sharon O'Mara Chronicles, and planned sequels, please visit and connect with Greg online:

www.gregorycrandall.info

See his blogs:
http://www.writing4death.blogspot.com

Other books by Mr. Randall:
Fiction
The Cherry Pickers

The Sharon O'Mara Chronicles
Land Swap For Death
Containers For Death
Toulouse For Death
12th Man For Death
Diamonds For Death
Limerick For Death

The Alex Polonia Thrillers
Venice Black
Saigon Red
St. Petersburg White

The Tony Alfano Thrillers
Chicago Swing
Chicago Jazz
Chicago Fix
Chicago Boogie Woogie

Max Adler OSS WWII
This Face of Evil
Pawns in an Ancient Game

Science Fiction and Slipstream
Sector 73
Seven Hours to Barstow

Nonfiction
America's Original GI Town, Park Forest, Illinois

Additional copies can be purchased through Amazon.com.